THE LAST
SUMMER
of
HER OTHER
LIFE

Also by Jean Reynolds Page

THE SPACE BETWEEN BEFORE AND AFTER
A BLESSED EVENT
ACCIDENTAL HAPPINESS

THE LAST
SUMMER
of
HER OTHER
LIFE

JEAN REYNOLDS PAGE

AVON

An Imprint of HarperCollinsPublishers

FIRST AVON PAPERBACK EDITION PUBLISHED 2009.

Designed by Diahann Sturge

Library of Congress Cataloging-in-Publication Data
    Page, Jean Reynolds.
        The last summer of her other life / Jean Reynolds Page.—1st ed.
            p.   cm.
        ISBN 978-0-06-145249-9
        1. Teacher-student relationships—Fiction. 2. Women teachers—Fiction.
        3. North Carolina—Fiction. I. Title.
    PS3616.A33755L37   2009
    813'.6—dc22   2009003392

09 10 11 12 13   OV/RRD   10 9 8 7 6 5 4 3 2 1

For Rick,
my husband, my partner,
and my best friend

Acknowledgments

None of my books would exist without the indulgence of my family, so once again I must thank Rick, Franklin, Gillian, and Edward. Your love and patience keep me going.

Along those lines, none of my books would be in print without the efforts of my fearless (and seemingly tireless) agent Susan Ginsburg. Susan, you are my friend and my champion and I am forever grateful.

Many thanks also to Lyssa Keusch, an editor with both the heart and the good eye to make this book better at every turn. I am grateful to have a home at HarperCollins. Special thanks must go to Aurora Hughes, for getting the word out there; to Wendy Lee, for keeping me on track; to Lauren Naefe for giving me a presence online; and to Johnathan Wilber for the early groundwork. And finally, thanks to Carrie Feron, Pam Jaffee, and Adrienne Di Pietro for all the energy and enthusiasm they've shown on my behalf. It takes a village and, thankfully, I have one.

Another resident of that village is Bethany Strout at Writers House. Problems are handled. Questions large and small are answered with such good cheer. Thanks, Bethany.

I would be a nervous wreck (or even more of a nervous wreck) without readers who give advice and support at every stage of the manuscript. For this book, I must thank Ken Patterson and Ian Pierce who gave shape to the early drafts. Their insights and valuable suggestions made a huge difference. Rick Lange, extraordinary physician and meticulous proofreader, saved me toward the end with his careful eye. My Texas writers group comes through every time. Mary Turner, Jeanne Skartsiaris, Kathy Yank, and Ian Pierce (reading a second time!) offered advice and corrections and I am so thankful to all of you. Lou Tasciotti and Chris Smith, on a reading sabbatical, offered support nonetheless. And love to my dear husband, Rick, who reads first and last. He never fails me.

Robby London patiently answered all questions about sound studios. For all the parts I got right, my thanks to him. (Anything I got wrong, remains my fault, unfortunately.) Tim Page, gave me Lincoln's playlist and advice on the life of a musician. Many thanks, Tim. Marc Farre took time out of a really special day to give advice on a crucial copyedit, and for this I am grateful. My good friend Bill Lynch offered much appreciated shelter and hospitality in New York. Also thanks to Andy Ziskind. The books change, but the photo remains.

Moral support is key at so many times in the writing process and fellow HarperCollins author Diane Hammond has been there in more ways than I can name (including switching hats to Web guru to get my Web site up and running!). Thank you, my friend.

As always, I must say thank you to Colleen Murphy and Victoria Skurnick, for the early support that brought me here to book number four. And to Hilda Lee, who believed it could happen before I dared to hope.

And finally, since life and work are closely tied together in a writer's existence, I must thank my larger circle of family: sister and brother, Joyce Ross and Ralph Reynolds; almost-sibling and dear cousin Lynn Saunders; Aunt Frances Thompson and Uncle Bob Reynolds; and all the other Reynolds and Blues out there who remain so dear to me.

THE LAST
SUMMER
of
HER OTHER
LIFE

Prologue

May 2002

Marnee sat on the edge of the claw-footed tub, her naked body down a third from the size it had once been. The day was gray outside, but warmth from the full bath rose up around her and she smelled the lavender bath oil Jules put in the water. She wished she could get in and soak, but the effort to climb in and out would be too great—for her and for Jules. For modesty's sake, she still could not bring herself to let Lincoln help her with the bathing part of her routine. He was a wonderful son, and would certainly have been willing. But old conventions died hard and, in the end, she was more comfortable with her daughter.

For everything else, Jules and Lincoln were equal partners in her care. Jules arrived first, had been with her for nearly three months. Lincoln came in from New York soon after, as soon as he rearranged his schedule of concerts. They'd both come without hesitation when she'd told them she'd taken a turn for the worse. Many mothers could not rely on loyal children. Even so close to death, she felt blessed.

She once thought God would deny her the privilege of children, but all that had changed with Lincoln. Then Jules followed, and Marnee saw her family complete. It had happened under different circumstances than she expected when she was young. But even so, all her hopes for motherhood had been satisfied, her prayers answered.

"Is this too hot?" Jules asked as she raised the sponge to Marnee's back.

"It feels good," Marnee told her. "I'm so cold all the time now. Anything warm is a comfort."

Jules rubbed the soft sponge over Marnee's neck and shoulders, down her spine and over her arms.

Marnee looked at the rise of her daughter's breasts inside the cotton sweater she wore, and saw the hint of thickness, now even more prominent than before, at Jules' waist. She'd been noticing the changes for about a week, and wondered if Jules would tell her. Obviously not. There was so little time, and if she wanted to talk about a baby—a grandchild—she would have to bring the subject up herself.

Jules had left that strange man she'd been dating in Los Angeles, said she wouldn't be seeing him again. If the baby was his, Jules didn't want him to know about it. Maybe she didn't want Marnee to know, either. Still, Marnee couldn't let it go unsaid.

"How long have you known about the baby?" she asked her daughter.

Jules dipped the sponge in the water again and squeezed out the excess. But then she stopped short of bringing it to Marnee's flesh. She sat down on the porcelain edge of the tub beside Marnee and closed her eyes for a moment. When she opened them again, Marnee saw moisture in her daughter's eyes.

"Oh, honey, I didn't mean to upset you," Marnee said. "I just thought we should talk about it."

"I'm glad you said something," Jules told her. "I figured it out just before I came here. I wanted to talk to you, but . . ." She wouldn't look up, and a sudden fear seized Marnee.

"You are . . ." Marnee stopped. Should she ask? Did she even want to know? "You do plan to have the baby, right?"

Jules turned to her suddenly. "Oh, Mom. Yes, I do. It's not that. Don't worry." She touched Marnee's arm. "I've always known that I wanted to have a child—eventually. And I'm thirty-eight. This isn't how I hoped it would happen, but, well, it *is* how it happened, so . . ."

"Nothing ever works in quite the way you expect," Marnee told her daughter, thinking of her own life as much as Jules'. "Thomas. The baby's his? Is that why you broke up?"

"I left him before I knew. He's got some problems. I think it's better if he doesn't know there's a baby. I don't know if that's the right thing or not, but . . ."

"What sort of problems?" Marnee asked.

Jules sat for a moment, just breathing, as if trying to build up the energy to answer the question.

"It's okay," Marnee began.

"No, no," Jules interrupted. "I want to tell you." She stood up and got a soft towel from the hook on the door. She put it around Marnee's shoulders, then sat down again and began.

"Thomas called me one day on a job and asked if he could come by and borrow my car," she said. "I said fine, as long as he came back and gave me a ride home. I figured his was in the shop or something. Two hours later, I was on the freeway with him, screaming my head off for him to stop while he drove over one hundred miles an hour."

"Dear Lord." Marnee didn't even like imagining her daughter in that kind of danger.

"He was laughing the whole time. He said if we crashed and died, our souls would be married on the way to some star system he seemed to be obsessed with at that moment.

I fished out my cell phone and he grabbed it and threw it out his window."

"Oh, Jules . . ."

"I finally got him to slow down enough for me to get out," she said, "although he never fully stopped the car. I was walking in flip-flops on I–405. Somebody stopped and I called the police, but by then they were already chasing him. He wrapped the car around a pole before it was over. He got bruised up, but walked away from it. Thank God he didn't kill anybody. That night, I got the unique experience of seeing my poor little Honda come to its end on the local news."

"Was he arrested?" Marnee asked.

"A psych evaluation," Jules said. "Charges are pending treatment. I talked to his ex-wife after that. She filled me in on his problems. He's bipolar. Apparently, he has a history of deciding to go off his meds without warning. God knows why no one told me before. When I found out about the baby, I already had my flight here scheduled. It seems wrong not to tell him, but I'm really scared for the baby."

"You have to think of the child first," Marnee said. "First and last, if it comes down to it." Marnee understood firsthand. She wished she could have left Jack Fuller to raise Jules and Lincoln alone. But she had her reasons for staying.

Jules stared at the squares of tile at her feet. "Are you ashamed of me?" she asked Marnee, not looking up.

"Oh, Jules. No, baby. You're a grown woman. I expect you to have a life." Marnee leaned over, raised her arm around the small of Jules' back. Even this gesture carried such effort. She wished she could slip free of her body, but still remain with Jules at the same time. With Jules *and* Lincoln. They needed her, and she couldn't stay much longer. She'd made peace with all of it— except that. It was her only lingering regret.

"Julie Marie," she gathered all her resources and began again,

"I have never once been ashamed of you. I understand that your choices come from a different point of view than I had growing up. The world has changed since then. I know that."

"A lot of people in this town don't think that way," Jules said. "A lot of your friends."

"Well," Marnee said. "One lovely thing about dying is that all that nonsense gets put into perspective. I do wish that you had a situation that would make this easier for you. But even in the worst of circumstances, babies are a blessing."

Jules leaned into her, forgetting for a moment, it seemed, Marnee's frailness. It took every ounce of strength Marnee had to bear Jules' weight against her, but she found such comfort in the effort. When Jules pulled back, Marnee took her hand, not wanting to relinquish the feeling of her daughter's presence. She fully intended, even in death, to stay near her daughter. Believed it possible with her entire mind and soul. But the touching . . . Oh, she would miss that.

"What does it feel like?" Marnee asked, surprised to feel a smile come to her face. "The little one in there."

"Not much yet." Jules smiled back. "Sometimes I think I can feel it, but that has to be my imagination at this point. You remember how it was with Lincoln, don't you?"

"No," Marnee answered her truthfully. "I don't."

"I guess when it's over and you go back to normal," Jules said, "it seems like it happened to a different body."

"Do you have a doctor?" Marnee changed the subject.

"I've been once. I'm supposed to go back next week."

"That's good," Marnee told her. "You have to keep up with that. No matter what's going on with me. Like I said, the baby comes first."

"I need you, Mom," Jules said, her eyes now wild with tears. "I don't know how to do this. I'm a daughter. I've always been a daughter. I don't know how to be a mother."

If Jules had known the raw pain her words brought to Marnee, she wouldn't have said them. For the first time in weeks, Marnee felt the anger return. The anger that this thing, this cancer, had claimed her life. She wanted more than anything to see Jules through. To meet her grandchild. But she couldn't. And there was no way to change that. For the first time, she wouldn't be there when one of her children needed her.

"Lincoln will be with you." Marnee was barely able to say the words. Jules' grief would come later, but Marnee's had suddenly arrived in full measure. Still, even inside her disappointment, she felt it. The small kernel of joy that a baby was there. A baby would be in her home again. And all the love she gave to Jules and Lincoln would get funneled into a tiny, new life.

"What do you say we finish the bath later, Mom," Jules said. "You look pretty spent."

Spent. That's how she felt. And there would be no reinforcements. No replenishing of the energy expended. She was simply using herself up day by day. So she had to choose wisely, deciding what to do with the scarce reserves she had left.

Jules slipped Marnee's gown over her head and Marnee struggled to find the holes for her arms. At sixty-four, there should have been more time. Still, she wouldn't complain. Her parents waited for her on the other side. It struck her as funny that there, she might even become a daughter again. Thank the Lord she wouldn't be Jack Fuller's wife for a second time. Wherever her husband had traveled in the afterlife, God would have the good grace not to send her there.

"It's better what you're doing," Marnee said as they made their way back to the bed. "I know it'll be hard. But it's better to have the baby alone than with someone too damaged to be a good parent."

Jules would understand what she meant. That was probably why she'd made the decision in the first place. If Marnee had been blessed with a choice, she would have done the same thing.

Jules curled next to her on the bed like a young girl, and Marnee reached over and pulled her daughter close. Jules and Lincoln both had been doing that a lot, lying by her side. Even though her children were grown, holding them the way she had when they were young still seemed as natural as breathing.

"Julie Marie," she said, her chin resting on the top of Jules' head. "You've been loved every day since the moment I laid eyes on you."

"I know it, Mom," Jules said, wrapping her fingers around Marnee's hand.

It was the middle of the day, but time didn't have a place in their schedules anymore. They would sleep and then talk some more when they woke up. Marnee's senses had been doing funny things since she'd been so sick, but, in the air around her, she smelled something lovely. Baby skin smell. It had to be in her mind, but she didn't want it to go away. She drifted to sleep thinking of tiny, perfect fists—little hands taking hold of her, determined and tugging at her skin, insisting on love.

Chapter One

When Jules was seven, Marnee sat down with her on the den couch after school one day.

"Julie Marie," she said, "we need to have a momma-girl talk." That's what Marnee called it when Jules needed to listen carefully, to be her most grown-up self. "You know why Mrs. Tucker has such a big tummy, don't you?"

Mrs. Tucker was Jules' teacher. She had a baby that lived only two months before he went to sleep one night and didn't wake up. But while she was pregnant, the second-grade teacher became a source of great fascination for the class, especially the girls, who had some vague idea that this might be their lot in life someday.

"She had sex with Mr. Tucker and made a baby," Jules said, parroting her friend Jamie's words. Jules knew the words to be true—Marnee had confirmed this—but had little understanding of what they meant, exactly.

"That's right," Marnee told her. "That's how babies get into the world. They grow in mommies' tummies and when God says it's time, they get born."

Jules nodded, wondering where the Mrs. Tucker tummy discussion was headed.

"Well, my girl," Marnee continued, "I think it's time that we had a talk about when you were born."

"Did your belly button pop out the wrong way when I got big before I came out?" Jules asked. "We could see Mrs. Tucker's belly button when she had on a shirt that was kind of tight one day."

"That's the thing," Marnee said. "You didn't grow inside my tummy."

Jules wondered where she might have grown. Could babies start off in jars like her friend Laura's sea monkeys?

"There was a lady who found out you were growing in her tummy. She didn't live here in Ekron. In fact, I don't know where she lived." Marnee seemed to get lost in this question for a moment before she came back to the discussion at hand. "But anyway, she went to a place in Raleigh where they find the right mommies for babies when the ladies they grow inside can't take care of them."

Jules imagined a lady shaped like Mrs. Tucker. But her face had a fuzzy quality like a picture too out of focus to recognize anyone.

"When they told me you were there at that place," Marnee said, "I knew that I was your mommy." Marnee looked into Jules' eyes. All momma-girl talks got to that point—the time when her momma would stop talking and look at Jules directly in the face. This was the important point. "I loved you before I even saw you," she said, "just like Mrs. Tucker loves that little one she hasn't seen yet. Do you understand all this?"

"Yes, ma'am," Jules said, but a question gnawed inside her head. She was almost scared to ask it. "Momma?"

"Yes, baby."

"Who named me?"

"What do you mean?" Marnee treated the inquiry with proper regard. She never dismissed anything Jules asked.

"Did the lady who grew me inside her have the name for me when you got me or did you get to make up a name after I was with you and Daddy?"

She based her reasoning on her experience with pets. Jules had seen dogs who'd lived one place and had a name, but then had to go to new owners. After the move, the animals came off as a little confused, as if they might want to hear another voice calling for them. Jules thought it had something to do with who named them, and she felt scared after she'd asked.

"When we went into that big room where you were waiting for us," Marnee told her, "I had no idea what you'd be called. But the second I saw you, it came to me. *Julie Marie.* I said it out loud before I'd even touched you. You turned your head toward me, just like you'd heard your own name. I guess I claim to have named you, but I think God whispered your name in your little ear before I even got into the room, the same way He whispered it to me when I saw you. That way, He figured you'd know the one who called you by that name was your momma."

Jules quit worrying after that. She never wondered once where she'd spent all those months growing inside some stranger's body. The notion of a birth mother seemed as relevant to her life as the women in her Bible stories in Sunday school. They'd existed at some point, but had no impact on what she ate for breakfast or what she got for her birthday. She had everything she needed in Marnee. And regardless of what her mother believed about God's whispers, Jules believed she came into being the second Marnee spoke her name. Before that, nothing mattered.

It had been a week since Marnee's funeral. A week and three days since Jules' discussion with her about the baby. About her grandchild. Jules had no idea at the time that it would be the last conversation she'd have with her mother.

After their talk, Jules and Marnee lay down for a nap. When Jules woke up two hours later, Marnee was on the floor by the window. Jules yelled for Lincoln and the two of them got their mother back on the bed. She was breathing, but would not wake up. She lived for three more days, but never opened her eyes again.

Still, Jules and Lincoln *felt* their mother with them. Her presence was stronger than consciousness. Stronger than words. They stayed with her around the clock. Sometimes together and sometimes just one of them at a time. When she finally stopped drawing any breath, they were both there, and the emptiness seemed to encompass the known world.

Lincoln had gone down to the cemetery every day, but it took Jules a week to go back to Marnee's grave. As she walked away from the still-fresh burial plot, her mother's long skirt grew stained where the hem brushed over the loose, red clay.

While caring for Marnee, Jules had taken to wearing her mother's clothes. For one thing, she hadn't brought much with her when, several months before, she left LA. Her plans had been made in less than forty-eight hours after Marnee's cancer began to worsen. Jules packed one big suitcase and a carry-on, leaving everything else behind.

At first, when Marnee still felt well enough to go to church, she loaned Jules clothes for the services. It was cool then, so the outfits were mostly skirts and sweaters with darker wintertime hues. Marnee seemed to like seeing Jules in her things. She'd suggest something that would look good on her, tell her to try it on.

Marnee kept two closets. One for summer and one for winter. Every spring, when she moved to the clothes in her summer closet, Jules would see a tightness in Marnee's features ease. She seemed to *wear* happiness itself as she put on her short-sleeved dresses.

When Jules arrived to take care of her mother, she'd traded the Los Angeles sun for a bleak coastal winter in North Carolina. Weeks later, warm weather was still late coming, and the strain of that, coupled with her physical worsening, showed in Marnee's eyes. Then by late April, when the season skipped spring and went straight to summer, Marnee was spending her days in nightgowns. Still, she made a ceremony of opening the summer closet.

"Why don't you see what fits you," she told Jules.

"I'm fine, Mom," Jules told her. "I've got some clothes."

"Why don't you let *me* see what fits you, then," Marnee said.

And Jules realized that the suggestion wasn't for her benefit. Marnee wanted to know that life would go on. All afternoon, Jules took things out of the closet and tried them on. At some point, Lincoln joined them, and sat in the chair by Marnee's bed. For all the pleasure it brought Marnee, Jules would have kept it up until night came and turned into day again, except that eventually hunger and fatigue began to take a toll on all of them. But after that day, it became second nature for Jules to look in her mother's closet for something to wear.

Since Marnee had been gone, Jules realized that the clothes had taken on a new significance. They felt good against her skin, as if some property in the fabric imparted onto her the best qualities of her mother. After the funeral, Jules found wearing the clothes a comfort, something tangible to carry with her. Because even though the preacher had devoted an inordinate amount of verbal real estate to the notion of souls and saints, Jules couldn't convince herself that the cancer left any part of her mother, flesh or otherwise, for heaven to claim.

If this was true of the devout Marnee, Jules figured she and her brother, Lincoln, must be in real trouble. There was more immediate concern for Lincoln, given his problems. Jules tried not to think about her brother's health. Seeing Marnee through the past months, Jules had experienced enough worry for a lifetime.

"Watch out!" A boy's panicked cry.

Just steps from the cemetery in the side yard of the church, he appeared out of nowhere, his bike a red blur before pain shot through her hip and arm as she hit the ground. Her ankle forced into an awful twist.

"You all right?" He let his bike fall and ran over to where she'd sprawled in the patchy grass. He stopped short, leaned in carefully as if she might be toxic.

"I'm okay," she said. "I turned my ankle, but I don't think I broke anything."

Her hand went instinctively to her abdomen.

"Did you hurt your stomach?" the boy asked.

"No," she said, amazed that he'd even noticed the gesture. "I'm going to have a baby. But everything's okay, I think."

The baby would be fine, still tucked deep inside the flesh and muscle of Jules' belly. With Marnee gone, no one but Lincoln and her doctor even knew that she was pregnant—well, Lincoln, the doctor, and some random kid on a bike. Why had she blurted it out like that?

But the boy wasn't interested in her pregnancy. He stared at her leg, and she realized her skirt was up, bunched high on her hip from the fall. He fixed his eyes on her tattoo, a small rose on the inside thigh. She pulled at the fabric and covered herself. Still, he couldn't seem to take his eyes off the spot where he'd glimpsed the flower.

"Help me up, okay?" She smiled, breaking his momentary fascination with the body art.

"Sure!" He came closer and began pulling roughly at one arm.

The boy must have been all of nine, maybe ten, slightly younger than she was when she lost her dad. At that odd moment, it oc-curred to Jules that she was an orphan for the second time in her life.

"You're that lady who does movie stuff, right?" the boy asked.

Jules tested the foot. It was sore, but took some weight. "Yeah," she told him. "I'm a Foley artist. I put the sounds in movies once they're filmed."

From the look on his face, she might as well have told him she taught monkeys to play chess.

"You do that in California?" he asked, as if that might explain it.

"Mostly. I've been here for a couple of months. My mom lives down the road." She caught herself using the present tense, but couldn't bear correcting it. "I grew up here."

"I know," he said. He got back on his bike. "I've seen you at my granddaddy's sermons before, and my brother said you talk to his class at school sometimes. He's in ninth grade." The last part was said with a fair amount of pride. "My brother's name is Vick. He said you talked to him one day. Do you remember him? He asked you what you have to learn to get to be a movie star."

"Yeah," she lied, "I remember." She'd talked to the students in the school's drama course a few times since she'd been home, but the kids' faces, especially the boys, were a blur of bravado and acne.

The young boy smiled, stood looking at her as if there might be more to say. It being a weekday afternoon, they must have been two of maybe seven total humans in a five-square-mile radius. Marnee's house was just down the road, and like all the other homes along her rural route, it sat a wary distance from other neighbors.

"I'm really sorry, lady," he said.

"No problem." She tried and failed to rotate the tender ankle. It was swelling and, though she could hobble, pain shot through the entire foot. She hoped she could manage to drive the quarter-mile stretch to the house.

The boy took off in the opposite direction from where she intended to go. She glanced back again at the cemetery. She'd thought things couldn't get any lower, but as she tried to rotate the tender ankle and had to stop from the pain, she realized she'd been mistaken. She limped to the car so that she could make her way back home.

Chapter Two

Jules stopped by the grocery store on her way home from the medical clinic. She'd had two appointments in the three days since she'd fallen. Sporting a light brace that the doctor gave her, she entertained the notion that she could stand without pain again long enough to make a dinner that involved a stove rather than the microwave. The end of an aisle opened up at the dairy display, and she saw Sam Alderman looking at the yogurt selections with his back to her. In the twenty years since they'd been a couple in high school, he hadn't changed all that much. Maybe a little more muscle in the shoulders. She noticed an earring, new since the last time she'd seen him a few years before at the airport in Raleigh.

He picked up one carton of yogurt and then replaced it, and looked at another. She watched him. Short hair, still brown, but with a little gray mixed in.

"Sam?" Saying his name remained familiar. Her tone carried with it an implied intimacy, and she felt suddenly self-conscious. He might even be married again. Last time they'd talked—that day in the airport—he said that he and his wife had just split up.

"Jules." His familiar grin, large and easy, took up a fair portion of his face. He came closer to her. "I heard about your mom," he said, the smile fading. "I'm sorry. I thought about coming to the funeral, but . . ."

He didn't need to explain. Any time that extended members of her father's family were in attendance, it was a good idea for Sam to keep his distance. Marnee had never blamed Sam's family for Jack Fuller's death, but Jules' aunt and the two uncles on her father's side wouldn't let go of the idea.

"I thought about you, though," he said. "I should've come by." He looked down at the shiny store tile beneath his feet.

"It's okay. I've been up to my ears in visitors and casseroles. Things are just starting to settle down." He smelled good, like clean laundry.

"Yeah, I figured your relatives might be sticking around for a while," he said. "I know Mom dropped something by just after the funeral. She said she saw Lincoln. She didn't stay long. Apparently Aunt Noreen was giving her the evil eye from across the room."

"What the hell, my family's not always that keen on me, either," she joked, although it was mostly true. "And Noreen still scares the shit out of me sometimes."

"I get the feeling she could lay a mean hex on somebody if she got the notion," he said.

To Jules' family on her father's side, Sam was guilty by association. Even though his dad had done nothing wrong. A terrible accident. That's what it had been. After it, both their fathers were gone. During the years she dated Sam in high school, she knew better than to mention his name at the Fuller gatherings.

"You look great, though," he said. "God, it's been twenty years and you haven't changed at all. I guess you've traded that drawstring bag on your belt loop for a real purse, but that's about it."

She hadn't thought about that cloth pouch in years. She could have been arrested more than once for what was in that little sack. "I guess I traveled lighter in high school."

"Didn't we all," he said. His voice carried something like regret.

Her good ankle felt achy from standing. She leaned against the corner of the dairy display, and the air made her bare arms cold. As if sensing her discomfort, he took a step, coming closer to her than before. It still felt familiar to be talking with him, as if decades had not gone by since they called themselves a couple.

"Are you still working for the NIH in D.C.?" she asked.

"No," he said. "I'm medical director for a pharmaceutical company in Wilmington now. I don't see patients anymore."

"Is that weird?"

"Not really," he said. "I was always better in the lab anyway."

"I like the earring. That must have lit up the phone lines around here."

"I've had it for a while now, but yeah, Mom was not pleased." He smiled again. "At least she's happy that I've moved back to North Carolina."

"How about you?" she asked. "Do you like being back?"

"Yeah, it's good here. And I liked the idea of getting closer. Mom won't admit it, but hearing in that one ear is gone completely now. She needs more help than she used to."

Years before, his mother accidentally knocked a shotgun off a gun rack on the wall while moving some furniture around. The gun discharged, and the noise from the blast left Rena with a damaged eardrum. That had happened around the time of the boating accident with their dads. Just before or just after, she couldn't remember. Childhood memories from that period in her life tended to run together in an odd loop of images without context.

Jules felt guilty every time the subject of Mrs. Alderman's hearing came up because she'd once been caught mocking the woman in a store downtown. With a bunch of her friends, Jules imitated the way Rena cocked her head to one side so she could hear. It was a stupid thing just to get laughs, but Sam's mother had been standing in front of a store mirror, and she saw Jules behind her. The moment Jules made eye contact with Rena Alderman's reflection, she felt her whole body fire hot with embarrassment. The incident had never been mentioned, but Jules was pretty sure it had also never been forgotten.

"So, I'm taking off for a week or so to help Mom get the cottage opened up for the summer," Sam was saying.

"I thought you kept it open year round?"

"We do. The *opening* and *closing* of the season are more ceremonial than anything. We have to scrub down every inch of that place before Memorial Day, or she says she'll sell it."

"Can't let that happen," she said. Jules wondered if his memories of their frequent, clandestine visits to the cottage were still as vivid as hers.

"No." He smiled. He seemed to go shy for a second, looking away from her. "We certainly can't."

Yeah. He remembered.

The moment hung there briefly before he asked, "What happened to your foot?"

"I took a fall last week when I was out at Mount Canaan visiting Mom's grave. Really stupid. I feel like a rhino moving around in this thing."

He laughed. "You look like anything but a rhino, but I know it's a pain in the ass to wear that thing." He bent down toward her slightly, as if to share something confidential, but instead he asked, "Are you going to be around for a while?"

"I'll be taking some time to go through Mom's things. And I've picked up a little work in Wilmington. A couple of commercials and one TV show. I'll be here for a few more weeks, at least."

"You still work as a sound tech for movies?"

"Yeah," she said, not bothering to explain her job in any further detail than his assessment. No one really understood what she did, although to her, Foley work seemed the simplest of concepts.

"Well, if you're in town for work, we should grab dinner," he said. "Some great restaurants have opened in Wilmington and," he added, "I can show you my place."

"That'd be great." Okay. No new wife. She hoped not, anyway. She wondered what sort of invitation he meant to extend with that comment. Then, for the first time since she'd seen him standing there, she thought of the baby growing inside her. The baby seemed like a fairy tale, a lovely thought that had no bearing on reality. Very soon, in just months, it would dominate her world. Should she tell him? Too awkward for a grocery store encounter, she decided.

"I should get back," he said, as if sensing her thoughts shifting away from him. "Mom's always been a worrier, but she's getting worse. If I'm gone too long she'll have the law out looking in ditches for me."

It hit her again, the idea that her own mother no longer waited for her at the house. She *would not* get maudlin in the middle of the butter aisle. She had to think of something else.

"Try the key lime pie," she said, nodding toward the yogurt. "It's killer."

He picked up a couple of cartons and put them in his cart. She smiled, muttered a "Good to see you, Sam" before moving toward the frozen food section. The ache in her foot from standing, coupled with the creeping nausea in her gut from the baby, made her decide to microwave for at least one more night.

* * *

Jules negotiated the curves leading out to the house, hitting the brakes to avoid a deer with a fawn crossing the road. How many times had she driven that stretch of asphalt? She remembered one weekend when she decided to surprise her mother and come home during her junior year at Chapel Hill. She finished class early on Friday and left immediately for the drive to the coast. The interstate didn't go to Wilmington then, and the drive took the entire afternoon. She arrived the moment day tipped over into evening. When she pulled into the driveway, both Marnee's car and her old truck were under the carport. A newer car was parked behind them.

"Hey, Mom," she called when she came into the kitchen through the carport door.

"Jules!" Marnee sounded more startled than happy.

The oven was on and Jules smelled Marnee's roast chicken with lime baking inside it. A fainter aroma, some cake or pie that had been prepared earlier, lingered.

I wonder how she knew I was coming? The question went through Jules' thoughts so quickly, it almost didn't register, but it was immediately replaced by the realization that Marnee had company. She'd invited someone over for dinner, and judging from the man's jacket hanging on the back of a kitchen chair, the friend wasn't a woman. Marnee was on a date and Jules spoiled it.

"Did you try to call?" Marnee asked, coming from the den into the kitchen. Jules saw Mr. Harlow rising from the couch to follow Marnee. "I was at the grocery store for part of the afternoon, so I probably missed you."

"No, sorry," Jules said. "I thought I'd surprise you."

Marnee glanced back at Mr. Harlow. "Well then, you're a lucky girl," Marnee said, turning back to Jules and offering a hug. "Your favorite just happens to be in the oven."

At the time, Jules felt relieved that she hadn't ruined anything. Obviously from Marnee's reaction, no big plans had been in the works. Mr. Harlow came over for supper. Something casual. No big deal. That's what Jules saw at the time. After her initial surprise, Marnee acted like herself again, and that told Jules all she needed to know.

Later—years later—Jules of course realized she *had* interrupted something. Mr. Harlow, whose wife died when Jules was in high school, would have been a nice person for Marnee to have in her life. That night might have been the only effort Marnee ever made at an existence separate from her children. Walking in unexpectedly, Jules shined a glaring spotlight on her mother's attempt at a social life, and, inadvertently, made her mother choose. To Jules' knowledge, Marnee never invited a man friend over again.

She hadn't thought much about it over the years, but driving back from the grocery store, the memory stung her for the first time. How could she have not known? Worse yet, how could she ever sacrifice like that for the child she carried inside her? At thirty-eight, she felt too old to learn those tricks, and the baby would suffer for it. Just like Marnee before her, the baby would bear the brunt of Jules' shortcomings. Oh, God. She felt panic rising inside her.

Her last conversation with her mother had been about the baby. If Jules had known those were her final words with Marnee, she would have pressed for more advice. Some kind of guidance. But at least her mother seemed happy about the news. Jules had felt such relief that she left everything, all her questions, for a later time. Just after they talked, the two of them lay down for a nap. After that, everything changed for Jules.

The late afternoon had, again, turned hot, and she cracked her window, taking in the new-growth smell of all the trees. If someone asked her what "green" smelled like, that would be it. New leaves.

She thought of Sam Alderman, and wondered if his invitation to dinner and a tour of his place would still stand after she told him she was pregnant. Now *that* would be an awkward conversation.

As she rounded the bend in the road just past Mount Canaan, she saw the dark sedan in the middle of the driveway at her house. She didn't recognize the car and was doubly annoyed that it blocked her entrance into the carport. Probably somebody from the funeral home with Marnee's jewelry. She ought to be grateful if they were dropping it by and saving her a trip, so she parked on the road, got her groceries, and hobbled up toward two people, a man and a woman, standing on the porch.

"Hey," she said, making her way up the steps to the front door where they waited. They both wore dark suits, but she didn't think she'd seen either of them at the funeral home before. "Can I help you with something?"

"We'd like to speak with you for a few minutes," the guy said. When he spoke, she vaguely recognized him. Someone she'd gone to school with, she thought. The sun was in his face, and he squinted, looking past her and not making eye contact. The woman spoke up.

"I'm Detective Janaway," she said. "This is Detective Mills. We're from the police department."

Billy Mills. That was the guy's name. What the hell were two plainclothes police officers doing on her porch?

"I'm afraid we're going to have to ask you to answer some questions," the Janaway woman said. She looked at Jules with an expression that seemed like pure contempt. Since Jules didn't know her, she thought maybe the woman looked like that all the time. Some people had unfortunate faces. Then it dawned on her that something really might be wrong.

"Is it Lincoln?"

"Who?" Officer Janaway asked.

"Lincoln, my brother. Has something happened to him?" Jules didn't know why they would be coming to tell her anything about Linc, but she couldn't think of a better reason why they would be going all *NYPD Blue* on her porch.

"We don't know anything about your brother, Ms. Fuller," Janaway said.

Billy Mills made a little face. It was subtle, but definitely there, and Jules could quote his thoughts word for word. *Her brother's queer. I know that much.* That's what ole Billy was thinking. *Well, screw you, buddy.* She was getting generally pissed at both of them.

"What are you guys doing here?" she asked, sounding annoyed, but less annoyed than she actually felt.

"There have been some accusations that we need to question you about," Billy finally spoke up. "A kid . . . a minor," he corrected himself, "has alleged that you had inappropriate sexual contact with him."

"What!" Her first impulse was to laugh, but Billy—Detective Billy to her, she supposed—was clearly serious. "Are you *joking*? What kid?" She felt as though she should be protesting more, but it was too damn ridiculous to justify. "What kind of contact?"

"We just need to talk with you," the woman said, her demeanor softening a little. "There aren't any charges, yet. We need to sort through the allegations and figure out what really happened."

"Well, I wasn't around for whatever happened," she said. "And I don't think I should be going anywhere or saying anything without knowing exactly what's going on. Who's making the accusation?"

"You might want to get a lawyer," Janaway said, not answering Jules' question. "If you want to do that, we can set a time tomorrow for you to come in. That should give you time to find someone," Janaway said. "We can't go into specifics at the moment. And we're not arresting you."

"Why would you arrest me? The closest I've come to any kid since I've been here has been from the front of a classroom—with the teacher there. Oh, and then there was the kid who nearly ran over me with his bike." She lifted her bum foot. "That was pretty intimate."

"I understand that you're upset," Detective Janaway said, "but sarcasm isn't going to get this settled. Make the calls you need to make and then plan on coming down to the station—our offices are in the basement of City Hall—tomorrow morning at eleven. That okay?"

"Okay." The reprimand left Jules spent, and the woman was right. Getting pissed off and rude wasn't going to help. Someone had made a big mistake, and Jules needed to get it straightened out. "I'll be there tomorrow at eleven."

Janaway nodded, turned to leave. Billy followed behind her. Jules sat down on the porch swing. Shaking from the encounter, she stared out at the quiet yard. Flowers that Marnee had planted before she became too weak for yard work offered up color. Jules looked out at the road. Dust kicked up by the detectives' sedan lingered in the still air. And in the middle of the two-lane highway, Jules saw someone. A boy. He was watching her. She stayed completely still as if the kid might be a deer or a bird easily frightened by sudden motion. She stood up slowly, trying to decide if she should call out to him, but the second she was on her feet, he took off running, all her instincts confirmed. Soon he was well out of sight.

Had she imagined him? Maybe she'd lost her mind entirely. "I've got to find a lawyer," she mumbled to herself, going inside, melted groceries in hand.

She tried to think of someone to call. Of all the people that had offered help since her mother died, no one came to mind as a potentially lawyer-savvy individual. Her local relatives were the last people she'd want to hear about some crazy accusations made against her.

The only person she could think of who might be able to help was Sam. Before she ran into him at the store, she hadn't even known he was in town, and suddenly there seemed to be no one else. Funny, after spending three months with her mother, seeing the parade of church people and club ladies in and out of the house, there wasn't a single person besides Sam she truly believed capable of stepping up to help. Her few close girlfriends from high school had settled in Raleigh or Charlotte, maybe Atlanta. Lincoln had gone back to New York. She'd never been so alone.

She didn't have Sam's cell number, but she still knew the Alderman house phone by heart. Sam's mother answered, and the tone her voice took on after Jules identified herself suggested that the store mirror incident had not been forgotten by the half-deaf, but nevertheless formidable, Mrs. Alderman.

Chapter Three

Sam said good-bye to Jules, and before he had put the receiver back in place, his mother spoke up.

"You shouldn't get mixed up with that woman." Rena Alderman sat at the kitchen table. From the look on her face, Sam figured she had her whole speech prepared, and he'd have to suffer through it before he could make the phone call he'd promised to make for Jules. "What kind of mess has she gotten herself tangled up in now?"

"She just needs help with something," he said. "And if she wants to fill you in, I'm sure she'll call you personally." He took a breath, immediately regretting the way the words came out. "I'm sorry. I'm not getting *mixed up*, I promise. I'm doing a favor for an old friend. That's all."

"We both know she's not old, and you haven't been just 'friends' since middle school." She pushed her short hair back off her forehead, hunched forward and rested on her elbows, head cocked toward him so that she could take advantage of her good ear. Rena didn't look her age, he'd give her that much.

Except for hair that had gone more gray than auburn, she was the same imposing individual she'd been when he was a kid.

"I saw Jules in the grocery store a little while ago, and that's the only reason she even thought to call me. Besides, her mother just died. Cut her some slack, okay?"

"She's always been unstable, Sam. Everyone in that family had a screw loose except Marnee, and now she's gone. Without their mother to ground them, Jules and that brother of hers will probably head straight off the deep end. You don't need to be attached to her when that happens. You hear?"

He didn't know what to say. He certainly couldn't tell her that Jules had called to ask him if he knew a good criminal lawyer.

"What's so funny?" she asked.

"Nothing. Listen Mom, I'm thirty-nine years old and I should be able to help a friend—regardless of what kind of friend she is—without getting a lecture. Jules isn't unstable. She's unconventional by your standards, maybe, but in the big scheme of things, she's pretty damn normal."

"You don't need to curse."

"Sorry," he said, frustrated that, after twenty-plus years, he was still hearing the same broken record about Jules that he'd endured when he was in high school. "I know your opinions word for word, Mom, but they've never been mine. You need to leave this one alone, okay?"

She let out a long sigh. That meant she was done talking, but she wasn't happy about it. She got up and went into the other room. Fine. He had to deal with his own feelings about Jules' phone call. Why the hell *did* she need a criminal lawyer?

"I haven't done anything," Jules had told him, after she'd asked him to help her find someone. "But the police obviously think I did. I've got to talk with them tomorrow, and I really need to get in touch with a lawyer today."

"Let me think for a second," he said, his brain moving through a mental Rolodex of possibilities. "I have a friend who works for a firm. He handles land development issues, but he could maybe recommend someone." With his mother in the room, he tried to stay clear of the words "trouble" or "lawyer".

"Thanks, Sam. I promise I'll explain all of this to you soon. It's total bullshit, but it shouldn't be a phone conversation. And I really do need to deal with it right away."

"I understand," he said, even though he didn't understand any of it. "I'll see if my friend's still at the office. If not, I've got his cell. We'll get this sorted out."

"I'm sorry to put you to so much trouble. I just haven't kept up with anyone around here except my aunt and uncles—and they're the last people I want to call about this."

"Go have a glass of wine," he said. "I'll call you back when I have a number for you."

That had been the sum of their conversation. What the hell could have happened between the time she saw him in the grocery store and that phone call?

She wasn't unstable. His mother was wrong about that. But she *was* different. In high school, she wore skinny jeans, so tight the outline of a cigarette lighter showed in her side pocket. Everything else—cigarettes, gum, keys, lipstick, and money—she carried in that black velvet pouch tied to her belt loop. She hadn't looked or acted like anyone else and, God, he'd loved that about her—and he felt all the old stirrings at just the sight of her.

For three years running, sophomore to senior year, he rarely went five minutes without thinking of her, thoughts that invariably traveled the length of her, pausing with particular delight at the tattoo on her thigh. Most weekends, they would sit beside each other in church on Sunday. One week on the Fuller side of the church, the other on the Alderman side. On most Sundays, their bodies still hummed from the night before when, alone at the beach cottage, they'd been skin on skin for hours. At the time, Sam considered their visits to the cottage the holier of the two gatherings.

Standing before her in the grocery aisle, he once again pictured the tattoo—and the body that went with it. So much about her was the same: her wild hair, olive skin, and dark eyeliner. She wore a necklace that looked like some kind of talisman. She smiled, reached up and pushed a strand of disobedient curls behind one ear; and just at the moment he became tempted to consider her perfection, she pulled out a wadded-up napkin from her pocketbook and spat her gum into it. As she crammed the whole mess back in the overstuffed bag that hung over her shoulder, his brain said, *Jules.*

The woman represented everything he'd lost over the years. Everywhere he looked, pearls and Prada ruled the day. When was the last time he'd been with someone unpredictable? The fact that nothing came to mind told him so much. But life was never boring around Jules, and if she planned to stick around for a while, maybe she would shake him out of his complacent rut.

But everything he loved about her caused the rest of the town—especially Rena Alderman—to regard her with suspicion. People called her wild, but she wasn't. Not really. She just didn't give a shit what they thought. Maybe that was what they found so unforgivable in the end.

In the years since his time with her, he'd had one wife, countless girlfriends, and even more lovers. One thing he knew at thirty-nine that he hadn't known at eighteen . . . what he had with Jules—in body and mind—didn't happen very often. When they'd split up after going to college, he'd taken for granted that the feelings he'd had with her would be found again and again, in all his relationships. But he hadn't had the same thing since, not even with the woman he'd married.

He scrolled down the list of names on his phone until he saw his lawyer friend's number. He'd get her the help she needed with God-only-knew what kind of problem. Then one night soon, he'd meet her for dinner. That's all he had to think about for the foreseeable future. Then, in all likelihood, she'd get on a plane for California in another week or two, and they'd run into each other every five or ten years until they were both too old to remember being naked and seventeen.

Chapter Four

Jules felt like hell. She didn't know if it was the baby, a more general manifestation of grief, or, perhaps, the anxiety of being summoned to the police station, but something had her so nauseated she could barely sit up.

From the point in life she identified as her lowest, the world had gone into a free fall, proving her wrong. Given that, she didn't want to speculate on how bad it could get. *Inappropriate sexual contact.* Who could have said that? What did it even mean?

After the wave of sickness subsided a little, she made her way to the kitchen. The damn nuisance of her foot, even without the nausea, made the trip to the other room for tea barely worth the effort. She'd gone halfway when she heard someone coming up onto the porch. Looking out the window, she saw a boy, a young teenager, standing at the door. He had on jeans and a gray short-sleeved T-shirt. Straight, dark bangs stuck to his sweaty forehead. She couldn't tell if it was the same kid she'd seen in the road earlier.

He hadn't knocked, and he looked hesitant, as if he might change his mind and leave. Even with shadowed daylight that had begun tipping over to dusk, it was lighter outside than in, so she was able to get a view of him when he couldn't see her.

She decided against turning on the porch light. The sudden glare might frighten the bejesus out of him. She slowly opened the door, and he wore an expression that fell somewhere between extreme concern and abject terror.

"Can I help you?" she asked through the screened door.

He held up a piece of paper—from the looks of it, a sheet torn from a spiral-edged notebook. It was folded into a loose square. She opened the screened door slightly and he stepped back, still holding the note out.

"My friend asked me to bring it to you," he said, his voice shaking and high enough to be a girl's.

"Your friend?" She took the note. "Do I know this person?"

"He asked me to bring it," he repeated, not even trying to answer the question.

She wondered if this was the boy who'd said things about her. Had she ever seen his face before? She couldn't tell for sure. He looked like every other kid in the drama class, every other boy in the school practically. When had all boys under the age of twenty begun to look alike? A few stood out. The ones with sideburns and men's bodies, but this boy didn't fall into that category.

"Did you write this?" Jules asked as gently as she could manage. "And did you say some things about me to the police?"

"No, ma'am!" Abject terror won out, and he turned immediately and left. No Southern niceties to pave the way for that egress. An awkward encounter, at best. He took off on foot down the road, and she watched him go.

The phone in the kitchen rang, startling her, and she closed the front door and went back to answer it.

"Ms. Fuller?" a deep voice inquired from the other end of the line.

"Yes."

"Hunter Randleman here. I'm a lawyer. I think we have mutual friends once removed or something like that."

"Mr. Randleman," she said. The relief that went through her nearly brought tears. "Thank you for calling. I can't tell you how glad I am to hear your voice. I've got a problem and I don't even know exactly where it's coming from."

"Why don't you start from some logical point and tell me what you know."

"Well, all I know for sure is that some local kid has accused me of *inappropriate sexual contact*, whatever that means. I've got an appointment at the police department at eleven tomorrow."

"Well, that's certainly something to start with, isn't it?" He didn't sound alarmed. He was a man who talked to people all the time after they had talked with the police. "Go through everything you know step by step, and we'll get this sorted out."

She told him about her conversation on the porch with officers Mills and Janaway. When she was done, he said he'd be over the next morning and they could ride together to City Hall.

"One more thing," she said after plans for the morning were set. "How much do you charge? I have some money, but I'm not exactly rich."

"Listen," he said, "don't worry about it." The edges of his words softened out, the longer vowels suggesting that he was just a regular guy trying to do the right thing. "Honestly? This is interesting work, *and* you're innocent. I believe that. Both of those things make this case attractive for me. Besides, my friend in the firm here who gave me your number—a couple of months ago he saved me from a disastrous real estate deal. I owe him one. I'll go over my fees tomorrow. But one way or another, we'll make it okay for you."

She thanked him again and said good-bye, realizing that an awful lot depended on whether she could really trust Hunter Randleman. She remembered the boy with the note. She hadn't looked at it yet, and had forgotten to mention it to Randleman.

She opened the paper. Scrawled in pencil were words that made the situation even more confusing.

I'm sorry. I didn't mean to get you in any trouble. Your pretty and nice and I don't want anybody to think your bad. Your friend, Vick

Friend? Where the hell did this kid come off thinking she was his friend?

How could he spread all those lies and think she wouldn't be furious? She looked at the note again, and tried to figure out if it told her anything. Misuse of the possessives aside, it seemed literate enough. But the note and the sentiments wouldn't improve her case. Vick (why did the name sound familiar?) hadn't written, *I'm sorry I lied.* That would have been helpful. What he wrote could be interpreted in any way the authorities wished. *Vick.* The boy on the bike in the cemetery had talked about his brother—Vick. Both of them had to live nearby. She wondered if Vick *was* the kid who'd just been on the porch.

The room, the entire house, carried an eerie quiet, so devoid of sound that it became conspicuous. Los Angeles was never that silent; ambient noise always offered a soundtrack of voices, traffic, and, for the lucky, surf. For the first time ever, she felt uncomfortable in the house where she'd grown up. She needed someone with her. She needed Lincoln. Hunter Randleman said he believed her, but Lincoln was the only person on earth who would *know* down to his very bones that she didn't do anything with an underage boy.

But could she do that to her brother? Ask him to drop everything and come back? Lincoln had just gotten back to his life in New York, and he was going through the same grief over Marnee's loss that she was feeling. It wasn't fair to ask him to turn around and come back down. But she needed him. With Marnee gone, he was all she had to call family.

Jules and her big brother understood the best and the worst of each other's lives. When she'd told him about the baby, he'd only been concerned for her. He didn't once judge the screwup of getting pregnant with a total-mess-of-a-guy. On the flip side, Jules didn't judge Lincoln for drinking. Alcohol dulled the memory of painful episodes he'd endured with their father. She knew that.

And there was a lot of misery for him to forget. She remembered when she was a kid, about nine or so, which would have put Lincoln at twelve or thirteen, her mom had driven her home from a youth group meeting at the church. They came in the house, and Jules could smell the fish that her mother had fried for dinner hours before. As they were hanging their coats in the front closet, they heard a noise. Jules could still see her own small, red coat in her mother's hands, its journey to the coat closet interrupted by the sound of loud, steady thumping. The noise came from one of the back rooms of the house.

"What's that?" Jules asked her mom.

The look on her mother's face turned from confusion to fear as she dropped the coat and took off toward the noise.

"Get out," Jules heard her father say from inside her parents' bedroom. "Leave us alone." His voice was loud, but he wasn't really yelling. It was the way he sounded when he'd had too much beer.

"Stop it, Jack," her mother said, refusing to leave. "That's enough. Leave him be, now. You've been drinking. You're going to regret this."

"Get out," he repeated.

"I swear to God, Jack, I'll call the police if you don't stop."

Jules heard the door close, but she didn't hear any more thumping. Jules went into the hall closet near the room where her father, mother, and brother were. She waited and listened. But there were no more sounds. *What if Lincoln is dead?* It was the first time she'd considered how much emptier her life would be without her brother. The thought traveled back and forth through her mind until the door to the room opened again.

It seemed like a long time, but it wasn't, and when they all came out she felt a wash of relief, even though Lincoln looked like he'd been in a car wreck. He didn't go to school for the rest of the week after that. When she asked him what happened, he told her, "Braden Haley happened."

At the age of nine, she had no idea what the quiet, shy boy two grades older than Lincoln would have to do with their dad hitting her brother until the skin on his face and arms was more blue than white. It wasn't the first time Lincoln had taken a beating, but it was the worst. Even so, Lincoln had told her later, it *was* the first time it didn't matter. Ever since that day, the smell of fried fish made her sick.

She looked out from the kitchen and down the hall. It was hard to imagine that all of that had happened in the same rooms she saw around her. Unlike Lincoln, she'd cared about her father. But that didn't mean she was blind to the truth. The house had been a better place, a better *home*, after Jack Fuller died. And not for the first time, she wondered what kind of home she would make for her child.

She found the paper where she'd written down Hunter

Randleman's number. She'd call and give him the information about the boy on the porch. After that, she would call Lincoln and ask him to come back. God only knew what the next day would bring, but if Lincoln was in the house with her, it had to be better than the one she'd just had.

Chapter Five

Lincoln stared at the Maker's Mark bottle that sat beside the empty tumbler near his kitchen sink. He kept the bottle and the glass visible, not as temptation, but as a perverse reassurance that if he *had* to, he could pour himself a shot at any time; that he was in control of his own destiny, even if that meant destroying it.

He looked around. Though he'd had over nine months to adjust, the apartment seemed hollow, still, without Tanner there. A place where someone used to live. Maybe he'd been away too much in that time to fashion it back into a comfortable life. First he'd gone to Los Angeles to work and stay with Jules. Then he'd been back and forth to North Carolina to be with Marnee. This last year, he was little more than a squash ball sent flying by the angle of the wall as he slammed against it. He looked at the bottle again and laughed. He wasn't in control of a damn thing.

Even so, he managed to keep the urges at bay—for the most part. There had been just a little to get him through the worst of it with Marnee, and a little more before the funeral. His doctor laid down the law about what would happen if he kept up the drinking. But those last days with Marnee were too much for him to handle without taking the edge off.

Oh, God, he wanted a drink. He stared at the bottle, listened to his doctor's voice running in a loop inside his head.

"This isn't a maybe," Dr. Lange told him. "It *will* kill you if you don't stop—and not at some ripe old age. You're heading toward alcoholic hepatitis. If that goes full-blown, you'll be a sick man, Lincoln."

He stepped away from the counter. Went to the other side of the room. He could do it. He'd kept sober on the plane ride between North Carolina and New York, hadn't he? And an evening flight, no less, when it was almost a reflex to hand the flight attendant a five-dollar bill in exchange for the blessed liquid. And in the three nights since he got back home—not a drop.

In some ways, it helped that nothing seemed familiar to him in a post-Tanner, post-Marnee world. Even the colors and the smells were different somehow. He'd heard that if you wanted to break a behavior, the best way was to make your world less familiar. Do anything to avoid old patterns. With everything around him changed, giving up the booze should be easier. But the currents of compulsion were building again, and he could feel them gathering force.

He reminded himself that, unlike Marnee, Tanner wasn't dead. Tanner, who refused to listen to his rationalizations about drinking. Tanner, who saw through all his bullshit. Tanner, who, of the two of them, was the lively one, the one counted on to be fun. And still, he managed to steer clear of addiction. Lincoln marveled at the ability of anyone to stop short of *needing* a drink.

Tanner was gone before Lincoln's discussion with Dr. Lange. Before Marnee's illness. All in all, nearly everything Lincoln cherished disappeared in the space of those nine months—his health, his mother, and his lover. That left him with Jules and music. Those two should be enough to make him continue getting up every morning, but he wasn't sure. And then, there was Jules' baby. He had to factor in impending unclehood. His mother would have loved having a baby in her life. Timing was everything, and the timing of her demise sucked—for so many reasons.

Marnee's diagnosis had come close on the heels of September 11. It was only May and she was already gone. September 11 and Marnee's news—the two were forever linked in his thoughts. He'd been in California with Jules when he saw the smoking towers on television. He'd been frantic to reach Tanner, who'd moved out of their apartment only the month before.

"I'm not going to watch you kill yourself," Tanner had told him. "I won't do it."

Tanner saw Lincoln's problems before anyone else. Before the awful conversation with Dr. Lange. Even before Jules realized it, Tanner knew that Lincoln was destroying himself. Angry and too proud to give in, Lincoln let him leave. Before going to California, Lincoln hadn't talked to his partner of ten years since the day Tanner came to get the last of his things from the apartment. Then, with New York in flames and Tanner's office just blocks from the Twin Towers, Lincoln had never felt so helpless. Finally, after an agonizing twenty-four hours, he got a text message.

HOPE THIS GETS THROUGH. I'M FINE. T

Lincoln was drunk when the message arrived, and he'd barely sobered up when Marnee called a day later with bad news from her medical tests. The world he'd known before that week seemed like someone else's life.

"Hey, Fluff." One of his two cats came into the kitchen, curled around his ankle, and then hopped onto the table. Fluffernutter was her given name, after the marshmallow cream and peanut butter sandwiches he'd loved as a kid. "Where's your partner in crime?" As he looked around the room for Jezebel—they usually traveled as a pair—his cell phone rang and he saw Jules' name on the caller ID.

"Hey. What's up?"

Her silence on the other end of the line made him stop his hunt for the stray cat and focus on the call. "Jules?"

"How are you feeling?" she asked. Her voice carried a strange, defeated quality. He wondered what could have happened.

"I'm okay," he said slowly. "No worse than yesterday when I talked with you. Jules, what's going on?"

"I know you've only been home a couple of days, Lincoln," she said, "and you've got your own stuff to deal with, but . . ." She stopped, let out a sigh as if building the courage to go on. "I need you. I'm sorry. It's terrible to ask you to fly back down here, but . . ."

Is it Mom? The question almost came out. It had been the dominant question every time she called over the preceding months. But he stopped himself, suffered as he realized all over again that, as far as his mother was concerned, the worst news had already come and gone. "What's happened?" he asked instead. He wondered if she'd lost the baby.

"Some kid," she said, "started a rumor. One of the kids in that drama class I visited . . . anyway, this kid says that I . . ." She stopped again.

"Jules?"

"He's told people that I had sex with him. Or something," she clarified. "*Inappropriate sexual contact.* That's what the police said."

"The police? Holy shit, are you kidding? Why the hell would anyone say something like that?"

"I have no idea." Her voice shook. "Two plainclothes cops— some woman and that guy from high school, Billy Mills—were here when I got back from the grocery store."

"I knew that kid's older brother. A real prick."

"Yeah, well, the nuts fell all together under that tree," Jules said.

"So have you been arrested?" Lincoln asked. Could they even do that just because a kid *said* something?

"No," she told him. "They're investigating his story now. This is crazy, Lincoln. I couldn't pick any one of those kids out of a crowd. Not if you paid me. I don't know any more than that right now. I was pissed as hell talking to those cops on the porch, but the one who told me about it was actually pretty nice considering that she probably really believes I'm a pedophile. She suggested I get a lawyer before I talk with them. But I have to go down to the station . . . Sounds like dialogue out of a B movie, doesn't it? *Down to the station.*"

"Do you know a lawyer?" Lincoln said, trying to orient her to the situation. "This can't go very far. I mean, it's bullshit, but you do need a lawyer."

"I ran into Sam Alderman at the grocery store," she said. There was a pause, giving him time to comment, but he let it go. If she wanted to stir things up with an old boyfriend, that was her business.

When he didn't say anything, she went on, "So after the two cops left, I called Sam to see if he knows anybody. He got me in touch with a lawyer in Wilmington. That's where Sam's living now. The guy, he's a criminal lawyer, he just called me. He's coming in the morning to go with me to talk to the police."

"Can we afford him?"

Lincoln ran through his finances in his head. He'd postponed New York performances and canceled touring dates to be with Marnee. Although his work on a couple of recent movie soundtracks helped a lot, New York was expensive, and his money wouldn't hold out forever.

"Hunter, that's the lawyer's name, he said not to worry," she told him. "He told me we'd make it work."

"Okay." Lincoln began a mental list of things he needed to do if he was going to leave again. Poor cats; he glanced down at Jezzie and Fluff, both circling his legs. "Let me see how soon I can get down there. I'll call you back after I've booked a flight. Just hang in there. This has to get straightened out pretty easily. I mean, no one can think something like this really happened. No one who's known you for more than five minutes, anyway."

She was quiet. He might have thought they'd lost the connection, but he could hear her breathing. "Lincoln?" she finally spoke.

"Yeah?"

"I want Mom." She sounded like a kid.

"I know," he said, feeling his throat thicken. "I do, too. But you've got me. That'll have to do."

"That'll do," she said.

He could tell she was crying, but she mumbled some version of good-bye and hung up before he could say any more.

"Damn it to hell," he said to himself as he headed toward his computer to book a flight back to Wilmington.

Chapter Six

Hunter Randleman wasn't a lot taller than Jules, but a lean energy lent him the command of more than his share of space in the sparsely furnished interrogation room. He was about her age, but carried less body fat than a cheetah, with the hungry look of a compulsive runner. Jules found his intensity unnerving.

"Okay, what prompted this investigation? Exactly what are we dealing with here?" Randleman took charge of the discussion the moment they sat down at a long table that claimed the entire middle section of the room. Detectives Mills and Janaway sat across the table, the two of them flanking an older man who introduced himself as Sergeant Stands.

Janaway explained that an investigation was under way because a boy from the high school had told some of his friends at school and online that he'd been "doing it" with someone he described as "that California drama teacher," and adults had gotten wind of it.

"The boy made claims to friends when they were in gym class," Janaway said. "He then repeated the claim in an e-mail.

The alleged victim's parents called the department when the mother of another boy saw the e-mail and alerted them. We have copies from both boys' computers."

Jules felt invisible, the way she'd felt during parent-teacher meetings when she was a kid. People talked about her, but she was the least relevant presence in the room. How could she become somebody's mother when at any given moment she could still feel like such a kid?

"Are there any charges being brought against my client?" Randleman's query wasn't combative, but more in the tone of a mild inquiry. The fact that he framed the question in normal tones alarmed her. Could they actually be thinking of arresting her? Neither detective appeared to go on the defensive.

"Not at this time," Mills said, looking through several papers he had in his hands.

"The boy's meeting with a child psychologist. We're trying to determine his credibility before we take it any further."

Well, that was reassuring. Jules was shaking. The idea that they were deciding whether to *charge* her with a crime . . . That notion became all too real. In their minds, the purpose of the meeting wasn't simply to clear up a misunderstanding. Her trip to the station was part of a legitimate investigation. What a nightmare.

"Ms. Fuller?" Detective Janaway looked at Jules.

"It's okay to answer," Hunter said, nodding his encouragement.

"I'm sorry. I didn't hear the question," she said, wondering how long she'd been lost in her own thoughts. The nerves in her throat signaled nausea coming on. Throwing up would not impress anyone at this point. It occurred to her that she probably should have told Hunter she was pregnant.

"Have you routinely spent individual time with any of the students in the drama classes? Any private instruction or other opportunities that might offer confusion on the boy's part?"

"It's kind of hard to confuse having sex with anything else, don't you think?" Jules couldn't believe they were asking her if she gave a kid mixed signals. A *kid*! Could they actually think that?

Billy Mills let out a small groan, and she realized she looked like a real wise-ass.

"I . . . I didn't mean to . . ." She sounded guilty, even to herself. "The answer is no. I've never been alone with any of them. Boys or girls. I was in front of the classroom talking most of the time. Then they would split up into groups of three or four, and I would do sound demonstrations with each group."

"Sound demonstrations?" Detective Janaway asked. Beside her, Sergeant Stands listened. He'd barely mumbled two words.

"That's what I do for a living," she said. "I work in a studio that puts appropriate sounds into movie tracks." The faces around her registered no understanding.

"For instance," she continued, "if a guy on a bike runs into an open car door in a movie, they'll film the stunt guy doing it, but the actual *sounds* he makes when doing it don't come across, at least not in the way the audience thinks it should sound. In a studio, I figure out how to replicate the sounds that an audience will expect, and then I dub that sound in the movie to correspond with that scene."

They appeared less confused, but no more convinced that this was any way for an adult woman to spend her time.

"Anyway," she tried to get back on track, "on the days I worked with the kids, we took regular objects and tried to make sounds, then figured out what those sounds might correspond with in a movie. We did it in groups, so I never had any one-on-one work with any of the kids."

"Did you work with a boy named Vick Johns?" Sergeant Stands asked.

Hunter had the boy's note in his folder—Jules' case folder.

She looked over at him to get some guidance as to whether she should tell them about the boy on the porch.

"Ms. Fuller had a visitor at her door yesterday," Hunter said, again taking charge. "A boy who gave her a note from someone named Vick. It's my understanding—correct me if I'm wrong," he said, turning to look at Jules, "but as I understand it, Ms. Fuller didn't recognize the boy on the porch. He denied being the one who had made the allegations, but she doesn't know if he was telling the truth or not. In other words, it could have been this Vick individual, but he said he wasn't."

"And you would not recognize this boy, even if you'd taught him in a classroom?" Stands asked.

"I might if I saw him," she told him. "But I didn't know the boy on my porch. I just don't know."

Stands nodded. Janaway and Mills sat silently. Now that the sergeant had weighed in, they both seemed inclined to let him handle it. "What did the note say?"

Hunter took it out of the file and laid it on the table. It was upside down, but she could still make out the now familiar words in that ragged-looking handwriting.

I'm sorry. I didn't mean to get you in any trouble. Your pretty and nice and I don't want anybody to think your bad. Your friend, Vick

The three of them leaned over, reading the grammar-challenged missive.

"I wish this told us something one way or the other," Stands said. "But it doesn't."

They were once again talking about the situation as if Jules wasn't there. She said she didn't know the boy, and no one gave a damn. It seemed to her that, as an advocate, Hunter Randleman should have been protesting her innocence.

Jules remembered seeing a blond teacher on television, the one from Oregon, or maybe it was Washington, arrested for having sex with her student. The teacher said she was in love with the boy. Her speech and her mannerisms were those of an adolescent girl, but she was in her thirties. Women who did this sort of thing acted like children themselves. Jules wasn't like that. Wasn't it obvious?

"We'll have a report from the psychologist in a couple of days," Stands was saying. "Maybe sooner. Ms. Fuller, stay close by. At this point, I don't have any reason to keep you here."

The air caught in her throat and she heard herself phonating something, although no one seemed to notice. *Here?* He meant locked up? The whole situation was insane. Couldn't they simply look at her and see that she wouldn't seduce a teenage boy? Why the hell would she do something like that? Even if—as everyone in her hometown seemed to think—she existed outside the norm, there was an awfully long stretch of road between a free spirit and a pedophile. She felt light-headed.

"Are you in line with this, Ms. Fuller?" the sergeant said. "Will you agree to stick close by until we get this sorted out?"

"Yes, sir," she said, her voice barely there.

"Good." He stood up and his minions followed suit.

They left Jules alone in the room with Hunter, and when the others were clearly out of earshot, he said in low tones, "This is good. Really good."

She failed to see how the word "good" could apply to anything that had gone on in that meeting.

"Why?"

"Because," he said, "they're letting you go home. If they had hard evidence—hell, if that old guy even had a strong gut feeling that you'd done this—he'd find some way to keep you here. He doesn't want you in jail. That means, his instinct is telling him you didn't do a damn thing. We're going to be okay here. He's just got to make sure he covers his ass before he drops it. Otherwise he'll get himself fired."

Hunter's entire demeanor had changed since the meeting ended. He'd once again gone from lawyer-speak to the relaxed, good ole boy cadences indigenous to her corner of the world.

"Let me buy you a sandwich," he said. "Hell, I'll buy you a beer. What's good around here?"

She felt like empty skin. Every possible emotion had gone through her in the course of an hour or two, and suddenly she felt nothing—except a little sick to her stomach, again.

"There's a grill just down the street," she said. "If I can stand the smell of hamburger grease, the food is pretty good."

"Not a grease fan?" He stood up and gathered his papers together. "I consider it a food group."

"My appetite hasn't been normal," she said, "not since I got pregnant," she said, then waited, still sitting.

He sat back down. "Well, that's a wrinkle, isn't it?"

"I found out just before I left LA to come here and take care of my mother."

"And the baby's father?" he asked.

"No one I want to be in touch with anymore."

"Does he agree? Does he want for you to have the baby alone?" Hunter seemed to be organizing a file in his head. One question built on the next without any show of surprise or judgment.

"He doesn't know," she said. "And I don't want him to."

"Why?" And still, he simply asked, indicating no opinion on the matter.

She wondered if she was obligated to tell him. As her lawyer, he was bound to confidentiality. If the bizarre accusations went anywhere, Thomas could hear about the baby whether she liked or not. She thought about the awful, viral news stories that ran incessantly when teachers got caught with young boys. It brought her heart into her throat. Then again, maybe it was baby nausea again. Either way, the whole thing had to end soon and quietly, and the best way to ensure that was to let Randleman do his job.

"The baby's father is a man named Thomas," she said. "He's a screenwriter—and he's bipolar. I didn't know anything about his condition until he had a manic episode that scared the shit out of me. I went to see his ex-wife and she filled me in on his problem. She said he gets stubborn periodically and goes off his meds. He's shoved her around—more than once. Not really hitting, she told me. Just out of control. He never got violent with me, but there was some strange behavior along the way. And then one final incident." She shook her head. She wished she could shake the memories out. Just thinking of it made her nervous. "So I broke it off. If I'd been solid in love with the guy, I might've stayed and tried to make it work, but I wasn't. After I left him, I found out about the baby. Then I came here."

"Damn," Randleman said, shaking his head. "I'm going to be worth every penny you pay me—and then some." His expression suggested that, if anything, Jules had added an additional bit of fun to the mix. At least the man seemed to enjoy his work. "Come on. We'll scratch the beer idea, but let's go see what you can eat."

The basement of the police department building was a maze of halls. As they navigated their way out, they passed a woman sitting on a bench. She looked at Jules as they walked by and then, just as they passed, spat at Jules' foot.

"Jesus!" Jules shifted sideways, saw the blob of saliva on the floor. "Are you crazy?"

"That's my boy in there. They've got him talking with a head doctor, thanks to you," she said. "And I know who you are. You were ahead of me in school, and lately, you've been at Daddy's church with your sick momma."

Preacher Walker's daughter. Jules saw it then. She was a few years younger than Jules, but her face had a hard look about it. The large, tired eyes and uneven tone in her cheeks suggested that life, rather than age, had been her enemy.

"You may have seen me," Jules said, "but I promise you, I don't know your son."

Hunter had put himself between Jules and the woman, but the boy's mother made no move to stand up. Jules suddenly thought of the worst-case scenario. *Enraged mother of violated son goes berserk and shoots pregnant teacher who seduced her child.*

"I thought it was nice of you, staying with your momma like that," the woman said. "Well, I don't think you're nice anymore. How could you take advantage of a young boy? He's a child, for heaven's sake."

"Like I said, I don't even know your son." Jules recognized almost everyone at Mount Canaan Baptist. Marnee had been a fixture in that church forever, and Jules went to services with her mother whenever she visited. This woman and her son had not been there, not until recently. "Have you been going to your daddy's church all these years? I don't remember seeing you until this spring."

The question seemed to take the woman off guard. "I've been living outside of Myrtle Beach until this year," she said. "I married right out of high school and moved there with my husband, but he died just under a year ago. I came here with my boys in January to live with my brother, near Momma and Daddy. We're living with Walt. Walt and Tuni, his wife."

A typical Southern exchange; even in the heat of an argument, an extended frame of reference had its place. Jules had seen Walt Walker at church over the years. He'd started out a typical, rebellious preacher's kid. He was just ahead of her in school. His wife, Tuni, wasn't from Ekron. Marnee used to comment on the name, saying it must be short for Petunia because she'd never heard of anyone called that before.

"My Vick is a good Christian kid," the boy's mother said, trying to regain her momentum after getting sidetracked.

"I'm sorry, remind me of your name?" Jules asked, hoping to get her talking again. A conversation might lead to some insights about the kid.

"Cici. Used to be Cici Walker. Now Cici Johns."

"Cici," Jules continued. "I don't know why your son would say the things he's saying. I'm sure he's a *fine* kid. But I didn't do anything. I don't even remember talking with him."

"Then why did he come home saying you're going to help him be a movie star?"

Because he's delusional. "I don't know. I talked with a lot of kids in the drama class, and I tried to encourage them. I guess he heard what he wanted to hear. I'm a sound artist. I'm not friends with any movie stars."

Sergeant Stands came down the hall. "I think it's best if you ladies refrain from discussing things until we get a better idea of what's going on," he said. "You agree, Mr. Randleman?" He looked down, saw the glob of spit and made a face.

"We were on our way out, Sergeant," Hunter said.

"My boy's a good boy," Cici Johns said again, ignoring the attempt by the men to wrap up the interaction. She stared only at Jules' face. "He's a junior leader in his Baptist youth group, and he gets all A's and B's at school. You come here from Hollywood, getting him all stirred up with your tattoos and your tight jeans."

"Listen, lady . . ." Jules had had enough. She wanted to say that she hadn't touched the little son-of-a-bitch. "You don't have any business accusing me . . ." Before she finished, she felt Hunter pulling her away. Stands had walked over to the boy's mother.

"You don't have any idea what it's like to be a mother." Cici ignored Jules' protests. "You try to look out for a child's best interest. You raise them, and protect them with your whole heart, and then somebody comes along and takes all their innocence away before they're even grown. You don't know the first thing about how that feels. If you took that boy's innocence, you'll go to jail, you hear?"

"Come on," Hunter said, guiding Jules toward the exit sign down the hall. "Let it go for now."

"You're not a mother," Cici shouted as she walked away. "You don't have a child. You only have yourself and that's all you can think of."

Jules followed Hunter, pissed as all hell. Not because of Cici's words, but because she let them get to her. *You only have yourself and that's all you can think of.* Was that crazy woman right? Jules only knew how to be the protected child. How could she possibly be a mother herself?

I'm the one who's been wronged here. She had to keep reminding herself of that. She did nothing to the boy and he made up lies. He was crazy, and the mother no better. She felt like going back to tell this to the still-ranting Cici Walker, but the situation wasn't going to be settled by challenging the kid's mother to a girl-fight at the police station.

As they came out into the daylight, she took a breath, tried to stop herself from trembling. Sensing that the crisis had passed, her arms and legs went weak.

"Jules," Hunter said, taking a deep breath, "tell me you don't have any tattoos."

"What?"

"The woman mentioned tattoos. Do you have any?" He pulled a pack of Newports from his pocket and lit up a smoke.

"One," she said. "On my thigh." As she said it, she could see the boy on the bike staring at her leg after she fell. And the kid's brother was Vick—Vick of the composition paper note. That much of it made sense.

"Have the kids in the class had any occasion to see your tattoo?" he asked.

"No," she told him, feeling so tired all of a sudden, "But that woman's other son, a younger one, nearly ran me over with his bike. That's how I ended up with this." She raised up her braced foot. "He saw the tattoo when I fell."

"Well, let's assume the younger kid will admit that he told his brother about it," Hunter said. "You don't manage to take the easy route with anything, do you?"

"Julie Marie!" She heard her brother's voice call from down the street.

"Thank God," she said, going toward him as fast as her bad foot would allow.

He looked tired and his color was off, but Jules shoved the worry out of her mind as she made headway in his direction.

He stood by a rental car.

"My favorite felon," he said, when she reached him. He smiled down at her and let her hug him.

As she stood there on a street she'd known for her entire life, the pieces of her world began to form into a whole picture again. For the first time, she entertained the notion that everything—everything from this ridiculous situation with the boy to her impending motherhood—just might turn out okay, after all.

Hunter had driven her into town. He left her with an assurance that things were going in the right direction and a promise to check in the next day.

Riding back out to the house with Lincoln, she looked carefully at her brother, and tried to determine if he looked worse than when he'd left to go back to New York just days before.

"How are you?" she asked. "Really."

"I don't know," he told her. His voice was without the flippant dismissal of the subject she expected. "No worse. At least I don't think so. But I'm so damn sad about Mom, it's hard to tell why I feel awful."

"What does your doctor say?" She felt suddenly afraid. If he admitted to any uncertainty about his health, it meant things weren't good.

"I actually told him a bit of a fib a while back," Lincoln said, not looking at her.

"What?" She felt her heart racing.

"I told him I'd lined up a doctor here while Mom was sick. He thinks somebody in Wilmington is on top of things. He keeps bugging me for the records from here. Truth is, I have no idea what my bloodwork is like at the moment."

She didn't yell at him. She never yelled at him. They dealt with problems from the point of admission. No questions asked. No guilt trips allowed.

Without another word, she called Sam and made plans to meet him for lunch the next day. She wanted to explain about her unexpected crisis, anyway, and thank him for getting her in touch with Hunter. Lincoln's problem simply added another favor to the list.

"I've got some stuff to finish up at a studio in Wilmington," she told Sam. "I thought we could meet someplace before I head off to work and I could buy you lunch. My way of saying thanks for your help."

"Sure," he said. "It's a date." An awkward silence followed for both of them at his choice of words, but he recovered with a restaurant suggestion. "I know a little place on a salt marsh this side of Wilmington. Soul food. You'll love it." He told her how to get there, and it sounded easy enough to find.

When she got off the phone, Lincoln looked over at her and raised his eyebrows.

"Don't say it," she told him. "He's a doctor. He'll know somebody. *And*, I'm buying him lunch to thank him for his help with the lawyer—and for his help with this. That's all I'm doing."

"That may be all it takes," he said, looking ahead at the road. Then he added. "But thank you."

"You're welcome," she said, turning her gaze out the window to watch the familiar landscape of her town go by.

Chapter Seven

"So how's your foot?" Sam asked just after he and Jules sat down for lunch.

"Better," she said. "I can put weight on it now."

They sat at a porch table, outside a bistro called Jess's Place. It was an old house that had been converted to a restaurant. Sam liked the fact that the dining room and porch overlooked a tidal marsh, making the place seem far away from the city, though there was a shopping mall less than a mile away. High tide had peaked, so that the water in and around the sea grass caught the sun, lending an impressionistic quality to the view.

There was something different about Jules. Her clothes. For as long as he could remember she'd worn fitted jeans and tops that hugged her small frame. But for their lunch, she'd chosen a loose shirt; it looked like a man's button-down, with pants that were at least a size too big. Maybe she wanted to send him a signal of some sort.

"So you're finishing up some work?" he asked, tackling the lull in conversation after they'd settled in their chairs.

"Yeah, I need to put in a couple of hours on this one thing. I got behind when things got really bad with Mom."

Jules told him on the phone that she had the Foley studio booked in Wilmington that afternoon. She wanted to know if he could meet her for lunch before she went into town. Her invitation somehow sounded more substantive than social, and he wondered what her agenda might be. Part of him hoped that her motivations were entirely personal, but maybe it was a little of both—although her outfit didn't exactly scream seduction.

She hadn't filled him in on her crisis from the day before, but he'd heard a lot about Jules' problems that morning from everyone else. The accusations from the boy seemed ridiculous to him. He couldn't imagine anyone taking them seriously, but the people in town he'd overheard acted as if she'd been tried and convicted.

At the gas pump, in the grocery aisles, at the library . . . Every errand he ran for his mother, people were talking about how Jules Fuller had gotten herself tangled up with some young boy.

"I guess with Marnee gone," he overheard one woman say, "she's decided to just show her true colors."

What the hell did that mean? That she'd always been a closet pedophile, but kept it under wraps for her mother's sake? People didn't say anything directly to him about Jules, but they damn well made sure he was in earshot if at all possible, then looked at him with a sideways glance to catch his reaction. Most of the time, he'd let things go, but the statement about Jules' "true colors" was so outrageous that he ended up telling the woman that, unless the judicial system had been entirely rewritten, someone had to actually be charged and found guilty before they could be labeled a criminal.

"Samuel," the woman replied, "you can't be faulted for the mess your friend has made of her life, but don't go around fighting her battles. We all know that Rena's never liked that girl.

You'll break your momma's heart if you start making a fool of yourself over Jules Fuller again."

Again? "When exactly would you like for me to schedule time for you with Jules, Mrs. Dukes?" he'd asked.

"What do you mean?"

"So she can fight her own battle with you, ma'am," he said. "Will tomorrow work for you?"

She walked away without another word, but he imagined that his mother had gotten an earful by the time he got home.

All of this went around and around in Sam's head and he waited to see if she would talk about the kid, about the accusations. But she took a sip of water, and squinted into the sun.

He decided that it might be easier for her if he brought it up, so after the waiter's arrival with her tea and the arranging of various lemons and sugars on the table, Sam asked, "How did things work out with the lawyer?"

"You saved the day by getting me in touch with that guy," she said. "Hunter Randleman is his name." She paused, took a breath, then dove back in. "One of the kids at the high school where I've helped out in the drama class—a boy—has been making up stories about me, saying I . . ." She stopped, couldn't even finish the sentence.

"I heard," he told her. "The preacher's grandson." He wouldn't make her go through the ordeal in detail. He kept his voice low. "So why the hell is he saying all this?"

"That's the big question," she said. "I don't know where it's coming from. I guess I've worked with the boy in that class, but I don't remember anything special about my interaction with him. Nothing that would get him started on this kind of fantasy." She fiddled with the edge of the tablecloth. "It seems crazy to even say it out loud. Yesterday was surreal. He put it in an e-mail, for Christ's sake. I don't know why he would make up something like that."

He put his hand on her arm. "I'm sorry this is hitting you now, so soon after your mom." Kind of an idiot thing to say. When *was* a good time to be accused of pedophilia? "What does his regular drama teacher say about it?"

"Remember Mrs. Compton?"

"Our Latin teacher? She's teaching drama now?" he said. "She has to be a hundred years old."

"Give or take a year or two," Jules told him. "Anyway, she's nice enough, but she remembers me as one of the wild kids. In her mind, I *am* still a kid. I haven't talked with her, but I doubt she's doing me any favors with the police."

Sam could feel her arm trembling and when she looked at him, he saw her jaw set in an angry effort to keep her emotion in check. He didn't know what to say.

"What I really don't understand," she said, "what I can't *fathom*, is why the hell anyone would take it seriously."

"People love gossip. That's probably the bulk of it."

"This isn't even gossip," she said. Her fingers moved, thumb rubbing over her nails as if she needed constant motion to manage the outrage. "This is some kid's fantasy," she said, shaking her head. "And believe me, most of the boys in freshman drama haven't finished puberty. The idea is too ridiculous to justify with denial, but I've had to hire this lawyer. It's really a nightmare. Thanks to you I at least *have* a lawyer."

He wanted her to calm down. She'd flushed red, nervous energy keeping her body in a constant small rocking motion.

"Everybody's heard about it," she said. The statement itself implied defeat. "The records are confidential because he's a minor, but it doesn't matter." Her tone implied defeat. "First, I guess it was all over the high school and then made its way to the parents. They haven't even talked about charges yet, but I had to go to the post office this morning and people were whispering when I went by—and then refusing to make eye contact when I looked at them. They all think I ought to be in jail. The kid's mother spat at me at the police station."

"She *spat* at you? Are you sure?"

"Oh, yeah. She didn't have enough firepower for a direct hit, but there was no mistaking the intended target." She stopped, smiled as if just comprehending the humor of that image. The preacher's daughter sending a missile of saliva her way with her Wilmington lawyer looking on in horror. "If I'd returned fire," she said, "the woman would have been toast."

She pushed her hair back off her damp forehead. With her arm raised, her shirt lifted a little, and Sam caught a glimpse of elastic panel on the front of her pants. Was she wearing maternity pants?

"You've seen me in action," she said. "Remember?"

"Yeah right," Sam recovered, dismissing the thought. "I've seen you with a wad of chew in your mouth trying to keep up with the big boys. You couldn't hit a wall at two paces."

"I wasn't mad enough then." She was still smiling.

She had a great smile. She smiled with her whole face—dark eyes and white teeth.

"And I'm not entirely sure I was sober," she added.

She wasn't. He remembered that much. One of his baseball buddies had a bottle of Jack Daniel's, contraband from his parents' cabinet. Between the chew and the liquor, they'd all ended up sick.

"If I'm thoroughly pissed off," she said, "I can nail a tin can at ten feet."

"I'll take your word for it."

They were laughing, then the moment settled into an awkward lull. It felt weird, how they could ease into such familiarity, then two sentences down the line, be back to near strangers.

"I don't even know how long I'll have to stay," she said, as much to herself as to him. "I can't go to California until everything's settled. My whole life is stuck here in this bizarre mess."

The waiter brought their food. Sam watched a small motorboat navigate through the tidal creek before disappearing behind the tall reeds of sea grass. He tried to think of something, *anything*, to say that would be helpful, but nothing came to mind beyond the obvious platitudes. She deserved better than that.

"So that's it," she said, picking up her sandwich, a roll filled with barbecued pork made fat with mounds of slaw. "You wanted to know and I told you. Now we talk about something else."

"Last question," he said.

"Okay," she said.

"Are you okay on money?" They'd had a total of four conversations in a decade's time. The question was too personal, but he asked it anyway. If nothing else, she needed a friend.

"Thanks for asking," she said, to his relief, not offended. "I'm okay for now. I've sublet my place in LA through the end of the month, and she'll take it longer if I let her. I've been able to pick up work here. Your lawyer friend's lawyer friend is great. I'm not exactly a charity case, but he's not making much off this. Especially considering what a train wreck it is. And Lincoln said he will pitch in if I need it."

"Well, I don't think any of us should start feeling sorry for the lawyers of the world, but I'm glad he's working out. And money . . . if you start to run short . . ."

"Thank you." Her tone suggested the end of that topic. He watched her give up on holding the enormous sandwich. She took it apart and ate the shredded meat with her fork. "But listen," she said, swallowing a mouthful before she continued, "I do have a medical question to ask you. Another favor really."

"Shoot."

"What do you know about hepatitis?" She held her fork midway between her mouth and her plate.

Oh, God, Sam thought. *Does she have hepatitis on top of every-*

thing else? "Infectious?" he asked, trying not to sound alarmed.

She shook her head. "Alcohol-related," then added, "it's Lincoln. He's got a lot of fatty tissue in his liver and they say he's at risk. The diagnosis came a few months ago and he'd been under someone in New York. But then he dropped the ball on his follow-up while Mom was sick. He's stopped drinking . . . at least I hope he's stopped entirely . . . but he needs to be followed by a doctor, and now I've dragged him back down here to help me through this."

"I know a lot about hematology," he told her, "and not that much about anything else. I can find a specialist if he needs to see someone here."

"Lincoln can't get sick right now. With all we've been through, his resources aren't there to fight something big." Tears suddenly came into her eyes. She rubbed at them with the heel of her hand.

How much more could be happening with one woman?

"Well, the most important thing is to keep him sober," Sam said.

"Like I told you, I haven't seen any signs that he's slipped up." She took in a deep breath and managed to keep her tears from going full-blown, but a worried tone cast doubt on her assessment of his ongoing sobriety.

"As far as a doctor goes, I'll ask around," Sam told her, "find out the best hepatologist around here. Will Lincoln be staying with you for a while, you think?"

"We haven't talked about how long he'll be here," she said. "Until things get cleared up with me, I guess."

"So is he performing these days?" Sam wanted to lighten up the subject matter. He wanted to see her smile again. "Seems as if he's been doing real well professionally." Sam read about Lincoln Fuller not infrequently in the *New York Times*.

"He took some time off from concerts when Mom got so sick," she said. "He'd done those two movie soundtracks when he was staying with me in California, and they've brought in more income for him than all his other work combined." She looked tired, almost frail. He glanced down again toward her stomach, but her loose clothing yielded no more clues.

"I saw good reviews for both of the scores," Sam said. "One of them was up for an Oscar, right?"

"Yeah, the one Lincoln arranged. He could have gone out to the ceremony, but Mom wasn't doing well and he didn't want to be on a different coast entirely. You know, just in case . . ."

"He should have come to lunch with us today," Sam said, then regretted it. Again, he wondered if there could be anything personal in her motives for meeting him? Did he want her to think it *wasn't* a date?

"He wanted to stay at the house," she said. "It calms him to have the place to himself with Mom's piano there. Music is his work, but it's also his therapy."

He looked out past the tidal grasses. He could just make out the waters of the Cape Fear River in the distance beyond the salt marsh. He had to really work to associate that bright stretch of water between Wilmington and Ekron, a coastline he'd loved since his earliest memory, with the place where both their fathers had died. Her dad had been sitting in a small aluminum boat. Drunk, as usual, with a fishing line set. Sam's dad had been driving his thirty-six-foot cabin cruiser as it plowed over the smaller boat without any sign of slowing.

Officially, it had been determined that the fishing boat was below the cruiser cockpit's line of sight. But Sam knew the larger story. His father had T-boned Jack Fuller's little boat with full knowledge of what he was doing. In the process Lyndon Alderman had also been thrown out into the Cape Fear. He probably would have survived if he hadn't hit his head in the collision. As it was, both men were gone in minutes, dying from their injuries rather than from drowning, the coroner said.

Sam looked over at Jules, wondered what she would do if she knew the truth. He watched her eat and thought of all the ways their lives had been connected. First death. First sex. Even first real love. How could he not want to help her?

"Will you pass the hot sauce?" she asked.

"Sure," he said, passing the bottle her way.

She gave him a funny look, as if sensing there was more on his mind than he was saying. Then she smiled, and he let go of his concern. A beautiful day. A beautiful woman. It seemed like a long time since he'd enjoyed that combination over lunch. He smiled at her and they both went back to their food.

Chapter Eight

Lincoln opened all the windows to the screens. Smells of dry earth and new leaves took over the room. His mother hated cold air, especially the artificial kind. After his father died, the house stayed as warm as biscuits throughout the spring. She waited as long as she could to turn on the air conditioner in the summer—long after the place had become unbearable to everyone else.

He stood at the window and breathed it in. Breathed *her* in. She was still in every corner of the house. The night before, he'd been sure she was in the kitchen, could have sworn he'd heard her late night noises in there. If Marnee Fuller couldn't sleep, she baked.

He felt restless. Restless in the old way that used to come over him. When he was sixteen and had no idea of his place in the world, he would find himself walking the length of the house and back. The yard, too, if it wasn't raining.

Then one day when he was shopping with Marnee in Wilmington, he saw a flyer posted on a construction site. It didn't say gay bar. But Lincoln somehow figured out the gist of it. He drove there one night when he was supposed to be out with friends. As scared as he was, the relief he felt was incredible. He remembered the powerful emotions of finding others just like him. He was underage, but in a place where everyone was look- ing around to make sure they *didn't* see anybody they knew, a tall boy who looked eighteen didn't raise any questions.

Funny how the place that became the greatest liberation of his youth was also the place that held the roots of his down- fall. Booze. He struggled to equate the thing that defined the very essence of acceptance back then, with the thing that de- fined death at present. He looked over in the corner at his com- puter, thought of how much the world had changed. Boys now went online to liberate themselves. In some ways it was safer, in others, much, much more dangerous.

When the afternoon's silence became unbearable, he went over to the piano and sat down to play. "What would you like to hear?" He said it aloud, because it made him feel better to talk to her, not because he thought she was there. But the answer came to him anyway. With her it was always Chopin. She'd never heard a note of classical music before he began to play as a kid. She learned what she loved from listening to him. In that way, Chopin belonged to them.

At the very end, they couldn't get his mother warm. He and Jules took turns lying beside her, holding her. She shivered all the time. The woman from hospice said the shivering was her system shutting down, that she wasn't uncomfortable. Not like they thought. But her children knew different. Every day, her skin became cooler farther up her extremities. First just her hands, then her elbows, and on to her shoulders. She took a long time to die, once it all started. Three days. She stayed for them. They knew that much. As hard as it was to lose her, they thought it would be a relief when her body stopped trying to hang on. Only when she went still did they know that it was no relief at all. It was unthinkable that she would never be in her home again.

He wondered how long Jules would be gone. She had work to finish in Wilmington, and, before that, she was supposed to meet Sam Alderman for lunch. Lincoln didn't dislike her former boyfriend, but he didn't really want her involved with him again, either. Sam's presence reminded Lincoln of too many awful things—one awful day in particular—and he preferred to stay as far away from bad memories as he could manage.

Still, he owed Alderman's father a debt of gratitude. Lincoln felt the man should be canonized for his contribution to society. Getting Jack Fuller off the planet had been a noble way to end his own life. Whether he realized the latter would happen, no one could say for sure.

Lincoln began to play. Music and booze—the only two things that distanced him from the sharp edges of his life. And since his unfortunate conversation with the doctor, one of those options had been rendered off-limits. He tried his best to hold to that. But some days were harder than others.

He finished Mazurka in A Minor then moved on through the *Berceuse*. He'd started in on a nocturne when he heard a sound on the porch and stopped. As he lifted his fingers off the keys, he turned to see a boy standing on the other side of the screened door. The boy just stood there, not knocking or saying hello. He stared through the screen at Lincoln.

"Can I help you with something?" Lincoln asked.

"I come to see her," the boy said.

"Jules? My sister?"

The boy nodded.

"She's not home right now," Lincoln told him, standing up and walking over to the door. He opened the screen, and the child stepped back looking worried, as if an ogre had invited him inside. "Would you like for me to tell her something for you?" Lincoln asked.

The boy shrugged his shoulders, looked at the floorboards of the porch under his feet.

"Vick?" Lincoln asked. "Is that your name?"

"How'd you know?"

"I was just guessing," Lincoln said, "because you wrote her a note."

Vick finally looked up at him, at least, but hadn't come any closer to the door. The boy stayed midway back on the porch, the way students selling magazines are taught to do when they first come to your house.

"Vick? Is that short for Victor?"

Vick smiled for the first time. "No, but that's what people think. You see, my daddy was raised in Vicksburg, Mississippi, and Momma wanted to name me that after his town. But my daddy said that was about the dumbest thing he ever heard. And Momma said, 'Well, how about Vick?' and Daddy said, 'All right.' So it's just Vick."

Lincoln smiled. It seemed impossible, given the extent of their previous interaction, that all those words had come out of the child's mouth at once.

"Well, my name's Lincoln," he said. "After the car, not the president. My daddy always wanted a luxury car. I was the closest he ever got."

"Funny how come they name us the way they do, huh?" Vick said, seeming almost entirely at ease for the first time. "My little brother's Hobart."

"What's that for?" Lincoln asked.

"I don't know." The shoulder shrug again. "We call him Bart."

That seemed to have exhausted the subject of names. Lincoln didn't quite know where to take the conversation. If the boy had a guilty conscience about his monumental lie, Lincoln wanted to keep him at ease. Get him to talk more. He thought of inviting him in, but decided the porch was better.

"I know who you are," Vick said, looking troubled again. "You're a . . ." He stopped short, looked suddenly stricken.

"Pianist," Lincoln said.

"What?"

"You were about to say I'm a pianist?"

The boy went mute again. Just stared off to the side. Lincoln was suddenly very relieved that he hadn't given in to Tanner's suggestion several years before that they adopt a child. His former partner had been keen to do the family thing, but something held Lincoln back. Just as well, considering how things had worked out with the two of them. Besides, kids seemed nice and precious when they were little, but he was realizing that they turned into the damnedest creatures when they started to grow up.

"You make a living working at music?" Vick asked, finally.

"Yes," Lincoln said, "I do."

"You play for people?"

"Sometimes," Lincoln said.

"They pay money for that?" Vick asked.

"Sometimes."

Vick nodded, looked for a minute as if he was thinking something over. Lincoln wondered if he was pondering the notion of getting paid to do something that didn't seem much like work. That very thing had occurred to Lincoln more than once.

"I gotta go," Vick said out of the blue. "Tell Ms. Fuller I came by. Tell her I might come back some other time. She's real nice."

"Why did you say those things about her, Vick?" Lincoln decided that since the boy planned to leave anyway, he might as well take a shot at getting something out of him. "She's in a lot of trouble because of the things you said."

Vick's face had almost no expression. He stood very still, seemed to be thinking over what he should say. Finally, he looked across the porch at Lincoln. "What if it was an honest thing I said?" He looked hopeful, as if Lincoln might be able to make it true. "That'd be a reason, wouldn't it?"

He turned, walked at a quick pace down the porch steps and into the yard. He kept going across the driveway and into the road. Lincoln watched him round the corner going toward the church. The boy never once broke stride, never once turned around. Lincoln watched until young Vick had finally gone out of sight. Then he went back inside and began to play again, because it was the only thing he could think of to do.

Chapter Nine

Jules watched as her friend Craig slammed a cloth-covered mallet into the side of an old washing machine. The large mallet seemed as if it should overwhelm his skinny arms, but his thin body had surprising strength. He made a face, indicating that the result failed to do what he'd hoped, but Jules filed it away in her inventory of auditory options. She'd liked the satisfying thump, even if it wasn't quite the right sound to signify a body hitting the roof of a car from two stories up.

"Any ideas?" Craig asked. He liked to take on smaller jobs—television ads and PSAs. Sometimes he'd sign on for a season of shows, but, for the most part, he tired of longer collaborative projects. His attention span was better suited to jobs that allowed him to finish quickly and move on. This one was a credit card commercial.

"Bigger mallet?" she offered. "Maybe against something more hollow."

"Maybe," he said, before going to the other side of the room to rummage through more stuff.

Craig was younger than Jules but had established himself early in the business. A few years back he moved to the East Coast to take advantage of the expanding film industry in North Carolina. A rush of business coming his way over the previous months had worked out perfectly when he asked Jules to work with him. She was grateful to him for keeping her employed. Lately, she'd been getting calls outright, without the referrals.

She had a couple of hours' work to finish up a small project, but Craig was booked into the studio before her and he was running long. As she waited on him to wrap up for the day, she thought of Lincoln back at the house. An unopened bottle of bourbon sat in the kitchen. He'd brought it with him. She'd tried to throw it out, but he insisted that it was part of his process of *not* drinking. She believed him. She had to. If she stopped believing Lincoln, too much was lost in her world.

"I'm going to try one more thing and then I'm about ready to call it quits for the afternoon," Craig said.

Jules and Craig had worked on a number of jobs together, back when he lived in LA. Early on, they'd slept together a couple of times before deciding they wouldn't work as a couple. They liked each other too much to play the mind games that came with occasional sex.

"So," he said from across the room, "are you going to fill me in on these legal problems you mentioned on the phone?"

"I will sometime," she said. "I really don't want to talk about it right now." The studio seemed like such an oasis. A place that existed outside of her City Hall interrogations and lawyer conversations. She wanted to preserve that somehow.

"No problem," Craig said.

Jules watched him pick up and discard a dozen items. She pulled again at the long hem of her shirt—a man's dress shirt that Marnee used instead of an apron when she cooked. She adjusted the tail of it over the excess material of her jeans. She'd given in that morning and put on expand-a-waist maternity pants for the first time, and the panel in the front had a clown-ish excess of material. But they were comfortable, and the waists of her regular pants, even her sweat pants, had gotten tight. At lunch, she was sure Sam would notice, but if he did, he didn't say anything.

She wondered if maternity clothes would bring her closer to the reality of her situation. Make her *feel* like a mother-to-be. She'd once heard an actor talk about preparing for roles. He said that if he could figure out what kind of shoes the character would wear—and then put on a pair of those shoes—he had the part nailed.

Jules first felt the transforming power of clothes when she and Lincoln were kids. One summer, when she was six and he was nine, he made up a game where they dressed as pirates. Their outfits consisted of Marnee's culottes (pinned at the waist to make them stay up) with a tucked-in nightshirt for her, cut-off jeans with one of their dad's old collar shirts for Lincoln. Ban-danas around their foreheads and eye patches fashioned from pieces cut out of paper plates completed the outfits.

Their Summer of Pirates, they'd called it. That was at the escalation of their father's outward disapproval of Lincoln. And every day, she woke up as Jules, an uncertain kid with a vague dread about what the hours might bring after Jack got home from work. But as a pirate, she felt emboldened. The swing set was their ship, and no one could touch them.

And it was true to some extent. As long as Lincoln remained in character, throwing himself into his game with Jules, their father treated them both with a favorable regard, for some un-known reason. Jack joked and played along—even pretending to fight swords with both of them once in a while. Jules always wondered why the pirate game engaged him in such a way.

Sitting on top of a huge, wooden textile spool, she felt a sense of calm come over her for the first time in a couple of weeks. She allowed herself to imagine what it would be like to hold a baby of her own. Just being in a studio again seemed to put recent days in perspective. Work continued, even as life had fallen apart around her. Work would be there still when everything settled out again. Eventually, a breathing-crying-eating-crapping-laughing child would be there, too.

The continuity of it soothed her nerves. For the first time, she entertained the notion that her present difficulties were a terrible interlude—a peak episode in the ongoing drama of her life. Troubles resolved one way or another over time and rarely tormented anyone forever. Even the pain of her mother's absence, she was told, would dull into a not-unpleasant longing, full of good memories. Everyone said this—that she would move on. She had to take them on faith because she couldn't imagine getting very far without Marnee in the world.

"So, I just got a call from a guy this morning." Craig came back across the room carrying a dense metal pipe covered in bubble wrap. "He needs some work done on a documentary, a piece some other guy botched. I've got three commercials lined up along with a couple of trailers, and I'm already behind, so I could use the help."

A few days before, she would have told him she didn't plan to be around that long. But suddenly, more work seemed like an excellent idea. She was getting a little extra from the sublet of her condo in LA, but with lawyer's fees, more income couldn't hurt.

"Thanks," she said. "I really appreciate everything you've done since I've been here."

"Well, you helped me plenty in LA. I'm just returning the favor. Besides, if I ever decide to schlep my ass back out West, I'll be on your doorstep."

"Count on it," she said, distracted. "This is a great place," she told him, looking around the space. The Foley stage was part of a post-production studio located in an industrial building on the edge of the city. It looked like a junkyard that someone had enclosed inside concrete walls. Recording and video equipment took up part of one wall. A makeshift room in the back had a bathroom, a hot plate, a couch, and a refrigerator. She'd lived in apartments with fewer creature comforts. The back room actually *looked* like a studio apartment in New York, only instead of a hall outside the "front door," there was a cavernous warehouse floor full of stuff most people would consider trash.

"So, you don't want to talk about the legal crap," he said. "How about the bambino? Want to fill me in on that one?" He pointed in the general direction of her belly.

So it *was* obvious. "I was hoping it didn't show just yet."

"Not so much when you're standing," he said, "but the belly has a bit too much pooch when you sit like that. Plus, when the bottom of your shirt bunches up, the groovy little elastic thingy shows on your pants." He adjusted the bubble wrap, then hit the heel of his hand against it, causing a staccato pop. "Whose kid? I'm guessing it's not supposed to be a secret. If it is, like I said, the expand-a-pants aren't doing you any favors."

She smiled, lifted the shirt enough to reveal the stretchy maternity panel across the front of her still-loose jeans. "No secret," she said. "But no daddy in the picture anymore, either."

"Man, I hear that. My dad was all too happy to make a deposit, but he wasn't interested in being a serious investor. I saw him, like, five times when I was growing up. So is it that guy you were with . . . Tom? The one I met out in LA last spring."

"Thomas," she said, wanting to change the subject. "Yeah, the same guy."

It had been all too easy to keep the news from Thomas. By the time she figured out about the baby, she was already a couple of months along. A few days later, she left LA for North Carolina.

"He freak when he heard the daddy news?"

"No. It didn't work out for us. He's got some problems and I think the baby and I are better off away from him. He doesn't even know I'm pregnant and I'm going to keep it that way." She thought of Thomas, wondered how he was doing. Every time she thought of him, she felt guilty about the deception. But then she replayed in her mind a conversation with his ex-wife. "He only pushes me around when he goes off his meds," the woman told her. "When he hops off the pharmaceutical train—even now, divorced and all—he'll still come back and go crazy at me once in a while." That information, plus one terrifying car ride, was enough to send Jules out the door.

These days, he was either back on his meds, still in the hospital, or sitting in jail. The police hadn't called her for information, so it was probably one of the former selections. Regardless of A, B, or C, she knew she was better off looking after the little peanut of a baby growing inside her all alone. Although raising a child by herself scared the life out of her.

"A squall's coming in." Craig stared through a large window that framed his view of the river. A slanted, gray cloud aimed in their direction claimed the sky over the water in the distance. "God, I love the weather here. How you can feel it coming first, almost smell it. Then you can literally watch a storm move over the water—heading your way. Cool as shit, don't you think?"

She suddenly wanted to cry for no apparent reason. The hormones were messing with her head again. First, a new sense of calm, then right back to the edge of tears. She wanted to hold on to the relief she'd felt just minutes before, but it was already gone, and any slight buoyancy of that moment had been a temporary fix.

Moods were temporary. Relationships were temporary. She

caught herself again, lightly touching the swell in her abdomen. Even for a baby that had months to go before being born, life and everything in it would be temporary. Before she gave in entirely to the melancholy, she reminded herself that, to her very core, she still believed that living mattered.

"Well, I'm done for today," Craig said, moving away from the window. "Oh, wait a sec." He went over to a scarred, 1950s wooden desk that looked like a prop from a *Perry Mason* set, and he picked up a brass ring with a couple of large metal keys attached.

"I meant to give you these before," he said. "They're a spare set to my apartment. I've got to go to Dallas for a few weeks this month, and I thought you might like to have a place to escape now and again. Also, if you're working here late, it will save you the drive back—and from getting stuck sleeping on that couch back there." He motioned his head toward the back room. "Anyway, these will get you in and out of my place. Even if you're not working, you can think of it as a little clubhouse of your own when you need a break from Mayberry over there."

"You're the best." She took the keys. They felt heavy and real in her hand.

"I'm fan-damn-tastic, and don't you forget it." Then his tone shifted to serious. "You need to chill more. You're looking tired."

"You have no idea," she told him.

After Craig left, she began her work. She felt the metal keys moving around loosely in the large pocket of her jeans. They hit against each other, and she could feel them against her leg. It gave her a sense of belonging. Even though the keys and the apartment they unlocked belonged to her friend, the jangling noise they made when they tapped against her body was something newly created and owned by her.

Even if it was no more than a sound, she had brought some-thing out of nothing—and every small act of creation defied sadness and fear. The noisy keys kept pace with her, joined with the other sounds she collected as she worked. At that small moment, the clear, resounding results of her efforts seemed to be enough to get her through.

Chapter Ten

Sam walked up the sloping stretch of lawn in front of the Fuller house. He'd spent hours of his time in high school either arriving at or leaving that same house. Decades later, the familiarity remained as he approached the porch. In those earlier days, Lincoln—already off at college—had rarely been there. Now Jules was the absent one, and her brother the one he'd come to see.

Lincoln opened the door before Sam reached it, and Sam felt unprepared. Standing in front of Jules' brother, he felt an involuntary shudder twitch through his neck and arms. It wasn't to Lincoln he reacted, but to the singular horror they had shared so long ago. He suddenly second-guessed talking to Jules' big brother about things he should address directly with her. But it was too late.

"Hey," Lincoln greeted him as he got to the stairs. "If you're here for Jules, she's not back yet. She'll probably be in Wilmington until after dinner."

"I know," Sam told him. "That's what she said at lunch. Listen, could I come in for a minute?"

Lincoln regarded him without answering for a moment, but stepped back to let him in. Sam didn't think the two of them had ever been in a room alone together in their entire adult lives. Sam wondered how quickly they would cut through the bullshit. They stood in the entryway. The house was quiet. Birds from outside offered the only distraction from the awkward moment.

"There aren't many reasons you'd want to talk to me," Lincoln said, "so I doubt this is a social call."

Sam felt relieved that he'd said it. With that much firmly behind them, he went into the living room and sat on the couch. Family photos, including some of Jules' dad, stared at him from a small table off to the side of the room. Pictures of a smiling Jack Fuller gave him the creeps. He wondered what it had been like when Jules' father lived there. Tense. Quiet. Jules seemed to have a different view of the man than the rest of the world. If you hadn't known him, listening to her you might determine that he was a good person, a regular guy.

"Son-of-a-bitch," Sam mumbled, almost forgetting that Lincoln was in the room.

"No argument from me," Lincoln said, sitting down in the chair opposite Sam. "You want something to drink?"

"I'm fine, thanks," Sam said, and Lincoln waited. Sam knew his turn had come to launch into his concerns, but he didn't know where to begin. The problem was theoretical. A what-if scenario. But he felt he had to do something—say something—just in case. "This trouble Jules is having," he said, "might lead them to dig up some of the old stuff between our families. My mother brought it up, actually. She got me thinking. But I don't think she realizes what it could mean."

There'd been an incident, the day their fathers had died. Sam was only a kid at the time, but Lincoln's father, drunk and angry, had gone after Sam anyway.

"What is there to dig up?" Lincoln asked.

"That day," Sam said, "the day your dad decided I'd make a good punching bag. My mom filed a police report. It got buried after news about the accident came in. But it's still there somewhere."

"So," Lincoln said, "why is that a problem now? There was an accident report, and the coroner's findings with both our dads. That should be that. And even if it went deeper, hell . . . Everybody knows what Jack Fuller was."

"But Jules doesn't know about that day," Sam said. "Not everything." It was all so complicated.

"She's a big girl," Lincoln said. "If it all comes out, then we'll deal with it."

Sam wanted it to be as simple as Lincoln made it sound. He wished to hell it had been an accident—the way Jules thought it was. But he and Lincoln understood a different reality about that day. Lyndon Alderman had run down Jack Fuller with a steady purpose in mind—to kill the man.

"My mother talked to the police that day," Sam said, "after everything happened. She gave a statement about what your dad did to me. There was a report, I guess. Official enough that they couldn't just toss it. But when word came in about the boats colliding, and about both our dads—" He stopped. It hadn't been so hard in years to talk about it. "The police chief was a friend of Dad's. He and my uncle dealt with it. The two of them decided that the report should just get filed away. Somewhere."

"Why didn't they just toss it?" Lincoln asked.

"I don't know," Sam said. "There were no charges at the time, but the chief said we needed to have it around in case anyone ever tried to dig up a wrongful death suit against our family."

"Who would do that?" Lincoln asked.

"The Fuller family," Sam said. "Your dad's brothers. If they dug up anything and tried to make a case that the accident was a murder-suicide, we'd have something to show that my dad wasn't in his right mind when he did it."

"So it's still there." Lincoln shook his head. "That's not great, but it happened twenty-five years ago and your dad's dead, too."

Sam took a moment to order his thoughts. "There are two things, I guess," he said. "One is that we don't want Jules to find out about this at the police station—or God forbid, in court. The other is my mother's insurance claim."

"Insurance?" Lincoln again shook his head. He didn't understand. God, Sam didn't want to be talking about that day. Reliving it. Jesus.

"So what was in the report?" Lincoln asked.

"Everything," Sam said. "Everything that happened that afternoon."

Lincoln let out a deep breath, settled back in his chair. "Still, what are they going to do? Accuse a dead man of murder? My uncles won't mount a lawsuit against your mother."

"It matters if the insurance company comes after my mother for fraud. That boat wreck was determined to be an accident. She got a lot of money. If they figure out my dad plowed into the smaller boat on purpose . . ."

"Your mom lied to the insurance company?" Lincoln asked.

Sam shook his head. "My uncle handled everything with the insurance company. She didn't know what was involved. She still doesn't. Right now, she's only afraid of making my dad look bad. Lyndon Alderman's good name and all that. She doesn't know that they could come after her house. Her bank account. I don't know. Jesus. After all this time, can they do that?"

"I don't know," Lincoln said. "But why would they even think it was relevant to what's happening with Jules?"

"The old police chief—my dad's friend—is gone. If someone comes across the file, think of what's in that report." Sam told him. "What your dad did—it's not sexual, but it *is* abuse. And it involves a minor. A pattern in the family? I don't know what they might come up with if it gets to that point." His head was swimming. He wanted out of the house, away from the pictures of a happy Jack Fuller that sat just inches from him, mocking him.

"What do you want me to do?" Lincoln asked.

"Just tell me, I guess." Sam stood up. He had to leave. "Tell me if you hear anything about a report. I don't know what we'll do from there, but I can be proactive, at least. I might call this Hunter guy. Jules' lawyer. See what he says."

Lincoln nodded and followed Sam to the door. He stood on the porch as Sam walked away.

"Sam?"

Sam turned from the edge of the porch to look at Lincoln.

"About my dad. That day with my dad. I'm sorry," Lincoln said. "I'm sorry I couldn't do anything. I should have been able to do something."

"It's ancient history," Sam said. "Let's just try to keep it that way." He started to walk again but then stopped. As long as they were on a roll with honesty, he had another question for Lincoln. "Can I ask you about something?"

"Shoot," Lincoln said. He looked tired.

"Is Jules pregnant?"

Lincoln took his time responding. The silence itself was the answer Sam needed, and he wished he'd had the nerve to just talk with her. He was putting her brother in a tough spot, asking him to confirm it.

"I'm sorry," Sam said before Lincoln spoke. "It's out of line for me to ask you. It's just, well—at lunch today, when she raised her arms, her shirt came up a little and it looked like she had on maternity pants. I didn't want to say it to her in case . . . Women are always worried that they look big."

"You'll have to talk with her," Lincoln said. There was no judgment in his tone. It was simply a statement.

"And if I do that," Sam said, treading carefully, "I'm not going to offend her?"

"No. You won't offend her."

Sam shook his head. "She's got too much going on right now. I'm worried about her. Your mom's death, the legal problems, and . . ." Sam stopped. He couldn't even bring himself to say she was having a baby. He wondered who the father could be. Was she that deeply involved with someone in California?

"You're right to worry," Lincoln said. "And you were right to come to me about this report. If she gets blindsided by the whole story at the police station . . ." Lincoln stopped and Sam understood. Neither of them wanted to think about it.

And then, the conversation was over. The only two topics they had in common—Jules and their dead fathers—had been exhausted.

He stepped off the porch, but then remembered what Jules had told him about Lincoln. There *was* one more thing to discuss. No wonder the man looked tired.

"Jules mentioned some health problems," Sam said. "She didn't go into a lot of detail, but if you need a resource while you're here, I'd be happy to help."

The small beginnings of a smile came to Lincoln's face. Sam didn't know why the offer would amuse him.

"Small towns are amazing, aren't they?" Lincoln leaned against the porch rail. He seemed to have stepped right off one of his album covers in that pose. "Secrets can't survive forever. They always come out."

"Are you talking about your health or this business with our fathers?"

"All of it," Lincoln said. "It's all part of the same story anyway."

It occurred to Sam that Lincoln's life had never been easy. At least Sam had some memory of what easy was like.

"I'm not prying," Sam said. "I'm just happy to help if you

need me. I told Jules I'd find a good specialist for you to see while you're here."

"Thank you." Lincoln said. "That would help a lot."

"My pleasure," Sam said. He stood for a moment more, thinking of all the times he'd brought Jules home, sat on that porch with her. But with Lincoln there alone, it seemed like a different place entirely. Memory was a funny thing.

Sam made his way back across the yard to the driveway, realizing that there was truly nothing left to say.

Chapter Eleven

Back in town after driving in from the city, Jules decided to pick up hamburgers from the Sea Breeze Grill on Broad Street, Ekron's equivalent of Main Street. When she walked in, the scent of sizzling fat on a hot griddle smelled good to her for the first time in weeks. Maybe she'd turned the corner on her nausea. She sat on a seat at the counter and waited to order.

Around her, regulars filled booths and counter stools, settling in for dinner. A group of teenagers crowded the back booths. They'd probably been around since school let out.

The place stayed full all day long. Breakfast, lunch, and dinner were served at the usual times, with kids filling in the afternoon lull ordering fries and shakes. Jules had gone there herself nearly every day after high school. Randi Meeks, the owner, had been on her feet taking orders and filling plates for at least thirty-five years. She wasn't an attractive woman, but she'd kept what looks she'd started with, changing very little from the time when Jules was a kid.

As she waited, Jules could hear low snickers from the back of the dining area. The high school kids mumbled and laughed, all the while looking in her direction. *Let it go, Jules. They're kids, acting stupid.* That much hadn't changed since she was in school, either. She thought of herself making faces behind Rena Alderman's back—then the horror of making eye contact with the woman in the mirror. That was one difference with the kids at the diner, she decided. They didn't care if she saw them.

On the other side of the counter, Randi finished writing down an order. She moved over to where Jules sat.

"Jules, I know you're going through a rough patch at the moment, but it might be better if you didn't hang out here right now," Randi said, glancing back toward the kids' table.

"What do you mean?" Jules' ears felt hot.

"With the kids in here and all," she said, looking down at her order pad, "and with all that's happened, some parents might not like you hanging around their kids."

Jules figured that the gossip in town had gone a little crazy, but even that was an understatement if she was getting kicked out of the town burger joint because of what the kid had said. Unbelievable.

"Randi," she said, trying to keep her voice quiet, "I didn't do anything. This is total bullshit. I don't know why that boy said those things, but I haven't been charged with anything. And nothing happened. I don't even know him."

"That older lady who teaches the drama class," she said, "old Mrs. . . ."

"Compton?"

"Yeah, that's her. She was in here the other day and said you did act awfully casual with those kids," Randi said. "At the very least, you put yourself in a bad position, Jules. Now I'm not passing judgment here." Randi looked her in the eye, even bolder now that the initial confrontation was over. "I'm just saying that, if you lay low, it'll be better for everybody." She glanced again at the kids in the booth. Jules followed her gaze, saw one of them making a gesture that looked vaguely obscene.

"Laying low will make me look guilty," Jules said, refusing to slink out of a public place because of a few teenagers. "This isn't right, Randi."

"It is what it is, Jules." Randi remained unapologetic.

Jules would have pegged her for a different response—one with a little more backbone. But then she realized, it wasn't a lack of resolve that led Randi to behave the way she did. Randi *believed* that Jules had done something wrong.

Jules would have considered Randi an old friend. How well did she know the woman? How well did she know anyone in town anymore? She felt her heart racing, felt the kind of anger that brought on tears. She couldn't let that happen. Crying would increase the humiliation tenfold. Adding to her misery, her ankle had begun throbbing again, and she wanted nothing more than to get home.

"Make me a couple of cheeseburgers to go," Jules said, more out of pride than hunger. Her appetite was gone. "Everything but onions. And an order of fries."

Randi let out a sigh. She'd obviously hoped for an immediate departure on Jules' part, but seemed content to compromise with a take-out order. Jules felt her nausea returning, but she managed to wait it out. Sitting on a stool at the counter, she might as well have been on a stage. Everyone in the place looked at her. Some openly, others casting sideways glances as they ate. After ten or fifteen awkward minutes, Randi handed her a white paper bag, fat with burgers. Grease soaked through the edge at one corner.

"How much?" Jules asked.

"Eight thirty-eight with tax." Randi answered, moving toward the cash register at the end of the counter.

Jules put a ten down and, with all eyes still on her, walked out the door.

With the days getting longer, it looked earlier than it actually was. Driving the last stretch of road toward home, Jules slowed down as she came to the church. She pulled into the parking lot and turned off the car. It was peaceful, sitting there facing the cemetery. Before, she always thought of graveyards as depressing, but since her mother's funeral, this Mount Canaan had become comforting.

"This is one place where no one will kick me out if I want to eat here." She spoke out loud, getting out of the car and heading toward the tombstone marking her mother's plot. Her dad rested beside her mom, but his was the only name on the stone. Her mother's would be added whenever she and Lincoln got around to calling the monument guy.

She sat on the stone pedestal of her parents' plot, leaned back against the headstone. Salt air stirred thickly in the slight breeze. The granite, warm from the day's heat, felt good against her back. She pulled one of the cheeseburgers out of the bag and took a bottled water from her purse. The first bite tasted like heaven. She was crazy hungry, and too angry and nauseated to realize it until the food was in her mouth. A calmness settled over her, leaving her momentarily euphoric. In some sick way, she felt more optimistic than she had in weeks. There was no practical reason for this. Her world had hit unimagined lows since the last time she'd visited her mom.

Maybe it was the baby. Marnee's illness dominated her time and her thoughts through the first months of the pregnancy. And then came the death itself, the unthinkable absence of her mother. She'd had no time to think about the baby. Really *think* about becoming a mother. But she was showing, and for the first time, she let thoughts of the baby fill her consciousness. Fingers, toes . . . A small beating heart. As everything stopped for Marnee, it began for Baby Fuller. Marnee found joy in that, if only for one night.

Jules raised up her shirt, stared at the bulging bump that her belly had become. She was having a baby! That—for the moment anyway—trumped all the other crap that had polluted her life since the boy's accusations. It also terrified her. How could she possibly know what to do for a kid when she couldn't even keep herself out of trouble?

"Smells good." A man's voice came without warning. Jules jumped, nearly dropping her food. With her free hand, she quickly pulled her shirt down, then looked up to see him approaching. He came from the direction of the back entrance to the church, and when he came close enough, she recognized him. Walt. The preacher's son. Vick Johns, the source of all her recent upheaval, was his nephew.

"So is it?" he asked.

"Is it what?" She felt flustered. A freshman again, talking to the varsity captain of . . . what? All the teams, best she could recall.

"Is your burger good?" He stood before her now.

"I think it might be the best damn cheeseburger I've ever tasted." She smiled and took on a bravado she didn't feel in an effort to hide her nerves.

Since high school, she'd seen him at the church over the years when she visited, but they did little more than nod and say hello. She always noticed him, but doubted the same level of keen awareness was reciprocated. Besides, he'd been married forever.

"Sea Breeze Grill?" he asked.

Jules nodded. "Randi booted me out of the place," Jules told him, deciding it was best to be as open as possible about her predicament. She'd lost her patience for keeping up appearances. "I'm a bit of a pariah, it seems." Besides, she couldn't make it any worse by acknowledging it. "You might want to keep your distance if your good name means anything to you."

"Yeah, I heard that," he said, sitting down beside her on the granite pedestal of her parents' headstone. "I guess I'll take my chances."

Walt was two years ahead of her in school. A year below Lincoln's grade. But they'd all gone to youth group together at the church when they were kids. The closest Jules ever got to him as a teenager was the summer before freshman year of high school. A group of them hung out together in the neighborhood and at the town pool. She'd had a wild crush on him, but knew that he still saw her as a kid, almost a little sister. Still, three months in close proximity to Walt Walker had been the stuff of dreams for her back then.

"I can leave if you want to be alone," he said.

"That's okay," she said. "I don't have many options for company these days. Being an untouchable limits one's social life considerably."

He was so tall—taller, even, than Lincoln—and still in the shape of a varsity athlete. In high school, Walt had been part of the hell-raising, jock crowd. Always surrounded by a bunch of football player types who were his friends—and the cheerleaders who hung with them constantly. Jules had *not* been a cheerleader.

Even sitting, he towered over her, and she felt small. She scooted over and made more room for him. He leaned forward, rested his elbows on his knees, and breathed in deeply, as if he, too, had just noticed the pleasant feel of the warm air.

She opened the white bag, tilted it in his direction. "Cheeseburger? I bought two, and I can only finish one. There are fries in there, too."

"Thanks." He took the burger out, the wrapper soaked with grease. She handed him a napkin out of the bag, took the fries out, and put them on the space between them.

After two bites, he'd nearly finished. He held the remaining piece in his large hand and looked over at Jules.

"Vick is my nephew, you know," he said.

She wondered if he would bring it up, or if she would have to. She felt relieved that he said something first.

"I know," she said. "Your sister spat at me. I've never elicited that particular response from anyone before."

A slow smile spread across his face and he shook his head. "Cici's a piece of work. High-strung," he said.

Jules thought that was an understatement when describing the saliva-wielding creature from the police station hall. "She said she's living with you and your wife."

"Yeah," he said. "She and Tuni have gotten thick as thieves. I come out here to get away from the hormones sometimes."

You came to the wrong place this time. Jules smiled at the thought of all the estrogen raging through her system. Instinctively, she placed a hand on her belly. "You and Tuni have a couple of girls, right?" Jules asked, offering her water to him.

He took a sip from her water bottle and handed it back. "Eleven and six," he said. "Now we've got Vick and little Bart with us, too. Can't scratch your neck without bumping into somebody in that house these days. Speaking of bumping, I hear little Bart 'bout ran you over here the other day. You okay?"

"Fine," she said. "Just a sprained ankle." She shifted the position of her back to ease a cramp coming on. "So you come here to escape the crowds at your house, and I come here to find folks who won't ask me to leave when I get here."

"Yeah. There may be lots of folks here," he said, gesturing around the graveyard, "and they're agreeable types, but they leave you be."

"Sorry I messed up your plans for a little peace and quiet."

"S'all right," he said. "I'll trade peace and quiet for one of Randi's burgers any day. I'll even put up with a social reject if I get fed." That smile. Slow and genuine, as if they shared a private joke. "Got any ketchup?" He eyed the fries.

She handed him the bag. "In the bottom, I think."

He put ketchup on the fries and ate in silence. They sat without talking for a while. She even leaned back against the stone and closed her eyes for a moment. When she opened them, he was looking off toward the woods. He seemed content with his own thoughts.

"I didn't do anything, you know," she said, finally.

"I know it," he said, still looking away from her.

"I don't understand why your nephew came up with that story, but I've barely said two words to him before. He's made all of it up. I swear to God."

He seemed to be staring at the spot where the groomed cemetery grass met a line of pine and old-growth trees. "Boy's had problems for a long time," he said. "His daddy's passing made things worse."

"I wish people around here knew that," she said. "They think I'm some kind of pedophile."

"People don't want to go against a kid. He'll get the benefit of the doubt until they sort it out."

"Will they sort it out?" she asked. "What happens if I get arrested?"

He turned to look at her. His eyes were kind. "I've had a couple of conversations with Stands," he said.

"The sergeant at the station who met with me?"

"He's a hunting buddy of mine," he said. "I told him what I think. Nothing I can say for sure, just my take on it. I'm probably not supposed to say so, but he's come to most of the same conclusions with his own gut feelings. The man's smart. I think it'll be okay."

He'd gone to see Sergeant Stands on her behalf. That kindness in the face of everything the town was saying about her . . . She could recall with amazing clarity how she'd felt that summer before high school. Of all the qualities that contributed to her crush at the time, his kindness trumped the rest. One day in particular at the pool, he'd been a real hero when a group of sophomore girls randomly singled her out as a target for ridicule. Walt had come to her defense. He had no reason to be nice to her. Then or now. But he was.

"I've tried to talk with the boy myself, but he won't have much to do with me." He took the bottled water from her again. Drank deeply.

"Why do you think he's done this?" she asked.

"Couldn't say. Kids pick on him sometimes. His mother thinks it's the interest in theater that makes him a target, but I'm around a lot of kids. Some of them simply have a thin shell emotionally. Makes them easy to hurt. Funny thing is, he can fistfight with the best of them, but he still seems fragile. I can't put my finger on it."

"So he said that about me to make kids think he's cool?" She still didn't understand.

"Maybe," Walt told her. "But I get the feeling pieces of the puzzle are missing. I don't know what's really going on with him."

"Did he get in trouble at his old school? Fights and stuff?" She wanted to know what the boy was about. It was the only way she could make her problems go away.

"Yeah. He was mixing it up with some of the kids there even before Henry, his dad, died. From what I gather, he and his daddy were getting into it pretty good, too. Henry didn't like Vick's interest in theater. Lot of things could make a kid act out. I don't know what this latest is about, though. Maybe I'm overthinking it. Boy's hitting puberty. Could be that it's not *about* anything, really."

It suddenly seemed to Jules as if their meeting wasn't really a random occurrence at all. She got the feeling that Walt Walker wanted an opportunity to talk with her.

"Were you just here by chance?" she asked. She looked at his eyes. Even with the light fading, she could see that they were blue. "Were you really just getting some *space*?"

"No. As a matter of fact, I wasn't." He took another sip of her water. "I was over at my daddy's helping him move some boxes to the basement."

The parsonage was across the street from the church. Jules could see a light in the kitchen window. Preacher Walker's figure was a dark silhouette, and she wondered if he could see them.

"Your momma's car was here," Walt was saying, "so I figured I'd come say hello."

"Well, hello then." She smiled at him.

He looked at her, unapologetic in his regard of her face. "Try not to worry too much," he said. "It's kind of delicate. But I think this thing will go away before it comes to much of anything." He stood up. "I got to get on home. Should have been there an hour ago."

"Where do you work?" she asked, realizing that she didn't know anything about him.

"At one of the high schools on this side of Wilmington. I'm a guidance counselor."

"A guidance counselor?" It seemed too ironic to be true. "You raised holy hell all through high school."

"Beats all, don't it?" That slow smile again. "Good thing is, I know all their tricks."

She laughed. And they called *her* unpredictable. Some things you couldn't guess. Walt seemed like the hardest sort of puzzle, a lot of pieces showing a little, but not too much. She gathered the trash from her meal and put it in the empty bag.

Walt held out his hand to help her up, and she accepted. When she stood up, she saw him looking in the vicinity of her belly.

"Yes," she said, "I am expecting a baby."

"How far along?"

"Over four months," she said, "almost five." She smoothed her shirt over the rise of her stomach. "Pretty soon I'll have the perfect place to rest a cocktail here, and I can't even drink. So unfair."

"Life's a bitch." He looked at her left hand as it rested on her middle.

"No," she said, "I'm not married. There's no father in the picture. It'll be fuel for the fire when people begin to figure it out."

"It's all words," he said, as the two of them walked together toward her car. "People can't remember what they talked about yesterday or the day before that, so I expect they'll talk about it one day and forget it the next."

"I wish I was as sure of that as you seem to be." She took her keys out of her pocket. "Can I give you a ride home?"

His laughter startled her. "No, ma'am. If you want gossip, let's the two of us go riding around together. Besides, my wife sees me get out of your car, and I'm an hour late home from work? I'll have myself a situation at home, too. It was good catching up with you, Jules."

"You too, Walt." She got in her car. "And Walt?"

He turned back toward where she sat with the door still open.

"Thank you." She didn't know what else to say, so she left it at that.

He nodded, then turned and walked in the direction of his house. She watched him make his way down the road, and thought about the irony. The one person who had managed to make her feel good—the best she'd been in months—was the married uncle of the little jerk making all kinds of trouble for her. She shook her head, put the Buick in gear, and headed toward home.

Chapter Twelve

Jules was pregnant. For any guy with sense that would be a major red flag but Sam couldn't get her out of his head.

He remembered all those years ago, holding the two acceptance letters, one in each hand. They arrived a day apart. First Yale, then Duke. He remembered being tired. Tired of arguing with his mother about Jules. Tired of lying to her. Tired of feeling guilty that Rena was alone, raising him without his dad— and he was treating her like shit with all the lies. He'd told her he and Jules decided to break up when they went to school, when in fact, they talked of just the opposite. He planned to go to Duke. Jules would be at Chapel Hill, just eight miles away.

But by the time the letters arrived, he was so damn exhausted. In some ways, his mother was right. Life *would* be less complicated without Jules, he reasoned. So he'd lied to both of them, his mother and Jules. He said that he'd been rejected by Duke.

Thinking back, looking at how his relationships had turned out, that decision might have been the worst mistake he ever

made. It felt right to sit with Jules again at a restaurant. To talk
with her, laugh with her . . . But as the old feelings came to the
surface, so came the arguments with his mother.

"He's just a boy, Sam. If she's capable of something like that,
she's got to be entirely unhinged." Rena carried a bag of potting
soil from the garage to the back porch, refusing to let Sam take
it for her.

He drove around for a while after talking with Lincoln, then,
he rode out to the cottage and sat looking at the water. Nothing
made him feel any better. Finally, he gave in and went home
to his mother's, but he was beginning to wish he'd stayed away.

"Who says she's capable of something like that?" He sat on
the glider at the far wall of the porch. "A California address
doesn't make you *unhinged*."

"It started way before that, and you know it." His mother had
seven pots in a row lined up on a canvas tarp inside the screened
porch. She was on her knees in front of the planters with the
large bag of dirt beside her. With dusk coming on, the warm
porch lights bathed her, gave her a rosy glow.

"What are you planting?" he asked, hoping to distract her
from the subject of his ex-girlfriend.

"An herb garden for the porch," she answered him, but returned immediately to the subject of his ex-girlfriend. "I remember those clothes she used to wear. She looked like a street
performer some days, a *street walker* on others. And every week
a new phase. Buddhism. Vegetarian food. Ukulele lessons. And
those obscene shorts with a *tattoo* on her leg, right there for all
the world to see." The last part she said as a whisper, as if body
art should not be discussed at full volume.

"That was a long time ago, Mom. We caught the tail end of
the seventies. I was into most of that stuff then, too. Everybody was."

"Whatever you were into, she led the way."

He sat down on a cushioned wicker chair, leaned back, and closed his eyes. "Could we talk about something else? Please?"

"That report," she said, keeping her voice low even though no one else was around, "what if it comes out?" She'd called him earlier in the afternoon with her concerns, just after he left his lunch. He didn't tell her he'd been with Jules. What was the point? He hadn't even thought about the old police records until she brought it up.

Rena had a full accounting to the police of the assault on him by Jules' father on the day it happened. If the insurance company got wind of it, his mother might very well be cited for fraud. That part hadn't occurred to her yet. She was only worried about the mark it would make on her dead husband's good name. The fascination the town had with the accident at the time would return tenfold if they realized Lyndon Alderman had hit Jack Fuller's boat on purpose.

"Your father doesn't deserve to have his good name dragged through the mud at this point—not after what that man did. And we don't deserve Jack Fuller's brothers getting all riled up again. They're thugs. Just as bad as he was."

The smear on Lyndon Alderman's name was intolerable to her. She'd adored her husband in life, but in death, he'd become something of a deity. Sam suspected she prayed to him as often as she did God.

He, on the other hand, worried about the practical concerns that hadn't occurred to her. As long as the report remained filed away, no questions would come up about an insurance claim that was filed as a boating accident. With his mother distraught, his uncle had taken care of the paperwork, and she never knew the issue existed. When Sam, twelve at the time, overheard his uncle talking with another man about making the paperwork disappear, he understood that what his mother had unwittingly done was criminal.

Even Jules' mom must have known the collision was no real accident. But surely, Marnee had witnessed more of her husband's temper than anyone. By the time he died, she'd probably wanted the ordeal over.

"And dope," his mother was saying, somehow back on the subject of Jules' vices. "She was into dope, too. Don't deny it."

He and Jules both smoked pot, but what his mother referred to was some incense Jules bought at the mall and left in his car beside her purse. To Rena, the two were somehow equivalent.

"It wasn't dope, Mom," he said, standing up. He gave up trying to have a normal conversation.

Rena had eaten early, left food out for him in the kitchen when he called to say he'd be coming in late. He went back into the kitchen to warm something up. Green beans and some kind of nonspecific gray meat. Beef roast, most likely, although it might be pork. He couldn't tell—never could, with Rena's cooking.

He'd call his uncle tomorrow, he thought. And then Jules' lawyer. He'd sort out whether there was a statute of limitations. Whether it was better to be proactive, or let it play out, quite possibly, to nothing. But all those questions could wait. For the time being, he would eat and then sleep. He wouldn't even set an alarm for the morning. He was taking vacation time from work, after all. If he was lucky, he wouldn't even dream.

Chapter Thirteen

"Your boyfriend came by while you were gone," Lincoln said as she walked in the door.

At first, she thought he meant Thomas had come to North Carolina from California, and she felt panic rise inside her. But her brother had a wicked grin on his face, and he knew that Thomas's arrival would be no laughing matter.

"Technically, two of them came by," he said, still somewhat amused, "but the kid's attachment to you is purely delusional, so I don't think that counts."

"The kid? Vick Johns came here?" She threw her purse on the couch. "Jesus, Lincoln. I'm going out of my way to prove I don't even know the kid. If he's showing up at the house, that's not going to help my case here. Thank God we don't have neighbors right on top of us."

"He's one seriously unbalanced child," Lincoln said, settling down into the den chair holding a cup of something. "I kind of felt sorry for him."

"What did he want?" She sat down on the couch, rummaged

through her pocketbook for gum. "Did he at least say something that might help us sort this mess out?" She stretched out full-length with her feet up to take the pressure off her back.

Lincoln cupped his hands around the mug. "He wanted to see you, but he didn't seem to really know why. He's got something going on. Maybe the court-appointed shrink will get to the bottom of it. I'll be damned if I could figure it out."

"But did he say he'd take any of it back?" she asked.

"Trouble is, little sister, I think he might have convinced himself it's all true." Lincoln took a sip of his drink, then winced as it burned his lip. "He seemed to believe his little stories."

"Then I'm totally screwed."

"So to speak." He raised his eyebrows.

"God, you're in a weird mood."

"Strange times call for strange behavior, I suppose."

"What's that?" she asked, trying to sound casual. His odd demeanor had her on edge.

"Earl Grey," he said. "I'm a Brit at heart."

"How can you drink something hot when the air is already sticky?"

"All the Maker's Mark I ran through my system over the years," he said, cutting his eyes in her direction. "Can't get my blood to thicken anymore."

"That's not funny."

"Might as well laugh as cry." The sardonic edge in his voice worried her. She knew the signs, like weather changing. She'd stay close, she decided. When he got sour and sarcastic, it meant he wanted a drink. She worried he was headed toward a binge. The irony was, he was a genuine puppy dog after he'd had a few. It was the craving that turned his world dark. Just the opposite of her father, who could be a nice man, but was a mean drunk.

"So who was the other one?" she asked, trying to put worries about Lincoln out of her mind.

"The other who?"

"Boyfriend. You said two came by."

"Oh, just Sam . . ." He stopped, as if catching himself from saying more.

"He knew I was in Wilmington all afternoon," she said. "Why'd he come here?"

Lincoln hesitated, didn't look her in the eye. "Must have forgotten," he said, finally.

She'd find out what he wasn't saying. Lincoln hated secrets. If something was close to the surface, it was only a matter of time before he spilled. She closed her eyes again and let it go for the moment.

She'd dozed off, exhausted, and awoke when her cell phone rang. She pulled it out of her purse, answered, trying to come fully awake.

"Hey there," Hunter Randleman's voice greeted her. "I just got a call from Sergeant Stands. We need to meet him back at City Hall tomorrow morning."

"What about?" She was instantly alert at the mention of Stands.

"He's got the report in from the psychologist who met with the boy. He also mentioned some other report that he thinks may or may not be relevant," he told her.

"What other report—and what does that mean?" she asked. "It may or may not be relevant?"

"Don't know," he said. "Guess we'll find out tomorrow. Why don't you meet me downstairs at the station offices where we were before. I'll be there by ten-thirty. Okay?"

"Are you sure they're not going to arrest me?" Anything was possible with the crazy turns her life had taken.

"I get the feeling he's a reasonable guy. Not out to prove something that isn't there, so I wouldn't worry. Get some sleep tonight and try not to think about it too much," Hunter said before moving on to his good-byes.

Try not to think about it. It would take a distraction of biblical proportions to think about anything else. But Hunter's easy demeanor gave her some reassurance.

She got up. Lincoln was no longer in the room and she felt momentarily relieved. He'd been bordering on unbearable. She heard the television on in the kitchen. He'd found some droning news channel to distract him.

But rather than savoring the solitude, she felt an overwhelming yearning to hear Marnee's voice. Her singular brand of reassurance. Marnee had been happy about the baby. Jules hadn't intended to tell her about the pregnancy, but when her mother figured it out on her own, it came as a huge unburdening. That memory served as a thin bridge between her life as a daughter and that as a mother. She felt grateful she'd had it, but she wanted more. More time. More Marnee.

For the first time in her adult life, Jules wanted to believe the Bible stories about reunions in heaven's mansions. She wanted to know that, someday, she could introduce her child to Marnee Fuller.

She would never long for Jack Fuller to meet her baby. Even though she loved him in her own way and even though she believed he loved her, she couldn't deny a threat existed every minute that he lived. Her baby shouldn't know that feeling. The feeling that danger existed inside his or her own home. They said that no matter how long wild animals lived with humans, they never stopped being wild. Instinct could override domesticity at any moment. Jack Fuller had been like that.

Marnee, on the other hand, personified steady. She was the sun and the moon.

Jules went into her mother's room. Scarves hung over the closet door. Shoes lay scattered on the floor below them. Dark had finally come while Jules slept on the couch, so she turned on the lamp and opened a window to let in fresh air. Tree frogs and cicadas sounded Vespers. Marnee used to tell her that these creatures were like the birds of the night, only better, because they made no attempt to get anyone's attention. The chorus was all, a communal hum of life.

Jules wished Marnee could have lived to see one more summer. Marnee loved the hot season. For this reason, when Jules first moved to Los Angeles, she'd been sure that her mother would take to that city, the land of birds, sun, and trees—perpetual June. But from the moment she arrived, Marnee had registered dislike for the place. She compared it to Orlando, where everything, even nature, was designed for effect.

"It's like Disney World out here," she said, sitting on Jules' apartment balcony one afternoon. "It is such an ironic display, this *creation* of the illusion of a natural state—when, in fact, what they want is the most predictable environment possible. There's far too much at stake for places like LA and Orlando to actually leave things alone. Back home"—Marnee gestured as if her own unkempt yard was just behind her—"there's so little to lose by conceding it all to whatever growth and decay may come."

The one thing Marnee had liked about California was seeing celebrities. To be someone who expounded the virtues of the natural state, she had a contradictory fascination with movie stars. Once, she and Jules were invited to a reception where a number of A-listers showed. To everyone's surprise, Meryl Streep made an appearance, and Marnee babbled like a teenager the entire way home.

"It's just that I've spent years watching her in those fancy gowns, collecting Oscars like they're bowling trophies. I couldn't get over standing in a room with her right there. I heard her tell someone she needed to go to the ladies' room. Movie stars like her, it's hard to believe that they have to get up and go take care of bodily functions like everybody else."

Jules began to aimlessly root through her mother's drawers. The best thing about the bedroom was the smell. Everything in it carried Marnee's scent, and, for a time, she seemed no farther away than the grocery store.

Amid the clutter on Marnee's bureau, an envelope stood propped upright between the jewelry box and the lamp. Jules pulled the note out to read it.

Dear Rena,

I can't tell you how much good it did me to sit with you today. It's been so long, old friend. I know that our lives have been—not in opposition. I never felt at odds with you—but, by necessity, in strange parallel. Sitting with you today, I realized how much we've both missed in that circumstance. But your visit brought our friendship full circle. Back to the closeness that I feel—have always felt—when I think of you.

It is with gratitude that I write this note.

Yours,
Marnee

Jules stared at the paper in her hand. She knew that her mother and Mrs. Alderman had been close friends. They'd been best friends all through school and then as young married women. The boat accident with Jules' dad and Mr. Alderman changed that. Bad blood between the two families made friendship too hard to maintain. That's what Marnee said once. Jules had never known how much her mother regretted the rift.

In the second drawer down from the top of the bureau, Jules found a white envelope filled with pictures. Beside it was an open pack of Salem Lights. There were five or six cigarettes left, and the sight of them hit her with an unexpected punch. Not because they likely contributed to her mother's illness, but because Jules had stumbled upon the one pleasure, with the exception of her children, that Marnee Fuller relished more than any joy during her time on earth.

Jules picked up the envelope and the cigarettes and sat on the edge of the bed. Cradling the objects in her lap—evidence of an absent life once lived—Jules allowed herself to cry.

Chapter Fourteen

"I need to tell her," Lincoln said to Sam over the phone.

He sat in the ladder-backed desk chair in his old room. His childhood desktop was frozen in time from his high school years. Pictures, a Beta Club mug, and even spiral notebooks full of Latin conjugations and math equations sat as they had for twenty-five years. Only the neat arrangement of the items gave away the fact that it was a diorama, no longer an actual teen-ager's domain.

"You should wait," Sam was telling him. "She really doesn't need another big shock."

"She's not fragile, Sam. And it'll be worse if that report tells her most of it," Lincoln told him. "She'll put everything together pretty fast, if she sees that."

Lincoln had overheard Jules talking with her lawyer on the phone. He gleaned from her side of the discussion that new information had come to light. There was no reason why the old report would have anything to do with the current problems

Jules was having, but still, he couldn't take any chances that she'd be blindsided by some police sergeant down at City Hall. Better to prepare her.

"Do what you need to do," Sam said. "Call me if I can help."

Lincoln hung up the phone. He sat in the dark and tried to fashion the words in his head, but they all sounded like a prepared speech. Better to just talk with her. Wing it. How do you tell someone that their father was murdered? Worse yet, how to convince her that the bastard deserved it?

Jules sat in a wrought-iron chair on the patio. She had her back to him, her arm propped on the table at her side. As he drew closer, he saw a lit cigarette in her hand, smoke curling up toward the low-hanging branches of a nearby Japanese maple.

"What the hell are you doing?" He went over and sat down at the other side of the table.

"I just found these." She held up the package of Salem Lights in her other hand. Old pictures were spread out before her.

He saw one of himself as a toddler, smiling, sitting on his father's shoulders. It was like looking at someone else's childhood. He had no connection to that moment, could not recall anything like it.

"I wanted to feel close to Mom," Jules said.

"Yeah," he said, "I can still see her sitting out here."

"It's weird." Jules threw her head back, exhaled a stream of smoke into the night air. "She loved these things so much, but she wouldn't smoke in the house. In the dead of winter, she'd come out here. This spot, these . . ." She held up the pack again. "I realized I couldn't get any closer to her than that."

"That's just sad on so many levels," Lincoln said, taking in the smell of the cigarette. "Put that damn thing out."

Jules ignored him. Black ash dotted the cement under her

chair, confirming that their mother had been there, cigarette in hand, countless times. Lincoln reached over and gestured for Jules to give him the pack. He took one out, lit it, and inhaled. A calmness descended, and he felt the slight bump of euphoria that, while entirely chemical, was nevertheless welcome. It wasn't booze, but it came pretty damn close.

"Be careful," Jules said. "You don't need to swap one addiction for another."

"You must be joking," he said. "You're fucking pregnant, and you're telling *me* to be careful with these things?"

She laughed. Really laughed. He hadn't heard that sound in weeks. Ever since she was a toddler and he'd first begun amusing her, he'd never tired of making her happy. In all his life, he had never felt small or unworthy with his little sister.

"There's a note in there that Mom wrote to Rena Alderman," Jules told him.

Lincoln thought of the irony of Jules finding that note when he was agonizing over the story he had to tell her.

"Did you know that Mrs. Alderman came to visit Mom when she was sick?"

"No," he said. "She never told me that."

"Wonder why?" Jules asked, but the question was rhetorical.

He hated what he knew he had to do. He took another draw on his mother's stale menthol and launched in.

"I've got to tell you something," he said.

She gave him her full regard with those big Holly Golightly eyes of hers.

"I haven't thought about it for a long time. Part of it I didn't even know until today. But there hasn't been any real reason to think about it for years, decades."

"What is it?" She asked the question but her mind still seemed off somewhere else.

"It's about Dad and something he did just before he died," he said. "Something he did to Sam Alderman."

"Sam? He barely knew Sam. We weren't even friends back then."

Well, he had her attention, at least. "The day of the accident . . . the wreck," he corrected himself, "Dad had been out fishing. And drinking . . . I guess I need to start before that. I was working as a camp counselor that summer at the park near the boat landing. Remember?"

Jules nodded.

"Sam was going to camp with his buddies. He wasn't in my group, but I knew who he was. Anyway, four of them, Sam and his buddies, slipped away from the group. I guess they goaded each other into skinny-dipping off the marsh creek dock while the other kids were crabbing down the bank."

Lincoln told her all that he remembered. Much as he didn't want to, he could still see it playing out in his head. The adult leader asked him to go look for the boys. Sam's friends saw Lincoln coming and scrambled out of the water. They'd taken off by the time Lincoln got to the dock. But Sam hadn't seen him, was oblivious.

"Get out of there," Lincoln called. "Are you crazy? Get your clothes on and get back with the group. Where'd your buddies go?" He looked around, but they'd disappeared.

Lincoln was annoyed with Sam. It was clear that the younger boy had little fear of his teenage counselor's anger. Sam knew that Lincoln wouldn't likely turn any of them in to the grown-up leaders, so Sam was laughing as Lincoln took his hand and helped him back onto the dock. He was laughing still when Jack Fuller surprised both of them.

Lincoln didn't see him arrive, but at some point his drunken father brought his boat up beside the dock. He got out and took a hard swipe at the younger boy's cheek before the bastard said a word. Sam went facefirst into the splintered wood of the dock, then raised his head, spitting blood, and Jack landed another punch to his head.

"You fucking little prick," Jack said before hauling Sam up and throwing him down again. "You teasing my boy? Making fun of him? Or are you a little faggot, too?" With no clothes to grab on to, Jack had a blood-stopping grip around Sam's arm just above the elbow. Lincoln grabbed at the boy and tried to pull his dad away. He could smell his father's stale breath, ripe with beer, but as hard as he tried, he couldn't get the boy free.

Jack hauled Sam off toward the parking lot, and when Sam stumbled, the crazy bastard continued his forward progress without regard to dragging the boy behind him.

"Stop it!" Lincoln screamed, running after them. He caught up once, and Jack shoved him hard. He hit the gravel and looked up to see Jack throwing Sam into his truck that was parked at the landing.

"What are you? Some damn lunatic?!?" Lincoln got up and started running again. "Let him go!"

But the older man hadn't let Sam go. Horrified, Lincoln watched the truck pull away and drive off.

"I ran after them," Lincoln told Jules. "I ran, but I couldn't get Sam away from him. Good God, Jules, I tried."

"Oh, Lincoln," she said.

"I ran to my car and followed Dad's truck. I hadn't been driving more than six months. It's a wonder I didn't end up in the Cape Fear. I lost them. I had no idea where they went. I went home and told Mom what happened. She called Rena Alderman, and by that time, Sam was with her. Dad had already brought him there in a rage and gone."

"Oh, my God." Jules shook her head. Lincoln knew it was

too much—too much to tell her at once. But he'd had it tightly contained for so long, and with it finally free, he couldn't stop. He had to get it all out. Everything he knew.

"Dad drove to Sam's house. Sam was just this little kid, all messed up, still naked. Dad yelled threats at Sam's mother, and she took a rifle off the wall."

"The rifle?" Jules said. "*The* rifle?"

"Yeah," he said. "That's when it happened, the thing with her hearing. I guess Dad tried to grab the gun and it went off. Sheer luck that it didn't hit anybody. Sam said his mother talked to the police, she was in the process of filing a report to have Dad arrested when . . ." He stopped. How to even say it?

"The accident happened," Jules finished. Still not really grasping that the two stories were really one.

"Dad didn't die because of an accident."

"Oh, so the splintered wreckage of both of those boats was . . . what? A movie stunt?"

"Don't be an asshole," he said. "This is hard for me, Jules. I'm trying to do the right thing and tell you about this."

"I'm sorry," she said, but he could tell she still didn't get it. She had no idea what was coming. The story of their father's death was so ingrained in her mental log of family lore that not even his preamble made her challenge it.

"Lyndon Alderman ran over Dad's boat on purpose, Jules."

"That's crazy," she said. "Even if he wanted to do that, how would Mr. Alderman have known where to find Dad?"

"When the police chief was with Sam and his parents, one of his guys went to track Dad down," Lincoln explained. "The officer came back in and told them Dad had been spotted out on his boat off Hunt's Point. That's when Mr. Alderman left the house. The next thing anyone knew, reports were coming in about two boats colliding." Lincoln shook his head. "Can you believe the bastard went back and started fishing again like nothing had happened?"

Jules stared down at the concrete below her feet. She didn't say anything.

"Do you understand?" He spoke slowly, hated the horrible look on her face. "It was never an accident."

"That's ridiculous." Her voice was barely there. "Mr. Alderman died, too. Why would he do that?"

"Maybe he didn't think his boat would take that much damage," Lincoln said, "Or maybe he had no idea he would be thrown. Or maybe he was so furious that he didn't think at all. Remember how Dad beat the shit out of me? Imagine finding out that someone did that to your kid? If Sam had been my son, I'd have run down the son-of-a-bitch, too."

"He really beat Sam?"

"It was bad, Jules." Lincoln could still see him on that dock. "It was really bad. And with swelling and bruising, God knows what he looked like by the time Mr. Alderman saw him."

"Damn it." Her cigarette had burned down to a line of ashes and singed her fingertip. She dropped it on the patio and crushed it with the toe of her shoe. "Why didn't you tell me?"

"Why *would* we tell you? You knew Dad could be a real bastard, and you loved him anyway. By the end of the day, he was gone. They both were, him and Lyndon Alderman. It didn't serve anything to make you feel more conflicted than you already did about him."

"So why now?" she asked, staring out past the dark yard and to the marsh beyond. "Why are you telling me this now?"

"The report Rena was in the process of filing that day—it was a statement of everything that happened—that report is still around somewhere. Sam was afraid they'd dig it up looking into your case. You just got a call about some unexpected information. That may be it. I didn't want you to find out by reading it in a file. Rena never had a chance to officially press charges before her husband took Dad out."

"Is that it?" she asked. "You and Sam had a powwow about whether or not to tell me?"

"Sam's got other issues. His concern is that they'll figure out that his father intended to kill our dad. Rena got an insurance settlement—a big one—based on accidental death. I don't think she thought about it as fraud. I'm sure she wasn't thinking at all. But Sam's uncle handled the insurance. And the police chief was a friend of the Aldermans. He kept it quiet and filed the report away so no one would put it together."

"You've known all this time?" She sounded more hurt than angry.

"Some of it. I knew he beat Sam up. And I knew the collision wasn't an accident."

"How did you know?" Her voice was flat. She still wasn't looking at him.

"The deputy called Mom when he was looking for Dad, and Rena told her she'd planned to have Dad arrested. They were friends back then. Mrs. Alderman told Mom that Lyndon left the station so angry she didn't even want him to drive. It wasn't real hard to put together what happened after that. I asked Mom point-blank and she told me the truth. I've wrestled with this all afternoon, Jules. I decided it was better for you to hear it from me now."

"Hearing it from you a couple of decades ago might have been even better," she said.

"Would it?" He wasn't going to apologize for protecting her from the story for all those years. He refused.

"I don't know." She sounded bitter and he didn't blame her. But she'd get over it. She wouldn't stay mad at him. She never did. "I thought you never liked Sam. I had no idea you'd been through something like that with him."

Lincoln lit another of his mother's cigarettes, gave Jules a drag when she reached for it. "He's an okay guy. I guess I just never liked to think of him one way or the other. It was a shitty day I didn't want to relive, and when I looked at him, it was hard not to see it all again. I don't know . . . Give me that thing." He took the cigarette from her. "Nostalgia's over. I'm going into Uncle Lincoln mode and cutting you off. The kid's going to have three arms if you keep this up."

Jules waved her hand through the smoke in front of her. "The smell is making me sick anyway."

Lincoln stood up, and she followed.

"Are you okay?" he asked.

"Not really," she said. "But I'll get over it. It's just a lot to think about." From the look on her face, he knew that the understatement wasn't lost on either on them.

On the way back to his room, Lincoln saw the furniture in the darkened den. If he squinted, he could almost see his mother there. He wondered if she would be relieved that he'd finally told Jules their story. Somehow, he doubted it. In general, her children's happiness, their protection, usually trumped full disclosure, he recalled. But he had no choice, really. There were so few choices, sometimes.

Chapter Fifteen

Jules went through the clothes in Marnee's summer closet. Most of what Jules had worn already lay scattered on the floor of her room. Some of them clean, some of them not. She made a mental note to take a load of things to the cleaner's. But for the meeting, Hunter had told her to look as conservative as possible. She searched through the hangers for something appropriate. Something dark. Marnee's summer tastes ran toward color and flowing fabrics. But there was one navy pantsuit, way in the back of the closet, that looked as if it might work.

She remembered her mother had worn it to a town meeting when she was trying to get the city council to put up funding for renovation of the senior center. Marnee had called it her lawyer costume. The center got its funding. Maybe that would bode well for Jules' legal woes. She took the suit out and put it on, leaving the shirt untucked to camouflage her growing belly.

She hadn't slept well, still shaken by her conversation with Lincoln the night before. It was as if an alternate reality had existed just beneath the surface of her regular life.

She thought of her dad, in the boat, watching the larger boat come at him without turning away, without slowing. Did he feel terror or resignation? Was he still too drunk to register any of that? He did horrible things, she knew. But she could never completely dismiss the gentle way he pulled her onto his lap when he watched TV. The way he took licorice from his pocket every Sunday in church, grinned as if he planned to eat it himself, and then gave it to her, rolling his eyes to say he wanted it, but he couldn't bear to refuse her.

He never gave Lincoln any of that attention. Sober, he pretty much ignored her brother. Drunk, he became someone hell-bent on damage of one sort or another.

"We're quite the ball-buster today, aren't we?" Lincoln said when she came into the kitchen in the suit.

"I can only hope." She poured a glass of orange juice. "I need to run a couple of errands on the way to town," she said, leaving out the specifics on purpose. "Do you want to just meet me there?"

Lincoln leaned against the counter by the sink. He raised one eyebrow to show her he was on to her, but he didn't ask any questions. "Sure," he said. "I'll drive the truck. You want to eat something before you leave?"

She shook her head. "Not hungry. Besides, Mom wasn't that much bigger than I am." She pulled at the waist of her pants. "With the baby growing, I can barely button these things as it is." She found her purse and her keys. "I'm off. I'll see you there."

Outside, she began to sweat immediately. The humidity turned her hormonally challenged glands into a sopping mess. She was going to look like Nixon debating JFK by the time she met up with Hunter.

"Hey!" a boy's voice called to her before she reached the car. "Hey!" he said again in case she hadn't heard him.

The boy stood at the road. He wore blue jeans and a white T-shirt and looked like any normal teenage kid. But he wasn't. She knew it was Vick, could vaguely recognize him from the days she spent in his classroom. Here was the kid who'd caused her a world of misery. She felt herself getting angry, just looking at him.

"Can I talk to you for a minute?" he asked.

Only if you're going to finally spit out the truth. "Sure," she said, trying to keep her temper in check.

He walked over and stood beside her at Marnee's car. "You look nice," he said. "Do you really have a baby in there?" He pointed to her midsection. "Bart, my brother, said you did."

"Yes," she said. "There's a baby." His gentle demeanor was disarming. "Vick, what are you doing here?"

"I wanted to talk to you," he said. "I came by a couple of times before, but you weren't here."

She looked at him closely, tried to remember if he'd ever done or said anything remarkable in the drama class. He'd been one of the crowd, nothing more. And nothing he'd done would have given her a clue about what was to come.

"Why did you say those things?" she asked, trying to keep her voice gentle. "You've gotten me in a lot of trouble. I've had to hire a lawyer and I'm going for another meeting with the police right now. I can't even go back home to California because of you."

"I told them it was me," he said, not looking at her directly. "I told them it was my idea."

"It doesn't matter. I'm the grown-up." Was she? In her thirty-eight years, had she ever thought of herself once as a full-fledged adult? She paid taxes, had a job. But she was also living in LA, which to many stood for Long-term Adolescence. She glanced down at the suit she wore, the matching pumps with heels. She certainly *looked* like an adult. "You need to tell them the truth. That I didn't do anything with you."

"It'll be okay," he said, still avoiding her eyes.

"No it won't, Vick. It won't be okay. What you said didn't happen. You have to be honest about that."

"No!" He looked up, his expression suddenly urgent. "It did happen."

Jules thought of what Lincoln told her, that Vick believed his story. It wasn't that exactly, but, at best, he was confused. In spite of herself, she felt sorry for the kid. Something was going on. Lincoln had said as much, and she saw what her brother meant.

"Vick, I've told them over and over I didn't do anything with you. That's the truth. Look at me. If you're in some kind of trouble, there are people who can help. But this lie isn't going to do you any good. I've told them that it didn't happen, and they *will* figure out I'm telling the truth. Do you hear me? You need to stop lying. We can help you if you tell the truth."

"You told them it didn't happen?" he said. He was breathing fast. His eyes had gone wild and unfocused. And to her amazement, she saw tears on his face.

"Even your uncle Walt knows it's not true," she said, hoping to bring him around to reality.

"You talked to *him*?" Vick's expression when he said "him" suggested that Walt was some kind of villain, the last person who should be told.

"Vick," she said, trying to keep calm. "What's wrong?" She was in way over her head. The kid had bigger problems than teacher fantasies. "Vick, go to your uncle Walt and tell him what's wrong. Whatever it is, he'll help you. You know he will. It doesn't matter what's happened. He'll help you."

She thought of Walt Walker, sitting beside her in the cemetery. She felt calmer just picturing his face. He was an ally. Someone her mother would call a good man. She'd known all of this within minutes of being near him. "Go to Walt," she said. "And we'll get this all straightened out."

"Walt's a son-of-a-bitch." Vick's voice changed. It carried such venom that she physically stepped back.

"What would you say that for?" she asked. "Vick, tell me what's really going on."

Vick Johns looked at her. He was nearly her height, but still had more growing to do before he matched the proportions of his feet and hands. Still, his expression had suddenly turned old. "I can make anything true I want. Don't you understand? I can even say I killed my daddy and it could be true. But one thing's for sure. Walt's not my daddy. Never was, never will be." He locked his eyes on her face for a split second longer, then turned and ran.

"Vick!" she called, but he kept running toward the low line of trees on the dry ground away from the marsh.

With her foot still weak from the sprain, she wouldn't catch him, even if she tried. *Jesus. I can even say I killed my daddy? What the hell was that about?*

"What's going on?" Lincoln was on the porch, looking out toward the trees where Vick had just disappeared. "Who were you yelling at?"

"Little man Vick was just here," she told him. "And you won't believe some of the stuff he said."

She told him about her strange interaction with the boy. "I started out being really pissed at him, but . . ."

"Now you feel sorry for him." Lincoln finished her thought.

"Yeah."

"Me too," Lincoln said, coming down the porch stairs to stand beside her. "Should we go after him?"

"He probably went home," she told him. "I know he lives down the road, and he was headed in that direction. And if I go running to his house after him, God knows what they'll say I was doing. I shouldn't even be talking to him. But something's happened to that child, that's for sure." She let out a long breath, hoped she was expelling bad energy and breathing in good. "I've gotta go if I'm going to run my errands and get to City Hall for this meeting," she said, still not telling him that she planned to go talk to Sam. "And I need to allow time to tell Hunter about all this. I'll fill you in when we're done there. Maybe the psych report will give us some clues. Man, does that kid have problems, though."

"You think?" Lincoln walked toward the porch steps, leaned on the banister. He'd lost some weight, but even so, his face looked puffy. It worried her. He offered a wave and attempted to smile as she laid the jacket of her mother's suit in the backseat of the Buick. Out the side window of the car, she saw him standing there, still, as she drove away.

Chapter Sixteen

Sam set his coffee cup on the windowsill and looked out at the surf. The cottage was closer to the beach than current building codes allowed. He wondered if a hurricane would come one day to claim the house and everything in it. Would he be there at the time? Some days he wished for that kind of excitement. Crazy really, but a hurricane, if he survived it, would make him feel more alive than he had in years. Hell, Jules made him feel more alive than he had in years.

Had Lincoln told her? If so, *what* had her brother said? Just how much did she need to know? He'd been a kid when it all happened. Still, he hated the thought of her imagining him like that. It was the most humiliating day of his life, and the most frightening. The worst he had ever experienced. Not many people had a single memory they could point to with such certainty.

It had been weird, talking about it with Lincoln. Having the conversation with the other living person who had been there made the whole thing immediate again. Sam could still see Lincoln as he had been that summer. Sam, so young at the time, had no real concept of what gay was, much less that the term applied to the older kid working as a counselor at the summer park program. And he would never have known about Lincoln—or at least not until much later when the general gossip began to circulate—except that he took the stupid dare to skinny-dip that afternoon.

Sam could feel himself in Fuller's truck again, huddled low near the floorboard, both because he was naked and because he was terrified. Over the years, a lot had gone fuzzy in his mind about that ride. But Sam remembered losing hope as he heard Lincoln's shouts fading in the distance. The drunk bastard, unsteady at the wheel, was driving him off to God-knew-where and the only other person involved had been left in the dust.

Jules' father had driven him to his mother's house. Naked, in the cab of Fuller's truck, Sam had no idea where they were headed, and his own home was the last place he'd expected to end up. He thought he might be dragged off to some shed and beaten to death. He'd almost come to terms with something that horrible. A strange calm came over him. Then he'd recognized his street and became terrified all over again. Somehow, facing his parents seemed like the worst thing that could happen. He didn't know why. He hadn't actually *done* anything but go skinny-dipping with a bunch of boys.

Fuller dragged him into the side door of his house without knocking. His mother came running into the den, where the man threw him down on the floor like an old rug.

"This little faggot of yours is prancing around in front of my boy at camp. I'm out fishing and I see him on the pier with my boy, laughing, trying to get something started. If you can't teach him to act decent in public, you best keep him at home."

Sam bled in a dozen places including his mouth. He could still taste it. His penis had shriveled to insignificant proportions from both fear and the blasting AC in the truck. The shame of it all was so huge that, even as an adult, thinking of it made him wince. His mother covered him with an afghan from the couch, and when Jack Fuller took a step toward the two of them—for purposes unknown—Rena had grabbed his dad's hunting rifle off the gun rack on the wall and leveled it at Jules' father. Without any fear that she would actually fire, the man stepped forward and grabbed the barrel, causing the weapon to discharge.

Sam remembered the next part as if watching it on video. His mother fell backward onto the floor. At first, he'd been afraid she was shot, but she'd fallen either from the shock of the noise—which left her nearly deaf in one ear—or the kick of the gun. Jack Fuller, now holding the gun, looked down at both of them, then placed the weapon carefully back on the rack. It was as if the gun deserved all the respect that he and his mother did not. Then the monster walked out the door.

First Dr. Fletcher arrived, then the police chief. Sam told them what happened, but he had no memory of this part. Repeating it made it live again in his head, so he blocked out even the telling of it. Rena reached his father at work and Lyndon Alderman had come home in time to hear the last telling. The deputy who'd come with the chief came into the room and said that Fuller was spotted on his boat. Shortly after, his father was nowhere to be found.

In the truck with a drunken Jack Fuller, Sam thought he was going to die. But by the end of the day, Sam had been very much alive. The same could not be said of Jack Fuller—or his own father.

"You're quiet this morning," Rena spoke over her shoulder to Sam as she brought freshly washed curtains into the room so she could rehang them over the small side window of the beach cottage.

He'd spent the early morning on the deck, putting a coat of

sealant on the teak chairs. The solitary hours on the deck had been calming, and he'd hoped to extend the calm through his coffee break. No such luck. His mother was right, he didn't feel like talking.

"I'm fine," he said. "I'm a little worried about work. Things pile up when I'm away too long." That was a lie. His job at Fenton Pharmaceuticals had none of the stress of academic medicine. Much of his work could be done by phone or e-mail, so he wouldn't even be that far behind when he returned.

Work barely entered into thoughts that were filled with Jules and police records. If the old report surfaced, everything his mother owned could be in jeopardy. He looked around the beach cottage. It was still in his mother's name, although she'd talked about signing it over to him and his younger sister.

"Sam?" His mother looked at him as if she was waiting for him to respond.

"I'm sorry," he said. "I didn't hear you."

"I said that your friend just drove up." Her icy tone left little doubt about who the friend might be. "Why is she *here*?"

"I don't know, Mom." But he did know. Lincoln had told her.

Jules wore a dark pantsuit that looked as if it had belonged on her mother. Likewise, the starched, white blouse, untucked with the shirttail out so that her belly was under wraps. It was sexy in a kick-your-ass sort of corporate way.

"Sorry to barge in like this," she said. "I called your house and Tessa said you were out here."

Tessa was the black woman who'd come in to help Rena with housework every Tuesday and Thursday since the Pilgrims landed.

"I don't have long," she explained. "I'm supposed to be at the City Hall in forty-five minutes."

Rena said a brief hello and then made herself scarce. Jules

looked over her shoulder as if Sam's mother might be hiding somewhere near, ready to jump out and say boo.

"Come on in. Sit down. Do you want some coffee?" He remembered that baby again and added. "Or water?"

"I'm good," she said. She stood near the couch, but didn't sit down. She reminded him of a lawyer getting ready for a closing argument. "You look really . . . adult," he told her. Outside, just beyond the thin strip of sea grass, the sun reflected off the water with blinding intensity.

"We're meeting with the psychologist today," she said. "Hunter told me to wear a suit or something. I found these in Mom's closet. Closest thing I could manage."

"Looks nice," Sam said.

She looked uncomfortable, as if trying to act normal, but not quite pulling it off.

They stood for a moment without talking, and she finally relented and sat down.

Unlike earlier times when a lull in words might have been part of the ebb and flow of their conversation, the silence between them implied hesitation. He sat in the chair opposite her and waited.

"Lincoln told me everything last night," she said at last. "At least everything he knows." Sam opened his mouth to speak, although he had no idea what he wanted to tell her, but she stopped him, continued with what she'd obviously come to say.

"You went all those years without saying anything about our dads—about what my dad did to you." She stopped, pressed her lips together, and took a breath. "All those times we were together. We had a lot of discussions about the weird stuff between our families . . ."

"We never talked specifically about our dads," he said. "I thought it was just understood that it should be left alone."

"The things the two of us believed about that day were entirely different. You knew and I didn't. We talked about the baggage, how we wished our families could get past everything," she said. "There were opportunities over and over for you to tell me and you didn't."

"Lincoln kept quiet," he said. "And your mother, for that matter. No one thought that telling you would have accomplished anything. Everything that happened was horrible, horrible enough without inflicting it on you."

"I'm not asking you to explain anything for Lincoln or Mom," she said.

"I know," he said, "but you can't separate them from this entirely. Everyone cared about you and wanted to do the right thing for you."

"What gave him the right?" she asked, as if the question made sense.

"Who?"

"Your father." She leaned forward, closer to Sam. The question wasn't really confrontational. She sounded more baffled than angry. "How could he do that? To my family. To yours."

"It wasn't a clear decision, Jules. He was angry. Did you not listen to *everything* Lincoln told you? My dad died. You think he wanted that? Your father set it in motion. Everything that happened started when he came onto that dock. My dad reacted to an assault on his family."

"I'm not trying to justify my own father's actions," she said. "My God, I knew he was capable of doing horrible things, but this . . ." Her voice shook at he watched her collect herself before she continued. "But that doesn't make what your father did okay. It doesn't make the fact that you kept quiet about it okay."

"Listen to yourself, Jules. You're not being fair."

"I don't want anything from you at this point, Sam. I just

thought we ought to have some kind of acknowledgment of the things Lincoln told me. Just so it's out there. It makes everything seem different."

"So at least acknowledge *everything* he told you. Your dad beat the shit out of me, then dragged me to my own house so he could scare Mom out of her mind." He was getting pissed. He wanted the conversation to be over. It couldn't end well, and he wanted to be done with it.

"I feel betrayed," she said, finally. "It's like every minute we spent together was a lie." She leaned in closer, so that she could speak even more quietly. "I don't blame *you* for what your father did." She expelled a long breath as if she'd been holding her lungs full in anticipation of something. "Honestly," she said. "I'm not even sure I blame *him* for running over Dad's boat. Lincoln certainly thinks your dad's kamikaze mission was some act of heroism. But to never tell me . . ." She sat back, putting distance between them.

"I would apologize," he said, fighting several emotions at once. "But that wouldn't be genuine. Not even close. I know you cared about your dad in spite of his flaws. I loved mine, too. And they were both gone. Telling you didn't seem to serve any purpose. I understand why Lincoln told you. The police station is no place to stumble on a story like this. But even now, I can't tell you I'm sorry for staying silent all these years."

"Well, I didn't come for an apology." She stood, her defenses up again. "And I'm not really trying to resolve anything. We haven't been *us* for a long time, so there's nothing to *get past* or anything like that. I guess I just needed some sort of moment when we spoke the truth about this."

He felt something collapsing inside. Something elemental and irretrievable. It wasn't the end of who they were, however new and undefined their current relationship might be. It was the end of who they'd been. Memories forever colored by the conversation they'd just had. The one they'd never had back then.

She picked up her purse, and he walked her to the front door. Then he watched her walk to her car. Even from a slight distance, she looked like Marnee Fuller walking away from him. But unlike her daughter, Marnee had understood the complexities of everything that happened. Maybe Jules was right. By keeping the secret, they had denied her the opportunity to see it in a larger perspective. To come to terms with how and why her dad died.

"She'll tell someone out of spite." Rena was suddenly there beside him, looking out at Marnee's car pulling away. "That brother of hers made a mistake in telling her. She'll use it to hurt us."

"She won't do anything to us, Mom," he said. He felt sorry for his mother. The bitterness made it impossible for her to understand anything about Jules. "She's not responsible for what happened back then. She's hurt, but she's not vindictive."

"Well then, that's another thing that's different between us," Rena said, going to an oak bookcase and wiping down the sides with Old English. "I hope they convict her for what she did with that child, and I hope they put her away until she's too old to care about having sex with anyone."

Sam wasn't sure he'd ever heard his mother utter the word "sex" before.

"What did she ever do to you?" Sam asked. "Honestly, why do you hate her so much?"

"That father of hers," Rena said, stopping with the oiled cloth draped over her hand, "didn't deserve the regard she gave him. She actually believes he was worthy of being considered human. She's got this idea that he might have been flawed, but that he wasn't evil. Even now—even after she knows what he did to you that day—she still thinks it. You can hear it in the way she talks about him. Well, Jack Fuller was a monster. And Jules? If she can't accept who he really was, she can join him in hell."

She turned to her work again. For the first time in his life, Sam wanted to sell the cottage. Ever since high school, the place had defined the best kind of happiness for him, and he understood that Jules had been central to that. Even when he'd been there with his wife, memories of his younger self fueled his imagination. But in an instant all seemed to have been lost. When he looked around him, he no longer saw himself at seventeen with Jules on the deck, laughing and sunning themselves—the flower tattoo on her thigh seeming to blossom as the relentless rays turned her skin pink. He no longer saw Jules waiting for him on the bed back in his room.

All of those memories had been replaced by Jules as he'd just seen her. Dressed in Marnee Fuller's borrowed clothes, laying waste to every good memory they ever had.

Chapter Seventeen

Lincoln walked out onto the porch and closed the door behind him. He thought of locking it, then realized how ridiculous that would be. No one would come in to steal anything. Even if they did, none of it mattered anymore. Without Marnee there, they could steal the whole lot of it—hell, even burn the place down—and he wouldn't care. Being around their mother's things made Jules feel better, but for him, there was no such comfort in silver and glass. The piano mattered, he supposed. That was about it.

The low sound in the direction of the woods took his attention away from feeling sorry for himself. He listened closely as a mewling whimper—something between a bird sound and a mammal in distress—suddenly escalated into a cry of sorts followed by silence. He thought it could be an animal, but it sounded human. He went down the porch stairs and took off running toward the noise. He heard it again, but the register fell lower than before, descending into a halting series of grunts. By the time he got to the edge of the woods, he had only small sounds, the barest of clues to go on as he moved in through the trees.

Nearby, in the low, thick branches, he saw the boy, his feet inches off the ground, with legs bare below his cotton boxers. Lincoln's adrenaline went into overdrive as he struggled on uneven ground to reach the child. Some part of him made note that blood seemed to be spattered on the boy's arms. But the urgent concern was to get him down. Vick hung from a tree branch. One leg of his jeans was tied to the limb, the other knotted in a loop around his neck.

"Vick!" he shouted as he approached. "Hang on. Christ!" Lincoln grabbed the boy by the hips and lifted to take the pressure off his neck. As he held Vick over his shoulder, Lincoln fought to loosen the denim, but the pressure of the boy's sudden weight had tightened the knot. "Oh, Christ," Lincoln mumbled again as he worked with one hand. The other arm supported the child, kept the material loose. After a minute or two, he was able to make progress. As he worked his fingers into the knot, he tried to figure out if the kid was breathing. The noises had stopped and he couldn't tell. Sweet Jesus. *He couldn't tell*.

As the noose came free, Lincoln lost his footing and the two of them went down hard. The boy's cry on impact made Lincoln giddy with relief.

"Can you breathe okay?" Lincoln asked.

Vick gulped in, hiccup-ridden bits of air, followed by coughing fits as he tried to expel each breath. He turned to look at Lincoln with eyes that seemed to barely comprehend that anyone was with him.

The boy's T-shirt felt damp with sweat. The boxers, also wet, had a distinct odor. From the smell Lincoln figured Vick had pissed himself. But there was also a vaguely metallic scent, and Lincoln scanned him quickly for signs of blood. On Vick's wrists, thin stripes of smeared red exposed his efforts. The wounds didn't look too bad and seemed to have stopped actively bleeding. "We've got to get a doctor," Lincoln said. He took a deep breath and began his efforts to get Vick to his feet.

Vick was mostly noncommunicative, but to Lincoln's relief, he held some of his own weight, but his head fell sideways at an unnatural angle. As Lincoln half pulled, half carried him toward the house, he saw a large Swiss Army knife lying on the ground by the tree. It had bits of blood in the serrated edge, and Lincoln forced down the nausea that rose in his chest. "Oh, God, Vick," he muttered as he made his way with the boy toward the pickup.

Somehow, through his own efforts and weaker attempts from Vick, Lincoln managed to secure him in the truck's cabin. As he drove, he wondered if his own heart would explode from the sheer terror of the ordeal. He felt the beats, coming fast and hard in his chest. The hospital was too far, would take too long. He could get him to the medical clinic in town. That's where he'd have to go.

When he finally saw the doctor's office in sight, he allowed himself to glance over toward Vick Johns. The child's head was still flopped to the side—his eyes wide with panic and his skin the color of putty.

"Stay with me, Vick," he said. "We're there now, you understand? Stay awake, you hear? We're getting some help, buddy."

Lincoln saw him try. Vick Johns offered the weakest of nods. That's when Lincoln allowed himself some small hope that everything might turn out okay.

He drove up onto the curve near the front door of the doctor's office, got out of the truck, and ran to the passenger door. As he moved, he yelled for someone—anyone—to help, and immediately multitudes of people came out of offices and storefronts.

Slowly, Lincoln felt the physical burden of Vick Johns begin to lighten as strangers took over, carrying the boy.

Lincoln bent forward with his hands on his knees. He thought he might fall, but miraculously stayed on his feet. That's when he finally gave in to the nausea, retching with hard, dry heaves that left him gasping for air.

Chapter Eighteen

Even through the bottoms of her shoes, Jules could feel the heat of the asphalt parking lot. The moment she stepped out of the car, the blacktop pressed hot into her mother's leather pumps, branding the soles with the grainy imprint of the ground below her. She looked around for Marnee's truck. Lincoln was supposed to meet her there, and since she had the car he would be in the pickup Marnee kept around to haul things. Seems they could do nothing without appropriating their mother's life.

Jules thought about the conversation she had with Sam. Why *did* she hold him to a different standard than Lincoln? He'd been right to ask, even though she was too proud to admit it to him. But there was a difference. Both Lincoln and her mother truly had been silent to protect her. Sam's motives seemed less pure. Her gut told her they involved his own need for self-preservation. That's why it hurt her to even think about it.

Jules looked around. She didn't see Lincoln or the truck. Maybe he'd parked on the street.

Inside City Hall, the cold, artificial air made her shudder. She took the stairs two levels down to the police station, and Hunter greeted her in the hall outside one of the rooms. Just inside, she saw Cici Johns, along with Walt and Tuni Walker. The boy wasn't there, but then, since he was a minor, they probably had rules about when he could or could not be present. Two other women were there as well. Maybe one of them was the boy's lawyer. The other, she guessed, was the psychologist Hunter had mentioned.

Walt made eye contact as she came in the room. His mouth offered that same slow beginning of a smile. Barely perceptible, but enough to make her wonder what he thought of her. She saw herself as he might see her and felt falsely represented in her mother's suit. Then she thought of Vick's reaction when she mentioned Walt's name. Maybe Walt was the one falsely representing himself. She made her way toward Hunter.

"So what are we doing here?" she whispered as her lawyer handed her copies of the papers everyone seemed to be holding.

"All by-the-book stuff," he whispered back. "The psychologist is here, she's finished her evaluation. Plus there's another report from Vick's old school that's turned up."

That was the *other* information that had come to light. The entire confessional by Lincoln had been unnecessary, after all. But that tight coil of truth that had sprung free the night before could not be untold. Just as well. It was about damn time she knew the truth. Adults accepted the truth and moved on. If she was going to be a mother, it had to begin with acting like an adult.

"So what do the reports say?" she asked, her voice still low.

"The school report was faxed yesterday so I haven't had a lot of time with it," Hunter told her. "The district was concerned with Vick's fighting. There'd been some before, but it escalated after his father died. The theory was that his ongoing arguments with his father made the death even harder on him."

Everyone seemed to be settling in to begin.

"Actually, there's something I should tell you." She was about to fill him in on Vick's visit to her house and the bizarre statement about killing his daddy. But she felt her cell phone buzz in her purse. "Hold on a sec," she said, glancing at the screen. "It's Lincoln. He's supposed to meet me here."

At the same time that Lincoln's agitated voice relayed to her some crazy story about Vick nearly hanging himself in the woods by their house, a policeman came in and pulled Cici Johns out into the hall. The wail that came from the woman just moments later told Jules that the boy's mother had heard the same story from the officer that Lincoln had told her. Vick Johns had apparently tried to commit suicide.

She felt herself go weak. Their meeting disbanded before it actually began, as news of Vick Johns' attempt on his life sank in. They headed en masse out of City Hall and down the street to the town's medical clinic.

Half the residents of Ekron, it seemed, crowded outside the medical clinic. Jules looked out the window and saw them milling around as if waiting for a parade. Lincoln sat beside her. His face registered the shock of the morning's events. She thought that he must look almost as bad as the boy, until the door to the examining room opened and she caught a glimpse of Vick.

Limp and shirtless, he was lying on the examining table; his ashen color sent a moment of panic through her. What if Lincoln hadn't gotten him there in time? But then Jules saw his face and his eyes were open and focused on the door. He looked at her and she had the impulse to run and hug the child, to tell him she was sorry she hadn't come after him when he ran away. *I didn't know how bad it was, Vick.* The boy had been to hell and back because of something or someone.

Preacher Walker and his wife sat in the corner, holding hands, with their heads bowed. Beside them, another, younger man joined in their prayer vigil. Jules had almost forgotten that the boy who had caused her such misery was her preacher's grandson. Cici seemed to belong somewhere else, not among the levelheaded Walkers. Even in his rowdy high school days, Walt came off as solid, reliable. Cici, on the other hand, seemed like a sudden storm, all strong air that laid things to waste and then moved on. She stood beside the praying trio and glared at Lincoln.

"Vick's going to be all right, Linc," Jules said, putting her hand on her brother's arm. "You did all the right things. He would have died if you hadn't gotten to him. But you did. You saved his life."

While Cici acted as if Lincoln was somehow responsible for her son's decision to use his blue jeans as a noose, Walt came over and thanked her brother.

"They're sending an ambulance to take him to the hospital in Wilmington. But it looks like he's going to be okay. I appreciate what you did," he said. "I knew my nephew had problems . . ." He glanced over at Cici, and Jules wondered if he was at a loss over his nephew or his sister's lack of gratitude toward the man who saved his life. "I just had no idea how bad things had gotten."

Lincoln nodded, offered a weak smile in response to Walt's efforts. But Jules saw that her brother was in his own private hell.

"You okay?" Walt turned to Jules.

"I think so," she said. She wanted to tell him no, that she wasn't okay. She wanted to offer him comfort and to feel that impulse reciprocated. But a scenario like that had no place in the current situation. In *any* situation. He had a family. "None of this makes any sense," she said, instead. She looked across the room and saw Tuni watching them. Jules had no right to turn to him for anything.

"Who's that with your parents?" Jules asked, changing the subject. She nodded in the direction of the younger man who'd been praying with the Walkers. She would engage Walt on more neutral ground and then end their conversation. She took a half step away, but her body remained conscious of the proximity to him. Even if she forced her mind in another direction entirely, she could not will the nerve endings at the edges of her skin to ignore him.

"That's Garrett," Walt told her. "He's Vick's youth group leader at the church. A little on the quiet side to be in charge of all those kids, but he's been good about helping Vick settle in here since the move. He and Cici have been seeing each other."

"Does Vick mind?" Jules asked. "Some kids get weird when their parents start dating." Could the key to Vick's behavior be that simple?

"Vick likes him, best I can tell," Walt said, "and since the boy doesn't seem to want anything to do with me, I'm glad Garrett has stepped up with him."

Jules was reminded of the boy's reaction when she brought up Walt's name. Vick's response seemed entirely at odds with the man standing in front of her. Was it possible that her judgment could be that flawed? If so, how on earth could she be ready, in a few short months, to make decisions for a defenseless child?

She had to ask him. She had to know. "What does Vick have against you?"

"I'm honestly not sure," he said. "His daddy and I didn't see eye to eye on some things. Maybe he picked up on that before Henry died and holds it against me. Other than that, I couldn't say."

"But Vick and his dad didn't agree, either," Jules said.

"I don't really know." Walt genuinely seemed at a loss.

Both Cici and Tuni glared at Jules from across the room. "I don't think the women in your life are too happy about you talking with me."

"I don't expect they are," he said, not even bothering to turn and look at them. "But we've all got more to worry about than whether the two of us have a conversation or not."

"It's still best if we don't make it worse," she said. "All of you are hurting over what's happened today."

"You're right," he said. His eyes were a color of blue she'd never seen before. And they were devoid of tears, but still full of misery. Vick's attempt on his own life had landed hard on the people around him.

"For whatever reason, Vick won't come to you, Walt," she said. "You can't help him if he won't let you. And you can't blame yourself for what happened today."

"I'm a counselor. I meet with kids all day long." He leaned back and rested against the clinic wall. "I listen to them and mostly make things better. At least I think I do. I should have done that for my own nephew."

She didn't have an answer. Maybe there were no answers.

"Some peace and quiet will make you feel better," she said. "Maybe a trip to the cemetery when the heat of the day starts to settle." She shouldn't have said it, but she couldn't help herself. She knew all of a sudden how Lincoln must feel when he needed a drink.

At first, she thought he hadn't understood, that he didn't know she was inviting him to meet her in the cemetery. Her remark had been cryptic, at best. But then he looked at her, and she saw that he knew exactly what she meant. The other thing she saw was that she wasn't helping him. From the look on Walt's face, God forgive her, she knew she was making things worse. She wanted to take it back. It was wrong from any angle. Why was she so drawn to him? God, she was an idiot.

After a moment, when her remark hung in the air with no place to go, Walt turned to Lincoln, who was still sitting, and said, "Thank you again for getting the boy here." Then he went to join his family on the other side of the room.

Jules lost track of time as they waited. The doctors were still in with the boy. They'd come out once and asked for the court-appointed psychologist to come in. Tuni Walker, Walt's wife, had left at some point and come back again, with Vick's little brother, Bart, in tow.

"Where are the girls?" she heard Walt ask Tuni.

"They're over at the church office with Rhonda," Tuni told him. "She said she'd stay and look after 'em as long as we need."

Jules recognized the boy standing with Tuni from the run-in she'd had with his bike. She was amazed at how her life had changed since the day that happened.

"How're you holding up?" Sam was suddenly beside her.

"Hey," she said, standing. "How did you know I was here?"

"Mom's still got that old police scanner in the kitchen," he said. "I heard the call go out when they were trying to find the kid's mother to tell her what happened."

Jules had forgotten that people in town kept police scanners in their houses—a precursor of the Internet for minute-by-minute local news. In the Alderman house, static could suddenly crackle, followed by some report of a crime or accident. It had startled the bejesus out of her more than once.

"How's the kid?" Sam asked.

"I think he's going to be okay," she said. "At least physically. But I don't know about mentally. Lincoln found him hanging there and somehow got him down before he strangled to death. We don't know why he did it."

"Damn." Sam glanced at Lincoln. "Your poor brother."

Hunter left the deputy he'd been talking with and came over to Jules and Sam. "This guy"—he motioned his head toward the deputy—"he's got a few questions about Vick Johns. About why he was on your property. I've explained that he showed up unannounced and had a brief conversation with Jules. Later, Lincoln heard noises in the woods and found him. There's no reason not to answer his questions. I'll stick around, in case you need me."

The deputy sat down beside Lincoln and began going over the details again with him.

"There's something else I was going to tell you," Jules whispered to Hunter. "I wanted to tell you without being overheard, but I didn't get a chance."

"Okay."

"Vick seemed really upset that I'd told everyone what he said about me wasn't true. I mean, he was really agitated—almost like he'd thought I might go along with it. I don't know. Then he said the weirdest thing. He said, 'I can make anything true I want. I can say I killed my daddy and it could be true.' And he looked kind of disassociated when he said it. I should've followed him when he ran off. I thought he was going home."

Hunter made a face that under other circumstances would have been comical. "The lawyer in me says that the worse he seems, the better for you, but the human in me wants to help the kid, you know?"

Sam listened in, and his expression mirrored her lawyer's disbelief.

"I wouldn't have just let him go if I'd had any idea he might hurt himself." Jules felt miserable.

"I know." Hunter tried to sound reassuring. "How could anyone predict this? The wiring is all different during the teenage years. I've read that, and I swear it's the truth."

Later, as they continued to wait, Hunter stood across the room and spoke with Cici and Vick's lawyer. The sound Cici Johns made left no doubt as to what information had been relayed to the boy's mother.

"He did no such thing!" Her voice would have registered on sonar if it had gone any higher. "His daddy died of an aneurysm while he was standing in line at the post office. Vick most certainly did not kill him. To say such a thing! She made that up. She said that to make the child look crazy. Shame on you!" Cici pointed an accusing finger at Jules. "You are a sick woman. You know that?"

It occurred to Jules that, in light of the day's events, Vick didn't need any help to make him appear unbalanced.

"I didn't say he did it." Jules' response barely gained whisper momentum. "That's just what he said."

"It's probably a Methodist thing he's using," little Bart piped up and spoke for the first time since arriving in the clinic waiting room. "He likes to do that."

"What in the devil are you talking about?" Cici looked at her son as if he was glowing neon green.

"At his old school," Bart continued, adamant that he had the answer. "The acting class teacher told him about Methodist acting. That if you wanted to do your best with being a movie star, you could pretend all the time that the character's life is like yours. Or something like that. Remember when Daddy got so mad and told him he had to quit going to that class, and Vick said no he wasn't never going to quit. That's what they were doing then. That Methodist thing."

"Bart, this isn't the time . . ." Cici tried to silence her youngest, but he hadn't finished and would not be denied.

"You remember. It was when Vick said he was in a Puerto Rican gang 'cause they were doing the *West Side* play, and Daddy said no boy of his was any Puerto Rican anything. He was a Baptist from South Carolina, and he ought to act like it."

The child stopped abruptly, as if he'd exhausted his recollection of Vick's explanation, but the bits and pieces of it were enough for Jules to understand at least part of what he meant.

"It's called Method acting," she said. "A lot of famous actors use it. Some of them stay in character the whole time they're filming their roles, so that they can come off as more authentic on camera."

"That's just the sort of Hollywood bull crap you would know. That business drove Vick's daddy out of his mind," Cici said, sitting down in a chair and running her hand up through her short, brown hair. "It's pure *bullshit*, he used to say," she muttered, then she seemed to catch herself. "Pardon my French, but that's exactly what he'd say. He thought that drama teacher was trying to turn Vick into a fruitcake with all that mess."

"You need to calm down, Cici." Walt's wife, Tuni, put her arm around her sister-in-law. "We'll be able to look after Vick when he gets home. There won't be anyone around filling his head with this kind of mumbo-jumbo and mixing him up anymore." She looked at Jules when she said this.

"Vick said that the Methodist, uh, I mean, *Method* thing worked real good," Bart perked up, in a pitch to extend his moment at the center of things. "Sometimes, if the kids picked on him or somethin', he said he could do that and they'd back off. He could nearly feel like he *was* someone else if he tried hard enough. He told me that."

Jules thought of Vick, pleading with her to go along with his story. The Method technique broke down pretty fast if no one else would play along. But what the hell was he protecting himself from with the charade? Why did he need that story about her in the first place?

One of the doctors came out, and Jules listened as he told Cici, Walt, and Tuni that Vick was going to be okay. He'd bruised his neck badly, but hadn't broken it. The doctor spoke about some cuts on the boy's body that seemed to be superficial. Gestures more than real attempts at harm.

"What cuts?" Jules asked Lincoln.

"His wrists," Lincoln told her, nodding down toward his arms.

"Holy shit." Jules didn't want to think about it but found herself unable to banish the images from her mind.

"As I was leaving, I saw a pocket knife on the ground by the tree. I left it there and told the police where to find it. I hope to hell it's gone when we get home," Lincoln said.

Jules' mouth went dry. A water fountain stood on the far side of the room, and she walked across to get a drink. A young guy she'd seen come into the room a few minutes earlier followed her to the far wall.

He came up beside her. "Excuse me?"

"Yes?" Jules saw that he had a pad of paper in his hand. "Can I help you with something?"

He couldn't have been much older than twenty-two or twenty-three. He wore a wrinkled dress shirt tucked into khakis that could have stood washing.

"I'm a reporter with the *Star-News* in Wilmington," he said. He seemed to be ill at ease, as if his mommy or daddy had made him approach her. "I understand that the boy has made some accusations against you," he said, not meeting her eyes. "Before all this . . ." he clarified himself. "He made accusations before all of this happened. I wondered if you had anything to say about the things he's said, and about his attempt on his life."

"I don't think you're supposed to be here," she said, struggling to locate Hunter's whereabouts in the room. "This isn't a public case. The boy is a minor, and I haven't had any charges made against me."

"I'm here because the kid's mother called my editor," the young man told her, almost apologetically. He sounded as if he was speaking for the first time as a real person, not a reporter. "He says if the mother is the one allowing it to go public, then we can print the story."

Jules felt her cheeks fire hot. Hometown gossip was one thing.

But if Vick's story landed in the paper, she couldn't even think about it.

"I really can't talk to you," she said, feeling a rise of panic in her chest. "You shouldn't be here." Hunter was talking with Sam. She finally caught his eye and motioned him over, and the two of them walked to where she stood with the reluctant reporter.

"I gotta tell you," the reporter said, before Hunter reached her. "The kid's mom is saying you might be pregnant with the boy's baby."

With that, Jules' knees went weak. "Are you joking?" She looked helplessly at her lawyer, who'd arrived at her side and caught the gist of the guy's remark.

"He's with the Wilmington newspaper," Jules told Hunter. "Cici Johns called them."

"You and Lincoln go on home," Hunter said. "I'll take care of things here. I'll call you later and fill you in on where we go next."

"But we have to tell him that's not true," she whispered in her lawyer's ear. "None of it is true."

"That's my job," he told her in low tones. "You don't say anything one way or another." He raised his eyebrows to make the point.

Sam looked angry. Jules was afraid for a second that he might hit the reporter, who, she was convinced, had only come under duress.

"Let it go, Sam," she said. "Hunter'll take care of everything. We should leave."

"She's right, Sam," Hunter said. "Ya'll go home. All of you."

The "ya'll" signaled to Jules that her lawyer was shifting into his we're-both-just-a-couple-of-regular-fellas-here routine. If that didn't work, he'd get hard-ass on the guy. Either way, she felt she was in good hands.

"Let's go, Sam," she said again, motioning across the room to let Lincoln know that she was leaving. Her brother, zombie-like, got up to come with her.

"Slimy bastards," Sam muttered as they moved away from Hunter and the young man. "They feed off garbage. But there's never enough of it to fill 'em up."

"It'll be all right," she said, in a strange juxtaposition of roles. But she wasn't sure she believed it, either.

"I'm going home, and since I can't have a cold beer, I'm getting in a cool tub of water," she told Sam.

"I'll have that beer for you," he said, looking as wrung-out as she felt.

Lincoln continued on toward the car, but Jules stopped for a moment to talk with Sam.

"I appreciate you coming here to help," she said. "I was pretty hard on you before. I wouldn't have expected you to show up."

"We're friends, Jules. Regardless of what's happened now or in the past. We have history. I'll always help if I can."

"No, I don't get off that easily with this one," she told him. "I was out of line with some of the things I said. It all came as such a shock."

"No apology needed," he told her. "Really."

"Thank you," she said. "For everything you've done over the last couple of days."

He hesitated for a second, and she wondered what was on his mind. Finally, he spoke up. "I noticed at lunch . . . Well, you seemed to be wearing . . ."

"I'm pregnant." She hoped her tone put him at ease, but he still looked ready to crawl out of his own skin. "I haven't announced it," she told him, "but it's not a secret, either."

"A boyfriend in LA?" he asked.

"Ex-boyfriend," she said. "By my own choice. I found out he's bipolar and I haven't told him about the baby. I don't plan on telling him."

Sam made a face, seemed troubled by her decision. "People do fine with the disorder, Jules. They've got great meds now."

"Which he's intermittently stopped taking," she said, not wanting to explain everything about Thomas to Sam. Even saying that he nearly killed her, driving like a maniac on the freeway, or that he shoved his ex-wife around during manic episodes, made Jules sound unstable for ever getting involved with him.

"He became frightening when he was off his meds," she said, leaving the details out. "And other people who've known him for a long time say he has a pattern of stopping his treatment on a whim."

"Okay," Sam said. "I wasn't trying to second-guess you. I just thought you might have misconceptions about the disorder. That's all."

"Thanks, Doc," she said, trying to sound light, but neither of them laughed. "I feel bad—wrong—keeping it from him. But I've seen what an unstable dad can do inside a family. If I can't trust him to stay on his meds . . . " another awkward silence followed. "Lincoln's waiting in the car," she said, finally. "I should go."

He offered a little wave as she went off to join her brother.

"Let's just leave the truck here," she said to Lincoln, who still hadn't shaken off the shock of the day. "We can get home and tackle what's left of this mess tomorrow." She pulled out the keys to the sedan.

"Yeah, okay," he said. "Tomorrow." He looked as if he'd forgotten about the truck anyway.

God only knew what another day might bring.

Chapter Nineteen

Sam returned to the clinic. Hunter had the reporter cornered, with his back, literally, against the wall.

"Do you understand, son," Hunter was saying, "that to print any of this is to open up your newspaper to legal action?"

"Yessir," the guy said, looking nervous, "but with all due respect, this is my first job, and I really want to keep it. I'm more worried about my editor's reaction today than I am about the paper getting sued sometime next month. I was told to write this story and that's what I'm going to do, with or without any information from your client. I won't say any of this is true, mind you. I'll use quotes from the mother, that's all."

"That's all?" Hunter said, his voice dripping with sarcasm. "That will brand my client a pedophile in a city newspaper. Do you really want to do that to an innocent woman?"

The reporter kept his mouth in a tight line. He was made of tougher mettle than Sam would have imagined.

Hunter shook his head and walked away from him, clearly realizing what Sam had figured out. The guy was going to write the story. Period. If it got squashed, it would have to come from higher up.

Sam went over to Hunter.

"Listen," Sam told him, "I've played tennis with the news editor a few times. He's the brother-in-law of one of the guys at the company. I'll try giving him a call."

"Chances of that working?" Hunter asked.

"No idea," Sam said. "But it can't hurt."

"Go for it." Hunter headed outside, pulling a pack of cigarettes from his pocket as he went out the door.

"Hey, Fred, it's Sam Alderman."

Sam stood on the covered cement stoop outside the clinic. The shade offered little respite from the heat that had come on in the previous few days.

"Listen, there's a reporter here you sent—a guy trying to dig up a story on the kid and the drama teacher."

"Not much digging to do, Sam," the man said. "The mother came to us."

"The mother's a whack job, Fred." Sam could already sense the resolve in the seasoned editor's tone. His efforts weren't going to come to much. But he pressed on. "The accused woman is a friend of mine, and she didn't molest anybody. She hasn't been charged."

"Way the mother tells it—according to my guy in there—the kid was so distraught over everything that he tried to kill himself this afternoon. That's news. I can't hold back because your friend doesn't care to have her name in the paper. Hell, I'd have a photographer there if the mother hadn't said she didn't want any pictures. Your pal got lucky on that end of things."

"You understand you're opening yourself up for legal action here," Sam told the man. "And I'm sure you've looked into Jules; you've probably decided that she doesn't have the means to hire the kind of ammo you have behind you. But she's already got a lawyer working with her from Thompson, Fields and Murphy. And when she runs out of money, I've got plenty to kick into her cause."

"You threatening me, Sam?"

"I'm trying to make you think before you do this," he said. "That's it, pure and simple. Think twice about the consequences, for you and everyone else involved. Hell, even the boy. You think this is good for him? The mother's upset, and she's trying to lash out any way she can. But she'll regret it in the long run, too, when she sees how embarrassed the kid is."

"In my experience," Fred Jakes said with an air of finality, "people love to get their stories in the paper. Doesn't matter much one way or the other what it's about."

After he got off the phone, Sam went back inside the clinic to tell Hunter that he'd given it his best shot and probably failed.

"That lawyer guy's already gone," the receptionist told him when he asked if she'd seen him.

Since there was nothing more to accomplish by staying, he turned around without speaking to anyone and headed back to his car. As he drove, he wondered what his real motivations were in petitioning the editor on Jules' behalf. Was he trying to make a grand gesture in the hope of winning her back somehow? Or was he simply doing the right thing for a friend? Either way, he felt his efforts had been futile. He purely dreaded seeing the morning's headlines when the paper arrived the next day on his mother's front stoop.

Chapter Twenty

It was no longer a surprise to arrive at their mother's house and see a kid sitting on the porch. Lincoln drove the car into the carport. He and Jules walked around front to see what the boy wanted.

As they came closer, Jules recognized the boy as the same kid who'd delivered the note from Vick on the first day of her ordeal.

"Hey, there," Lincoln spoke up, looking skittish as he approached the house. After the shock of finding Vick Johns hanging from a tree, Jules figured that the very sight of an adolescent boy gave her brother the jitters.

The boy stood and waited for them to approach. The rocking chair behind him moved back and forth as if some presence remained.

"Can we do something for you?" Jules asked. Dressed in a white T-shirt and blue jeans, the kid would have been interchangeable with Vick to her undiscerning eye just a week before.

"Is Vick okay?" he asked.

How did he know already? The online gossip factory must have already begun to disseminate Vick Johns's suicide attempt among the high school kids.

"He's doing better," she said. "They think he'll be okay. Are kids talking about Vick online already?"

"I don't know," he said. "My mom won't let me have a computer in the house. She says the devil's work is done on those things. I have to go to Vick's or my cousin's to look at anything on the Web."

"So how did you hear?" Jules asked.

"Mom called me in and told me," he said. "She heard it on the scanner."

Jules saw something close to a smile move across Lincoln's features. Thank God he still had some sense of humor after everything that happened. She and Lincoln reached the door, but the boy stayed in the middle of the porch. Jules thought of inviting him in for a cold drink, but she decided—recent events being what they were—inviting a young boy into her home was probably a bad idea. Even having him on the property wasn't great.

"You go on in," she told Lincoln. "I want to talk with him for a minute."

Lincoln glanced at the kid, nodded, and went in the house.

"What's your name?" Jules asked, sitting on the porch swing that hung from the ceiling, but taking care to keep a full length of porch between herself and the boy.

He sat in the rocker he'd occupied while waiting for them. "Arthur to grown-ups," he said. "Artie to my friends."

"I guess that makes you Arthur to me," she said, "although some people around here would challenge that call. Are you a good friend of Vick's?"

"Best friends. Him and me, we do stuff together all the time. Ever since he got here this year. I live right down the road."

"Do you go to Mount Canaan?" She wanted to get him talking in general before getting to the meat of her questions.

"No, ma'am," he said. "I'm Nazarene. Momma says Baptists talk too much about what they believe. Nazarenes just live it. But I do go with him on Sunday nights sometimes to his youth group meetings. Vick's a junior leader. Garrett, the real leader, says Vick could be a preacher like his granddaddy if he wanted. Says he's got the flair for delivery in a speech 'cause of his drama talents and all."

Jules wanted to say that his imagination was right up there, too, but she held her tongue.

"Momma don't know that I go with him there," Arthur added, seeming to regret his open admission.

"It's okay," Jules told him. "I won't spill the beans."

"I appreciate that," he said. The major religions had nothing over small-town denominations when it came to differences of dogma and practice of belief. Methodists and Pentecostals could get into it with teeth bared if they stayed in a room together too long.

"Why do you think Vick tried to hurt himself, Arthur?" She decided it was time to inch toward the topic at hand.

"I don't know," he said, without any trace of wariness toward her inquiry. "Vick gets crazy ideas sometimes. Maybe he was really sad about something. But it could be that he liked the way it looked on TV when somebody did the same thing. I wonder sometimes if he knows the difference between TV and what really happens."

"Is that why he made up stories about me?"

"He'll say stuff sometimes like it's a fact. It turns out true one time and wrong the next. He might be lying when he does that, or he might be mixed up. It's hard to say."

"Does he get upset at school about things?" she asked. She

was making stabs in the dark. When it came to Vick, she didn't even know the right questions.

"Sometimes. His temper can get up if something hits him wrong." He pulled a stick of misshapen gum out of the pocket of his jeans and, after pulling off the sticky wrapping, put it in his mouth. "The worst I've seen was the time he said that stuff about you. That was after some boys in gym called him a faggot."

Jules winced at the word, but tried not to show it. The kid had information and she wanted to get him to finish.

"So Vick, he goes ape-shit on those guys," the boy continued, growing more animated by the second and gesturing with his hands. "I mean some serious yelling and telling them he'd put their damn heads through a wall if they ever said that again. He might've done it, too. He's skinny, but he fights like a dang bobcat when he gets mad. Anyway, he was saying shit like that to them. Excuse my cussing."

"That's okay," she said, not wanting to break his momentum. "Did they back off when he did that?"

"Mostly they were just laughing," he said. "But I think they might have been a little freaked out, too. He didn't look quite right. I never saw him like that before."

"That's when he told them he'd been with me?"

"Yes, ma'am." Suddenly self-conscious, he looked down. His hands went still and dropped by his sides, as he stared at the paint-chipped floorboards beneath his feet.

"Did you believe him?" she asked, leaning forward and keeping her voice as calm as she could manage.

"Like I said," he told her, "it's hard to know the difference with him sometimes." He looked up at her then. "But he's my friend." The last part implied that it wasn't his place to decide. She had to admire that brand of loyalty.

"He's going to get better, Arthur." She tried to reassure him. "But I think he needs help with other things after his injuries from this heal."

He nodded.

"He'll be okay," she said again.

She sensed that they both knew that was far from a given.

Jules and Lincoln had gone back inside when she heard a car pull into their driveway.

Who now?

She looked out the window and saw a tan Eldorado, an older model, the kind that parked along the road and under the trees every Sunday morning at Mount Canaan.

A short woman, nearly as wide as she was tall, got out of the car. She opened the door to the backseat and took out a rectangular dish. Pyrex. On top of that, she put a metal bowl with Saran Wrap covering whatever was inside.

"Looks like dinner's here," Lincoln said, gazing over Jules' shoulder.

Jules went to the front door and, from that vantage, recognized her as Mrs. Dukes from church. She taught both of them in elementary school.

"Hey Mrs. Dukes," Jules said as the woman made her way up the porch stairs. "Let me help you with that."

Mrs. Dukes looked up at Jules, studied her face for a moment before handing over the dishes. "You'd think I'd be used to this hot weather after all these years," she said. "But I declare, it's coming earlier in the spring than it used to."

"Yes, ma'am," Jules said as they made their way toward the kitchen. "I believe you're right. Can I get you a cold soda or some iced tea?"

Lincoln followed them into the room and pulled out a chair for the older woman to sit at the table.

"Tea would be wonderful," she said. "Just put the sugar bowl on the table beside me. I drink it sweet enough to rot your teeth on the spot. But since most of mine aren't real anymore, I can get away with it."

Jules laughed. She occasionally said hello to the woman at church, but she couldn't recall ever having an adult conversation with her. As a third-grade teacher, Miz Pukes, as they cleverly called her, had been terrifying. Looking at her, Jules wondered how that could have been.

"I heard about your trouble here this morning," she said as Lincoln put a glass of tea and the sugar bowl in front of her on the table. "Thank goodness you were here and heard the boy."

"Yes, ma'am." Lincoln sat down beside her.

Jules wished her mother was there to entertain the church lady. It still seemed to her as if she and Lincoln should say their polite greetings and then be allowed to go play.

"I owe you an apology." Mrs. Dukes turned to address Jules at the end of the table. "I said some unkind things about you. That boyfriend of yours—well, I guess he used to be your boyfriend—but anyway, he called me on it in the grocery store. He reminded me that if I have something to say, I should say it to a person's face. He was quite rude about it, actually, but he was not out of line. I was miffed as can be at the time, but when I got home, I got to thinking about my behavior, and I realized he was absolutely right. I'd already decided to pay you a visit, but today's events seem to have underscored your innocence in all this. I am sorry, Jules. Buying into gossip is beneath me, and I'm old enough to know better."

Jules looked down the table at her brother. Mrs. Dukes faced away from him, and he shrugged his shoulders and put his hands in the air to indicate he had no idea how she should respond. He then sat back with an amused smile on his face and waited.

"I'm used to people making comments," Jules said. "This

thing that's happened . . . people don't know what to make of it. *I* don't even know what to make of it. There's no need for you to apologize, I'm sure."

"Oh, but there is," the woman said, undeterred. "From what I understand, the boy has a lot of problems. The preacher even said as much when I talked with him after church last Sunday. He took a moment to pray with me about my weakness for rumors and such. The child is his grandson, you know."

"Yes, ma'am, I know," Jules said, trying to imagine Mrs. Dukes and Preacher Walker bent over in prayer as she asked for forgiveness for gossiping about Jules. The scenario seemed surreal.

"And what happened today . . ." Mrs. Dukes added, shaking her head. "Horrible. Just horrible. I hope the child gets the help he needs. So anyway, I jumped to conclusions about you, Julie Marie, after I listened to unfounded rumors. That was not the Christian thing to do. I've asked forgiveness in the name of the Good Lord Jesus, and now I'm asking it from you."

Jules couldn't remember the last time her own name—her proper name at that—had been invoked in the same conversation as that of the blessed Savior.

"Of course." Jules attempted to channel Marnee's response to such an unusual request. "Whatever you said, consider it forgotten," she told her, hastily adding, "and forgiven." She wasn't sure if formal wording was required, but she wanted to cover all her bases. She glanced again at Lincoln, who gave her another shrug and a thumbs-up.

With forgiveness asked for and bestowed, Mrs. Dukes turned to ask Lincoln what he was up to with his music. Jules got up and found some Danish wedding cookies in the pantry that didn't look too old. She put them on a plate and brought them to the table. Then she sat back down to, once again, preside over the impromptu gathering.

"I taught both of you in third grade, isn't that right?" the older woman asked as she added copious amounts of sugar to the already sweet concoction in front of her.

"Yes, ma'am," Jules and Lincoln replied in unison.

"Lincoln," she said. "Even then, you played the piano like one of God's special angels."

"Thank you," he said, having distinct memories of butchering Mozart in the Fall Talent Show of that year.

"My thoughts are not in line with everything in your life, Lincoln," she added.

"I expect not, Mrs. Dukes," he said.

"I don't hold to all of the choices you've made," she said, not letting the subject end there, "but you have gifts that only God can give, and I'm very proud of what you've done with them."

"Well, Mrs. Dukes," he said, "it would be nice if everything in life was a choice, but I have been fortunate in my career, and for that I am grateful."

After the older woman and her brother both said their piece, Jules felt the regard shift to her.

"I don't mince words, Julie Marie," the woman said.

Dear God. Jules shifted to a different, but no more comfortable, position in the hard kitchen chair.

"You've gotten yourself into a pickle, it seems."

Jules thought they'd already covered the matter of her innocence in the Vick situation. She waited to hear where the woman was headed.

"I can't imagine what you are thinking, but at least you've made the right decision to give birth and not go that other route."

Jules realized they weren't talking about Vick and his scandalous claims anymore. She was surprised that Mrs. Dukes even knew about the baby, then realized she shouldn't have been. Snow in July had a better chance of survival in Ekron than a secret.

"Don't get me wrong," Mrs. Dukes continued, "your mother would have loved the opportunity to be a grandmother. But the circumstances would have left her heartbroken."

"The first of those things is true, Mrs. Dukes," Jules said, "but not the second. Mom knew about the baby and she was happy. Really happy."

"Is that a fact?" Mrs. Dukes seemed at a loss for the first time since arriving. She quickly rallied with part two of her mission. "I have to ask you, do you intend to marry this man?" She glanced down at Jules' belly and pointed, as if the father's picture might be stamped there for reference.

"No, ma'am, I don't," Jules said, trying to keep her voice from rising in frustration at the church lady's nosing around her personal life. "I don't plan to see him again."

"Your mother would not like that," she said.

"Again, my mother *did* know and she took into account the specific circumstances on which I made my decision."

Mrs. Dukes waited, apparently expecting Jules to up and share those circumstances with her, but Jules had had enough. "Mom was in agreement with me on this—Lincoln, too," she added. Lincoln nodded like a bobble doll. "I appreciate your concern, but, I assure you, we are fine here." Jules hoped her tone suggested that the discussion was over. Talking with Mrs. Dukes in that manner felt an awful lot like putting on Marnee's clothes.

"Fair enough," the woman said, smiling unexpectedly. "I'm an old woman, and I tend to get involved where I shouldn't sometimes. But I've said what I felt obligated to say, and now I'll tell you something else. If you need anything, any help with this child, I will be available to you. I have not had the privilege of children. Though Mr. Dukes and I tried and tried, the Lord did not see fit to bless us in this way, and therefore I have no *grandchildren* of my own. It is the one true regret of my life with Mr. Dukes," the older woman lamented.

Imagining their exhaustive efforts at procreation made Jules frantic to fill her head with other, less shy-making visions. She hoped Lincoln would jump in with some response so that she wouldn't have to, but he had apparently been rendered mute by Mrs. Dukes' deeply personal revelations.

"I appreciate your offer," Jules managed to say, feeling some respect for the woman's candor. "I'm sorry you've had that disappointment."

"Well, yes," she said, "but I've made the best of it by doting on my sister Maureen's children."

"Are they around here?" Jules seized her way clear to a more palatable topic.

"Sara moved to Atlanta," Mrs. Dukes said with regret, "so I see too little of her. She's tall and beautiful like Maureen, fighting off men left and right, but she's never settled on one particular beau. Colin, my nephew, lives in Wilmington and is good about visiting. I keep waiting for him and his wife to give me great-nieces and nephews, but they're both absorbed by their careers, so . . ." She stopped, finished with an exaggerated sigh.

"Well, I don't know how long I'll be staying around," Jules said, "but if I'm here with the baby, I'd certainly welcome your help."

"A baby," she said. "Those precious, little creatures. If you're here, you can count on me." Then her demeanor seemed to shift gears. "How are things," she asked, "with your *situation* with the Johns child?" She said the last word with such gravity that Jules had to suppress a smile.

Lincoln caught her eye and from behind the woman mouthed the word "situation" with exaggerated facial expression. Jules shot him a disapproving look that made her wonder, once again, if Marnee's spirit had taken possession of her body.

"Everything's looking better legally," Jules said. "People—well, everyone but the boy's mother—seem to be figuring out that he has real issues and that I just got caught in the middle somehow. But now Cici Johns has gone to the Wilmington paper, trying to drum up a story about me. If that gets into print, it doesn't matter what happens with the lawyers. I'll never get another job."

"Cici is too high-strung for her own good," Mrs. Dukes said, clearly irritated with the preacher's daughter. "She has always wanted every scrap of attention she could get. She was like that as a child, too. I had her for two years. That's when I switched from teaching third to teaching fourth, so I followed that class up a grade. Can't Preacher Walker do something with her?"

"It may be too late," Lincoln said. "They've already been hounding Jules, and apparently the news editor smells blood, so there may not be anything to stop it from running tomorrow."

"Tomorrow! My gracious, that's not right," Mrs. Dukes said, her mouth set in a scowl. "Not right at all."

There didn't seem to be any more to say on the subject. In fact, there didn't seem to be any more to say at all.

"Would you like some more tea?" Jules asked.

"No thank you, dear," the woman said, standing. "I should be getting back home. Horace is particular about his supper. He doesn't care what he eats as long as it's on the table at six o'clock." She glanced at her watch. "And he's headed for a disappointment this evening, I'm afraid. That's a seafood casserole," she added, pointing toward one of her dishes on the counter. "It's still warm, but when it cools you'll want to freeze it if you don't plan to eat it in the next couple of days. The other is a fruit salad. I stopped by the farm stand over on County Road, so everything should have just been picked today or yesterday. Berries are just about the only thing in season this early."

"Thank you, Mrs. Dukes," Jules said, surprised that, in spite of a few contentious words, she had warmed up considerably to the woman in less than an hour's worth of conversation. "I don't think there'll be any need to freeze anything. The two of us haven't been thinking much about groceries lately, and that smells wonderful."

"Well, I hope it's good," she said, patting Lincoln on the shoulder as she made her way back to the front door. "It was my grandmother's recipe, so it's fed a few generations of us at this point."

Lincoln and Jules walked her to the tan Eldorado, then watched her miss the ditch at the end of the driveway by just millimeters as she pulled out onto the road and drove away.

"You hungry?" Lincoln asked when she was out of sight.

"Starved," Jules said, following him back into the house to eat dinner.

Chapter Twenty-one

Even as a small boy, Lincoln had never met his father's expectations. He was not *all boy*. That's what Jack said. Lincoln preferred pretending to braid Marnee's hair to rough-housing on the floor with his dad. He had no interest in the trucks and toy guns Jack insisted were birthday presents appropriate for his son. As early as elementary school, he wanted classical records for the turntable he kept in his room.

"Why can't you just swing a goddamn bat?" Jack Fuller had said to Lincoln once when he was well into his second six-pack of the evening. "How hard is it? If you're coordinated enough to play those blasted piano keys, can't you keep your eye on a damn ball long enough to at least *try* to hit it without looking like a retard?" That was the milder stuff early on, before the violence and disdainful dismissals that escalated with every year.

Lincoln stood on the stoop that led to the backyard. Tomatoes, remnants of the garden that Marnee had tended the summer before, were coming up wild in the weed-stricken patch beside the house. Lincoln wondered if she would want him to try to do something with them. Clear the ground around them, stake the vines, and see if anything grew. He owed her that much—and more. As bad as it got with his father, it would have been worse without Marnee's intervention.

Oddly enough, Lincoln's release from the shame his father heaped upon him followed that awful beating. The one that left him too bruised and battered to go to school.

He thought of Vick. Strange as the logic seemed, Lincoln decided it was possible that the extremes of his own situation saved him from becoming as desperate and delusional as the boy. By all accounts, Vick's father offered an incessant disapproval, absent the violent explosions of Jack Fuller. The insidious nature of the man's disappointment in his son likely kept Vick forever blaming himself.

Even in Lincoln's guilt-ridden, adolescent mind, there was nothing—*nothing*—that could justify the beating Jack Fuller laid on him. For the first time, Lincoln was able to see that his *father* was the aberration, not him.

Jack seemed to sense the shift in his son, the loss of whatever hold he had on him. More bruises came, but bruises healed. Beyond that, regardless of his father's actions against him, nothing the older man did could faze Lincoln once he refused to feel responsible.

It went on that way until that last day, when seeing Lincoln on the dock with the fresh-from-skinny-dipping Sam Alderman triggered the worst in Jack Fuller. The worst and then some. Jack had been fishing—and drinking—out in his boat. Bad timing all around. Sam paid for it, catching every bit of the rage Jack Fuller felt at being marginalized by his own son. The thing Lincoln regretted most was that Lyndon Alderman hadn't lived long enough for Lincoln to shake his hand, to thank him for ridding the world of that monster.

Lincoln went back in the house and told Jules he wanted to take a walk. The sun barely hung on as the day waned, and the air had cooled just enough for him to spend a few pleasant minutes outside before light disappeared and mosquitoes took over. He felt the luxury of a full belly with real, home-cooked food for the first time in days. Whatever Mrs. Dukes' views were on his personal life, she was to be commended for a fine hand in the kitchen.

"Want me to come with you?" Jules called to him from the porch when he'd reached the yard.

"I'd like to be by myself for a bit," he said.

He wouldn't have minded Jules' company, but he planned to go to the spot where he'd found Vick earlier. He wanted to make sure the police had retrieved the bloody knife. The thought of it on the property bothered him. He had a half pint of Jim Beam Black in his pocket. Not his brand, but it would do in a pinch, if the need became overwhelming.

Images of the boy hanging from the branch, the thought of what he had attempted to do before he made his jeans into a noose . . . all of this haunted Lincoln. It made him wonder again what the kid had been through to cause such a destructive impulse. Lincoln was no stranger to self-loathing—his father had seen to that—but he had never wanted to do harm to himself.

Vick Johns' various demons were less clearly defined. If Lincoln could figure out what had happened to him, *who* had happened to him, he might be able to help.

Lincoln reached the tree. Nothing—beyond a few broken branches—indicated the horrors that had occurred just hours before. The blue jeans were gone. The pocket knife, too. Ekron's finest had done their job.

Lincoln turned deeper into the woods, away from the marsh that spread out toward the water. He walked with the shadows darkening around him, mosquitoes gathering in number. He walked until he came to the road. Instead of doubling back toward home, he turned in the other direction toward Mount Canaan.

Chapter Twenty-two

She'd made a simple comment. *Maybe some peace and quiet will make you feel better. Maybe a trip to the cemetery when the heat of the day starts to settle.*

She heard Lincoln leave, and without taking time to think, she found herself outside, walking in the direction of Mount Canaan. She wondered if Walt would come. For all she knew, he'd been and gone home. An argument raged inside her. She wanted to see him standing there when she got to the church, but she knew that it went against everything they both knew to be right.

Jules thought again of that summer before high school, the weeks of hot days that were spent with a crowd that included him. Gina, her friend from church, was a year older and on the drill team. She'd been Jules' entry into the group that summer. Talking with Walt then had felt both thrilling and natural. In twenty-five years, that part hadn't changed.

She remembered one day, the high point of the summer—hell, the high point of the year—when one of the awful sophomore girls pulled out her talons with Jules at the pool. Jules' friend had already left and Jules sat alone on her towel. The older girl, Kendra, whose father was president of the bank in Ekron, routinely made sport out of girls one grade below her. She saw Jules sunbathing by herself and wasted no time walking over with a couple of loyal suck-ups.

"Hey Jules," she said loudly enough for the entire pool to hear. "Aren't you afraid you'll get a sunburn on that skanky tattoo?"

Jules remembered the feeling of saliva flooding into her mouth. Tears could follow if she couldn't get herself under control. She willed all of the rage into a central, deep part of her chest. It felt like holding down a feral cat.

"Worry about your own tan, Kendra," she said, "and leave me alone." Jules was astonished that her voice came out so calm.

"Make me, freak." Kendra crossed her arms, and maintained a sickeningly triumphant smile.

Jules looked down at her magazine as if bored, but spoke loud enough for everyone to hear. "Sorry. I make a point of not trying to discipline other people's children."

She braced for what would come. *Would the bitch actually kick her?* Instead, she heard Walt's voice.

"Hey Fuller," he said, walking over from a nearby table. "Are you ready to go?" He stood there, skin glowing from the late season sun, looking, for all the world, like a deity.

Jules didn't know what the hell he was doing, but she planned to go with it, whatever it was. "Sure," she told him. "Let me get my stuff."

She caught a delicious glimpse of Kendra's astonished face—the lackeys suddenly nowhere in sight.

"Sorry to interrupt, Kendra," Walt said, "but Jules promised to get a milk shake with me this afternoon."

Kendra glared for a moment longer, then made her exit from the little scene. Jules walked with Walt to his car.

"Thanks," she said. "I really appreciate the Lancelot move in there. I can go to the pool office and call my mom."

"Forget it." He grinned. "I'm all psyched for a milk shake now."

They drove to the Sea Breeze, got a booth, and ordered. She wished everyone she knew could see them there together.

"I really do appreciate what you did," she told him.

"Nah, you were holding your own. I loved the line about other people's children." He shook his head, smiling.

She grinned. "I stole that from Lincoln. He's had a lot of practice dealing with shitheads."

They finished their drinks and he drove her home. When school began in the fall, she and Walt moved into their different circles. But even when surrounded by his jock friends, he made a point of acknowledging her, showing a respect that carried over with others far less inclined to kindness than Walt Walker.

She was thinking about that day when she reached Mount Canaan. She saw him before he saw her. He sat on a riding mower that was left by the side of the graveyard. She noticed that half the grass had been mowed, the other half waited for the groundskeeper to return the next day.

He stood up when he saw her, and, together, they walked to her parents' headstone. She so rarely felt that she belonged exactly where she happened to be. With Marnee, she'd always felt it. With Lincoln.

Walt's presence gave her that same feeling of comfort, of family, but nothing could be further from the truth. He wasn't part of her in that way. She barely knew him, *and* he was someone else's husband. Still, it was there. That feeling of wholeness. The elemental pleasure of it kept her from turning around and leaving as she ought to have.

She'd changed into a loose shift, something of her own. As she approached him, she scratched at her bare leg where a mosquito had been, and he handed over a small canister of something. Bug spray.

"Are you always prepared?" she asked, smiling. She sprayed the noxious stuff on her legs and arms.

"Not for everything," he said.

"Me either."

She sat beside him. It felt good to be off her feet. The smell of hamburgers cooking on a grill drifted over from the parsonage across the street, reminding her of the unexpected meal they shared the first time they met among the graves.

"Smells like Daddy's grilling out," he said, absentmindedly. "Hell of a day, but I guess they have to eat."

"Hell of a day," she echoed, and they settled into the comfortable silence of two people grateful for even a moment of peace.

Chapter Twenty-three

The white clapboard of the church stood light against the evening shadows. Lincoln knew the church would be empty at that time of day and likely unlocked. He let a car pass, then crossed the street and went toward the front door. Turning the handle to go in, he felt a flood of feeling as a piece of his childhood returned.

He'd been in the empty sanctuary at Mount Canaan countless times with Marnee. Sometimes, returning Communion items after she'd brought them home for polishing and laundering. But mostly, when she was shielding him from his own father. If Jack had been drinking, as his mood began to turn, Marnee would quietly slip on her shoes and motion for Lincoln to do the same.

"I'm off to the church for a quick errand," she'd call out as they slipped out the kitchen door.

Those outings with Marnee to the darkened church began when he was two or three, before Jules came into their lives. "Let's take a walk" became code for an escape to Mount Canaan. Marnee would pray while Lincoln sat in the corner with a book, or played the piano at the front of the church. Jack Fuller would not come into the sanctuary drunk. He'd barely set foot into the place sober.

Lincoln was safe there.

After Jules arrived, she'd come with them. First in her stroller, and later walking between Lincoln and Marnee, each holding her hand. There was no need for Jules to escape Jack. No need for Marnee to worry about her daughter. Lincoln had always been the only target. Over the years, he and Jules had tried to figure out why.

He remembered Jules, no more than seven at the time, taking fingerpaint and smearing it over the walls of her Sunday school classroom. The teacher was horrified, Marnee perplexed, but their father had only laughed. Lincoln understood immediately that Jules wanted to draw Jack's attention away from him.

Marnee eventually figured it out, too—Jules' uncharacteristic *acting out*. Kissing boys before she turned ten. Putting on fake tattoos. At the age of twelve, sneaking off to Wrightsville Beach to get a real one. Cutting holes in her jeans and stealing cigarettes from Marnee's purse. At least one day a week in middle school, she was sent home for violating the dress code in some blatant fashion.

Marnee halfheartedly punished her. Jack, if he was sober, thought she was cute. If he was drunk, he didn't notice at all. At some point, Lincoln realized that Jules had begun to do outrageous things out of habit. Even after Jack died, when she was in high school, Jules' persona was established, so she kept it up to some degree. She was that rarest of kids, the honor student who got hauled into the counselor's office with Jack Daniel's in her backpack. Lincoln didn't think she even drank it.

He knew that inside her head, Jules was a model citizen who had masqueraded for so long as a bad girl, she felt compelled to maintain the farce. The side bonus for her was that she seemed like she ought to be loose and she wasn't. Lincoln watched it drive boys wild, something she didn't seem to notice. By sophomore year, she'd paired herself off with Sam and that was that. Everyone wanted her. Sam got her.

Marnee never came down too hard on her daughter. In her gut, she knew Jules wasn't a rebel. She saw through what had become to her a poorly disguised ruse, a bird trying to draw the predator away from its nest. But the irony was it never worked. Never made a bit of difference to Jack. Until the day he died, he laughed and called her his little rabble-rouser, saving all his anger for Lincoln.

If Lincoln got teased for being a sissy, if he got called Piano Boy with disdain when he couldn't throw a ball far enough to go from mid-field to the pitcher, Jack became furious. When Lincoln began to show interest in other boys, the verbal abuse turned physical.

"I think it's because I'm not his blood," Jules told Lincoln once, not long before Jack died.

"Why would that make a difference?" Lincoln asked. "If anything, it seems like it would be the other way around."

"He's not responsible for anything he sees as disappointing in me. He didn't *make* me this way with his own DNA. Whatever he sees in you that he doesn't like doubles right back on him. You're part of him in a way that I'm not, and I think he fundamentally hates himself."

She was parroting something she'd read, pop psychology at best, but it was the most plausible answer either of them had come up with, so they left it at that.

Lincoln walked down the aisle to the altar. He thought again of the boy, of how tortured the kid must have felt to do what he did. Lincoln instinctively reached in his pocket. The small weight of the booze calmed him a little.

He sat on the low platform that separated the preacher's

domain from the congregation. The choir loft sat off to the side. Images of Vick hanging from the tree flashed inside his brain, images of bits of flesh on the serrated edge of the knife. He felt a delayed sort of panic quicken in him. Visions of the boy blurred with Jack Fuller's bellowing taunts, the voice that never completely vacated Lincoln's head. And then he felt it again, in his arms and in his chest. In his head. The wave of need eclipsed everything else. One drink. That bottle in his pocket would make the surging impulses go away.

He took the Jim Beam out, tilted his head back, and poured the liquid into his mouth. Relief came almost immediately. He closed his eyes, imagined it moving through his body. Banking up against the walls of blood vessels and moving like a flood of water to a gathering of parched and weary souls. One more. And again.

He opened his eyes. The pulpit loomed above him, and he felt a mixture of shame and elation. Odd roommates inside his thoughts. What had happened to Vick? What could make a boy fashion a noose from his clothing and try to exit his own existence?

In the dim light, Lincoln saw the black and white contrast of the keyboard. He got up and went over to the piano, sat down and felt the familiar completion of himself. Sitting by the keys, his body was whole.

He began to play Scott Joplin, realized a certain satisfaction in the incongruity of the ragtime echoes through the dark sanctuary. He started out playful and gathered momentum as the song progressed. By the end, the piece had acquired a nearly manic fury, and Lincoln found that he had tears in his eyes from the frustration that had run through his fingers and now echoed inside the sanctuary walls.

He'd been worried about Jules, about what the boy's accusations would mean for her. If the paper ran the story, it would make life hell for her for a while. Maybe forever. How long did it take to cast off the stink of that kind of insinuation? But he found that his tears weren't for his sister. She would find her way. She would be okay. He *knew* he could help her. His tears were for Vick Johns. He revisited the afternoon in his head, felt again the weight of the barely breathing child against his shoulder as he half dragged the child to the truck.

Again he asked himself, what the hell had happened to that boy? Had other kids done something to him? A teacher? Someone from the very church where Lincoln sat? Recovering from the day's ordeal was not going to make the reasons the child had done it disappear. Someone or something had taken that child to places an innocent boy shouldn't go.

By all accounts, Vick's father had been upset with the boy's interest in drama. As much as Lincoln hated to even entertain the notion, was it possible that the drama teacher at his old school—the *fruitcake* Vick's father had so loathed—really had been doing bad things? Just because homophobes were wrong in their bias didn't mean they were *always* wrong in their hunches. Lincoln felt the burden of the question on him. In his pocket, he could feel the nearly empty bottle, lighter than it had been when he arrived. He'd have to toss it before he got home.

He looked at the dark shadow of the altar that rose up beside him. Why didn't God always protect children? Hell, even some sick priests abused children. Lincoln wanted the comfort he'd felt in the empty sanctuary as a child. Instead, he felt a rising anger at whoever was responsible for Vick Johns's decision to tie himself by the neck to that tree. He wished the boy's mother had Marnee's powers of protection. But not every child had a Marnee to stand between them and the villains of the world.

"What was that song?" The woman's voice startled him, coming from the other side of the altar. "I heard you could play piano, but I never heard anybody play like that before. I liked it."

"Who are you?" Lincoln asked. She clearly knew who he was.

"It's Tuni," she said. "I came in from the back through the fellowship hall while you were playing."

"Why didn't you turn on any lights?" he asked, afraid she would smell the alcohol on his breath.

"Why didn't you?" She had no irony in her voice. No defiance. It was a simple question.

"Fair enough." He realized he was smiling. "I guess I just like the dark."

"Why are you here?" she asked.

"I came here to think some things through." He stood up and walked over to her. "How about you?"

She looked down at the carpet for a brief moment, then back up at him. She motioned for him to follow her, and she went to the side door of the church that led outside. Slowly, as if trying to be very quiet, she opened the door. She motioned with her head the direction he should look. At first, he didn't see anything. The cemetery spread out beside the church. A full moon had come up, making the stone markers look white against the grass.

But as his eyes focused, he saw what she wanted him to see. Two figures, sitting on the base of a headstone. From its placement among the graves, he knew it was his parents' marker. He recognized Jules as half of the couple, but he couldn't make out the other person, besides discerning that it was a man.

"Who's she with?" Lincoln asked.

Tuni Walker replied in a voice so small and broken that he had to lean in to hear her. "That's Walt," she said. "She's with Walt."

Chapter Twenty-four

The buzzing of cicadas gathered around Jules and Walt. In the distance, a tree frog's call sounded like the sharp breaking of twigs.

"Oh, I almost forgot," Walt said, picking up a greasy sack from the other side of him on the marble pedestal. As he handed her the bag, she opened it and peered inside. Warmth rose from tinfoil-wrapped packets. She didn't know what it was, but it smelled heavenly—deep fried with the heat of it meeting her face as she loosened the foil from around one of the objects inside.

"Apple fritters," he said. "Only thing I know how to cook. I made some at supper and cooked up the leftover batter before I came out here. They were too hot to eat when I started out. Should be about right now."

He handed her a napkin, then took a crispy cake from the bag she still held and laid it on top. Steam rose as her portion met the cooler evening air.

Marnee's mother, Grandma Kate, used to make fritters. Jules

hadn't had one in over a decade, she was sure. Walt's concoction tasted both light and substantial.

"This is wonderful," she said.

After she'd finished eating, she leaned back against the marble headstone. "What do you do all day?" she asked. "I mean, with your work."

He waited a few moments, as if considering his answer. "Mostly I sit in an office and meet with kids who have gotten in fights or called somebody a name. Once in a while you get a kid who's been aggressive with a teacher. Gotta nip that in the bud. Those people work too hard and are paid too little to put up with that."

"Sounds like kids are more tame than when we were in school," she said.

"Maybe," he said. "Sometimes there'll be a problem with drugs, but usually it's milder stuff. Dress code issues. That's a big one. I have to politely tell them that the cracks in their backside can't come up higher than their pants. For the girls, it's skirt length. I don't know why kids are so keen on showing as much of themselves as they can get away with."

"Oh, how quickly you forget what we were like." Jules smiled, thinking of her own issues in middle school. "I would have been in your office every other day."

"Yeah, I remember you," he said. "It was you against the world for a while. Then you and Sam against the world."

She knew she'd been conspicuous, but she'd never felt particularly outrageous inside.

"What'd you think of me," she asked, "you know, back then?"

"Pretty. And smart, I guess."

"How about wild? Everybody thought I was so wild." She took a sip from a bottle of water at his side.

"Yeah, I saw that," he said. "I don't know why, but I never really bought it."

"I didn't think you thought much about me one way or the other back then," she said. "You were really nice—a real hero at the pool that day. But you had girls coming at you from all directions."

"I watched you all the time," he said, suddenly serious. "When you were in the room, I don't think I could look at anybody else."

She felt something inside her give way, some defense, and hope flooded in. But she recovered quickly, finding the reality that would never go away. There was nothing to hope for with Walt Walker.

"Why didn't I know this?" She kept her voice light. "I mean, you had to know I had a crush on you. But you were this older, football star, so it makes sense that I would swoon when you came into a room."

"Swoon, huh?" He smiled. "I planned to ask you out, that fall when you started high school. But before I knew it, you were with Sam," he said. "You had your own thing going and I'd missed my chance. But I sure loved watching what you might do next."

"You said you didn't buy it—the whole wild child thing. Why?"

He shook his head and leaned back, taking in a deep breath through his nose. "I always thought you were like some rodeo clown."

"Well, that's pretty flattering." She kept her voice light, but felt stung by his assessment of her long-ago self.

"No, no." He leaned forward again, came in close, smiling at her. "I don't mean how you looked. I mean the reasons you acted like you did. I know that you and Lincoln have always been close. High school kids aren't a charitable bunch, by and large. I could be wrong, but it seemed like you didn't so much want people to look at you, as you *needed* them to look away from something else. The best way to do that is to distract them.

Rodeo clowns seem all happy and silly, but their job is dead serious. And they're fearless. Ask any cowboy." His gaze was leveled on her and she had to look away.

Jules couldn't find words. She felt naked. Exposed. But the oddest part was, she felt willing—glad even—to give that to him. She trusted him. And, God help her, she wanted him. But where could it go? He wasn't hers to have. She had to retreat, to remind both of them how steep the drop was just a few steps away.

"So how'd you meet Tuni," she asked.

"At Appalachian State." He shifted gears seamlessly, and Jules wondered if she'd read too much into all that came before.

"She came in two years behind me," he went on. "Quit school when I graduated so she could go with me. She wanted kids in the worst way. It took us a while, but we finally had the girls. They're something else, I have to say."

And just like that, he'd taken the conversation away from his wife. Jules barely noticed the segue into the palatable topic of his children. But she *needed* to talk about his marriage. She wanted to talk herself out of all the things she'd let herself think and feel about him.

"I know the girls are great," she said. "But what's your life like with Tuni?"

He looked off in the direction of his home. Jules could see the line of his jaw in a moonlit silhouette. "It's complicated," he said, finally.

"I'm pretty smart."

Still, he didn't answer right away. He waited, as if considering the words, ran his hand over his forehead and through his hair.

"My life with Tuni is what it is," he said. "We married young and have a family now. She needs me."

Jules heard regret in the tone of his words, but also the resignation she expected.

"She left me once," he went on, sounding almost wistful.

"Did she take the girls?"

He shook his head. "Left all of us. Stayed away about two weeks. She has problems with her nerves. I knew she'd come back, I just didn't know when. Doctor gave her something a while back that takes the edge off. She's been better since then. She's a good wife."

Jules heard it in that last pronouncement. *She's a good wife.* Men like Walt didn't leave their wives. Especially not a good wife. She felt herself aching for him, a longing that went through her body and touched on her soul. He must have sensed it in her—or felt the same thing himself—because he turned to her, came close, and bent his head slightly. She felt his lips brush her temple, and he stopped there, keeping his face near her. She leaned into the warmth of his breathing.

"You've got commitments," she said, weak with yearning.

He laid two of his fingertips lightly on the swell of her belly.

"You've got some of your own," he said.

"To the baby," she spoke in a whisper. "But no one else."

He didn't ask why. There was really no need for him to know. His own promises made to a wife and two daughters trumped any excuses he might have for breaking them.

"You've got a family full of commitments," she continued. "And we're not the kind of people to ignore that."

"We've just barely missed each other twice now," he said, pulling back from his close proximity to her.

"Timing is everything." she said. Her heart raced in her chest.

"Yeah," he said, letting out a long, deep breath.

"Is Vick home yet?" She forced her mind away from thoughts of Walt Walker.

"They took him over to the hospital in Wilmington," he said. "They want to keep an eye on him. The doctor said we need psych involved. We have to get to the root of his problems and make sure he's not going to do it again."

She thought of the baby growing inside her. What *psych* issues were already running through his or her DNA? The father's history did not bode well. Her heart went out to Vick Johns. Was it a faulty genetic lottery that landed him in the mess he was in or something else that happened to him? Maybe both. Either way, he was a victim, she just didn't know of what.

"Let me know how he's doing," she said.

"I will."

"You know Cici called the Wilmington paper?" She changed the subject.

"I'm sorry," he said. "I truly am. I would have stopped it if I'd known before she did it. I told the reporter she's too emotional to be a credible source on this. But I honestly don't think they care about anything but selling as many papers as possible. I've convinced her not to say any more than she already has, but I guess they'll go ahead and run what she's given them. I don't know. "

"My lawyer was getting into it with the guy when I left," she said. "Maybe he'll get it stopped. It doesn't matter. I'll deal with whatever happens." She felt too exhausted, all of a sudden, to think of how. "I should get back to Lincoln."

Walt nodded. They both knew he had people waiting on him, as well.

He stood and picked up the empty fritter bag. With the other hand, he reached out to help her up. His skin was warm, his fingers slightly rough. She prolonged the act of steadying herself so that she could feel the gentle press of his palm against hers. Then he stepped back away from her, his face lost in the shadows. A shame, she thought, to be standing so close to him and not see his face.

Without words, but as if by some mutually understood signal, they turned away from each other and went their separate directions. Back toward the places they called home.

Lincoln was standing in the kitchen when she came in the door. He leaned against the counter. A bottle of sherry, cooking wine from Marnee's pantry, stood on the counter.

"What's up?" she asked, eyeing the bottle.

"I'm thinking of making a batch of that crab pasta sauce that Mom used to make for us to have tomorrow. Old Mrs. Dukes' casserole reminded me how good it is to have real food in front of us," he said, moving the bottle a small distance away from him. "No worries."

She saw olive oil, a can of crabmeat, and fish stock off to the side on the counter. "Sounds good," she said.

He looked at her, stared at her, really, with an odd expression.

"What is it?" she asked.

"She was there," he told her. "At the church. Walt's wife was inside the church. She saw you."

"How do you know?"

"Because I was there," he said. "And I saw you, too."

Jules tried to muster a feeling of regret, guilt even. She felt like a horrible person, not because she'd been sitting with Walt, but because she felt no remorse at the pain it must have caused his wife.

"I could promise you I'd end it, but there's nothing to end," she said.

"I'm not judging you," he said, his face apologetic.

"You never do."

"If he told you she's a shrew, I'd think twice about believing him. She didn't strike me as particularly hard to take in any way."

"He said she's a good wife," she told him, not even bothering to argue otherwise.

"I guess he's as decent as he seems then." He walked toward her. "I just thought you'd want to know that she was there." He put his arm around her and pulled her in tight. She let him comfort her.

"Why were you there?" she asked, her cheek still against his cotton shirt.

"I don't know. I was thinking about when I used to go there with Mom when I was little. You did, too, remember?"

"Yeah," she said. "I remember."

"I just wanted to be there, I guess. But it's different without her," he said.

"Everything's different without her." She heard her voice catch and was glad when Lincoln suddenly shifted gears.

"Hey," he said, "I think we should ride over to the kid's old school tomorrow, see what we can find out. School's out for the summer, but the teachers and office people will be working another week or two. We might get some insight into what's going on with him. I'd like to help sort out this mess with the boy if we can."

"I've been feeling that, too," she said. "He doesn't seem like a bad kid."

The mood in the room lifted. They had a strategy, a mission of sorts, and it involved helping somebody else, rather than rehashing their own troubles. What made Vick desperate enough to end up as he was? The answers were there somewhere. Lincoln was right. Maybe some of them could be found with his old drama teacher or someone else at the school. Besides, a day trip to Myrtle Beach would distract her from what surely would arrive in the next morning's paper.

"Okay," she said. "We'll go in the morning."

"Sounds like a plan. Then we'll come home, and have crab pasta for dinner." His color had returned a little, and his mood was better than she'd seen it in a while. She had a flash of worry that his elevated mood might have something to do with drinking again, but dismissed it. She couldn't live in constant distrust. He was her brother and, until the little one arrived, the only family left in the world she felt eager to claim.

Chapter Twenty-five

Sam heard the thump of the newspaper as it landed on the stoop just before five-thirty in the morning. An hour later he had not gotten up to get it. He didn't want to read the horrible things the Johns woman had to say about Jules.

Why did it matter so much to him? His inability to stop the story seemed to represent some sort of failure to him. But more than that, he simply wanted to make things right for Jules.

Even when she was with him all those years ago, she seemed to be flying just beyond the scope of his understanding. Her approach to life, if not self-destructive, was naïve, and he was alternately thrilled by her and worried for her. He could never predict where she was headed.

In some ways, the baby she carried complicated things, but in other ways, the pregnancy made the picture very simple. Before, he'd never known what Jules wanted, what she intended for her own life to become. The way she'd embraced the notion of being a mother, even without the baby's father in the picture, answered a large part of that question. It was a decision he could understand. One he could respect. For the first time, he felt he possessed some small understanding of her.

And this time around, he wasn't a high school kid, too self-absorbed and too intimidated by his mother to be what Jules needed. He'd grown, and that fact alone might be enough. There was even that small glimmer of hope when she apologized for her overreaction about the thing with their fathers. She'd grown, too. The old Jules would have held on to that grudge forever as a matter of stupid pride.

If he could have done this thing, stopped this assault on her by that prick of an editor, he might be worthy to give it a try with her. That's what he'd thought. He didn't even realize that's what he'd thought until the moment had passed. And it didn't matter anymore. All the possibilities seemed lost.

When he got downstairs Rena sat at the table with a cup of coffee and the paper opened in front of her.

"Morning," she said.

"Good morning." He waited. If she hadn't seen it, she would, and it would begin. It would be as if the ridiculous words of some angry, unstable mother were enough to justify everything she'd ever said about Jules.

He poured his coffee, put an English muffin in the toaster.

"When do you have to go back to work?" she asked.

"Day after tomorrow," he said, taking the jam out of the refrigerator. Maybe he wanted honey instead.

"We need to finish up at the cottage today," she said. "That way we can relax tomorrow, and I can make you a nice dinner."

"I'm only forty-five minutes away during rush hour," he said, smiling at the way she treated every visit home as if he'd returned from another continent.

"I know, but this has been a nice, long stay. Feels like old times." She finished flipping through the paper and closed it, pushed it across the table for him to read while he ate his English muffin.

Praise God, she's missed it. It would buy him a morning's peace. Not much longer, he was certain. The stalwarts of the gossip mafia would call. But at least the morning could be spent in harmony.

"I'm going to get dressed," she said, getting up and kissing the top of his head before heading back to her bedroom.

He sipped his coffee, opened the paper page by page. Nothing. His worst fear, front page, was put to rest right away, but even on the local pages—not a word. Had he done it? Had he brought the bastard to his senses and gotten him to squash the story? He couldn't imagine it, but there it was, in the lack of black and white. He felt a near euphoria, went through each section headline to headline just to make sure.

Maybe he did hope there were still possibilities. But for what? He didn't let his thoughts go that far. For the moment, it was enough that Jules was safe in her bed. No waking nightmares to be found on her front porch.

Chapter Twenty-six

"You sure?" Jules hunched over her decaf while Lincoln looked through the *Star-News*. She'd been awake since dawn, but hadn't been able to bring herself to pick up the paper.

"It's not here," he said, standing at the counter with the paper spread out in front of him. "I've been through twice."

"Check one more time," she said, getting up from the table to have a look over his shoulder.

"Jules-y," he said, his voice impatient, "if it's not screaming at us, it's not in here. They hadn't planned on making it a subtle story."

Jules wondered what happened. Had Hunter talked them out of it? If so, he'd already earned a big chunk of his billable hours. "Maybe I should call and find out if they plan to let it go away," she said.

"And put it back on their radar?" Lincoln raised his eyes from the paper. "That's a good idea."

"Stop." She laughed. "Maybe they're waiting to make it even bigger," she said. "A Sunday feature or something."

"It's not a feature," he said. "It's news. They're not going to let it get old and then run it—or let someone else get it first." He got up to pour himself a cup of coffee.

"That's decaf," she warned him.

He made a face, but filled his mug anyway.

"Sorry," she said.

"That's okay. I can drink swill in solidarity, Little Momma." He sat across from her. "Anyway, I think you've dodged a bullet on this one."

"God, I hope so," she said. Relieved, she got up to shower and get dressed for their outing to Vick's old school.

The drive south toward Myrtle Beach reminded Jules of trips when she was in high school. If she and her friends wanted to decrease their chances of being spotted by someone who knew them, they would drive the extra hour into South Carolina. Only now did she realize what a bad idea the driving part was when they'd been drinking. She pressed her hand to her belly, hoped her kid would have more sense than she did when she was growing up.

"Did you reach anyone at the school when you called?" Lincoln asked. He was driving, so she settled back and tried to get comfortable in the seat.

"The school secretary said that the psychologist isn't around— and probably couldn't talk with us anyway because of their privacy rules. But the teachers will still be working full days this week and next. They begin half days next week. What's the drama teacher's name again?"

"Morgan Gaines," Lincoln said. "The school Web site listed him as the only drama instructor, so that's got to be the guy."

They drove down Highway 17. Crossed the state line just after Calabash, where the fried fish smell flooded into Jules' nostrils, calling up memories of that day her father went off on

Lincoln. It seemed appropriate, somehow, to have that memory so close. Vick was nearly the age of Lincoln when he survived that ordeal.

"Did you ever think about hurting yourself?" Jules asked. "You know, when things got so bad with Dad."

"He hurt me enough for both of us," Lincoln said, his voice flat. "But no, I never had those impulses. I felt guilty when I was younger, like everything was my fault. But by the time I was Vick's age, I was mostly just pissed off."

"That's healthier, I guess," she said.

"I don't know. It all sucks if you ask me."

Jules looked out over the low landscape that led out toward the ocean and wondered, not for the first time, what Marnee saw when she looked at Jack Fuller. But with a child of her own arriving in a few months, Jules understood the depth of conflict Marnee must have felt, seeing him mistreat her son. The lingering questions Jules had about why Marnee stayed rose again to the forefront of her thoughts.

"I wonder even more these days why she never took us and left," Jules said after a few minutes' silence.

"Who, Mom?" Lincoln seemed to have already moved on to other thoughts. Maybe that was how he survived all the early years.

They'd had the discussion many times before and the questions had become nearly rhetorical. But with her own maternal instincts looming large, Jules revisited the subject with new urgency. On the surface, keeping her own baby from Thomas didn't seem right, but the real answers ran deeper than face value and the alternative was unacceptable.

"It's never made sense." Jules searched for angles she might have missed. "It goes against everything I know about Mom. She would have stood in front of a moving train for us. Why would she have kept you in Dad's line of sight? When she found out what I was doing with this baby, she told me I had to think of the baby first. First and last, she told me."

"Maybe it was finances." Lincoln, one hand resting lightly on the wheel, kept his eyes ahead on the road. "She could have been scared of how we'd have to live. I don't know. I used to think she might leave him. I had to trust that she had her reasons."

Staying in the house with a man who had, even once, laid a violent hand on his son . . . How had Marnee reconciled that decision? Jules never before saw things so clearly as she did at that moment. As a kid, she'd gotten used to a skewed perspective of what was normal. As a mother, she didn't have that luxury.

"Here we are," Lincoln said as he turned into the parking lot of the school. The low building looked too quiet to be the hotbed of burgeoning hormones that was middle school.

They parked near the front and walked across the steamy asphalt lot into the cool entrance. The paint job was new, but otherwise the look of the building remained as it must have for decades.

Before she had a chance to get her bearings, they came upon the office. And Jules felt for all the world like a kid in trouble—again.

"Can I help you?" the receptionist asked.

"Yes, ma'am," Lincoln took the lead in responding. "We're looking for Morgan Gaines."

All her life, she'd been a good girl in bad girl clothes. Now she stood there in maternity clothes. Did that make her better or worse?

"Mr. Gaines' classroom is 11B," the woman said in response to Lincoln's inquiry. "If he's not there, try the auditorium. He was organizing some of the props in the backstage storage area yesterday, so he might still be doing that."

With that, they went off to find the man who had put notions of movie stardom into Vick's head.

Chapter Twenty-seven

Morgan Gaines looked nothing like Lincoln expected. He'd envi-
sioned a slight, youngish man with a distinct sense of fashion and
dramatic tendencies at every turn. Instead Mr. Gaines—as the
nameplate on his classroom door identified him—was an over-
weight man in his mid-forties, wearing blue jeans and a T-shirt
from the 1992 Chicago Pride Parade.

His classroom was empty, but a teacher passing by pointed
them in the direction of the auditorium. Gaines was trying with
some difficulty to put a box onto one of the loftier shelves in the
storage room behind the stage. Lincoln went over and helped
him lift the container high enough to slide it into place.

"Thanks," the man offered. His face was damp with the effort
he'd expended. "I'm not sure who would have won that fight—
me or the box—if you hadn't come along. Can I help you with
something?" The Southern vowels in his voice carried for miles,
even to Lincoln's North Carolina–bred ears. He had the tonal
quality of a tenor.

"Are you Mr. Gaines?" Lincoln decided he'd better confirm
what seemed to be a given.

"Just Morgan, please," he said. "I don't want to feel any older than necessary."

"Well, Morgan, I'm Lincoln Fuller, and this is my sister, Jules. We were hoping you could give us some information on Vick Johns. We grew up in Ekron, the town he moved to when he left here."

"Oh, my God," Gaines exclaimed. "Lincoln Fuller? You're Lincoln Fuller?"

A music lover. Lincoln spotted the "fan glaze" in the man's eyes. He hadn't made up the term. A friend of his, a famous baritone, had coined it as far as Lincoln knew. But it aptly described the goofy, wide-eyed expression people got when they'd heard you, or at least heard *of* you, and decided you qualified as a celebrity.

"I have all your recordings," Morgan said. "Including the movie soundtracks, which are brilliant. I have to say it again—*brilliant.* Hollywood doesn't usually have that much sense when it comes to music, but . . ." He shook his head in apparent awe.

"Thank you," Lincoln said, eyes averted to discourage any further discussion of his work. He never knew what to do when people threw compliments his way.

"I heard you play at Avery Fisher Hall . . . oh, it must have been ten years ago. Magical. An evening of Grieg and Chopin. Just magical."

"Thank you," Lincoln said again, looking at Jules to help him out.

"So Mr. Gaines," Jules said, "about Vick Johns."

Morgan Gaines looked at Jules as if he'd just realized she was in the room. "Again, call me Morgan. So, how is our boy?"

"Not so well. Vick's been going through a rough time in Ekron," she told him.

"I know some of what's happened," he said, his voice full of sympathy. "One of the policemen, a sergeant, I think, called me and asked some questions. Sounds like Vick has been indulging his imagination again. He had a tendency to do that." He gestured as he spoke. "The psychologist here thinks he uses it as a coping mechanism. She talked to me about it and I told her, 'Honey, that's what acting is all about. Where would we be in the theater without the ability to make up what isn't there?' But I guess young Vick has taken it a bit too far."

"I'm the one he's made all those claims about," Jules said.

"Oh, I see," Morgan said, nodding with a new understanding of their mission. "And is anyone buying it?"

"Some were," she said. "But yesterday, Vick tried to kill himself. He's in the hospital in Wilmington."

"Oh, sweet Jesus." Morgan seemed genuinely shaken. He sat down on the edge of a worktable, and the wood groaned under his considerable heft. "How is he?"

"He's probably going to be okay," Lincoln said, "but the issue is why would he do it? Will he try again?"

Morgan Gaines closed his eyes. It seemed that he tried to remove himself from the room by shutting it out. But after a moment, he looked at them again.

"He was teased quite a bit," he said. "Boys and girls alike. He had a true passion—and some talent, I have to say—for theater. But he was one of only three boys in a class of seventeen or eighteen girls. It wasn't easy for the fellows. That, plus his father objected, I know."

"Did he talk about his dad at all before he died?" Jules asked.

"What do you mean, exactly?"

"He said something to me that made it seem as if he almost *wanted* to take responsibility for his dad's death," she said. "He didn't do anything, of course, but why would he say that? Was there anything of that sort in the plays you studied or any of the books the class read?"

"Oh, Lord, the Greek stuff is full of it," Morgan said. "We

go through a full section on Greek tragedy. And then we did readings from *Twelve Angry Men*. Spent a little over a week on that. I don't know, though. Like I said, his father objected to his interest in drama, and Vick had a lot of anger about that. It's a little hard to tell what might be just normal teenage emotions and what would be a real red flag for bigger problems, don't you think?"

"Judging from the time you spend with kids," Lincoln said, "where do you think that line is? When does it cross over from normal angst to a kid trying to hang himself?"

"Good Lord!" Gaines flinched at Lincoln's words. "He did that?"

"He did," Lincoln told him.

"Vick had problems with the male authority figures in his life. First, with his dad, and then after his dad died, transferring all of it to the uncle."

"You saw that *before* he moved?" Jules asked.

"Yes, absolutely." Morgan adjusted himself on the table-top and, for a second, the groaning legs of the structure again threatened to buckle underneath the man.

Lincoln watched his sister, knowing she had more than a passing interest in finding out about Walt. Whatever this *thing* was between Jules and Walt, Lincoln feared it could only lead to more problems for her.

"His uncle Walt would drive down with his family to the school plays if Vick had a part. Vick always seemed pretty excited they were coming. But then, the last play of the year, the one that happened after his dad died, he didn't seem to want his uncle here. I said, 'Will your family be coming from Wilmington this time?' He said, 'Can't stop 'em, I guess.' I said, 'You don't like your family anymore?' He told me, 'I could do without Walt.' That's all I got out of him. But I thought it was weird. I wondered if something might be up with *Uncle Walt*."

He raised his eyebrows. "But the thing with his dad—we've all fantasized about settling the occasional emotional score here and there. Then suddenly, the father drops dead of a stroke or something. Maybe Vick thinks he willed it to happen."

Vick may have employed an overactive imagination to delude himself about his father's death. But he hadn't pretended to hang himself. That was all too real. Lincoln tried to gauge his gut feelings about Morgan Gaines. The drama instructor didn't give off the creepy vibe of a pedophile. You never could tell for sure, Lincoln knew, but he'd put money on the man keeping pretty decent student/teacher boundaries in place.

"Was there anyone in his life here at school who might have taken advantage of him in any way?" Lincoln decided to get it out there, see the teacher's reaction to such a question.

"You mean sexually?" Morgan asked.

"In any way," Lincoln said.

"If you're asking if I think he was abused," Gaines said, "I don't believe there was anyone here who would do something like that. Not any adult, at least. But the kids could be cruel. Verbally, to be sure. But more and more, you see kids get violent with each other. More than just the swinging fists we all had when I was in school. It's possible that something bad happened with another kid or kids. But that's just a hunch. We do our best to control bullying, but it's a losing battle sometimes. If I'd known of anything for sure, I would have responded."

Lincoln felt too pained to speak. He'd taken his own share of ridicule as a kid and had no desire to step so close to the fire of those particular memories.

"You know," Morgan spoke up again, as if something had just occurred to him. "He asked me once if I was gay. I told him yes. Then he asked me if I got picked on because of it. I told him yes, I did. Then he asked me if being picked on was why I was gay."

Whoa. Lincoln literally drew in a breath. "What did you tell him?"

"I told him that I'm gay because that's how I was born. That nothing anybody does could make a person be gay or not gay."

Lincoln suddenly wished Morgan Gaines had been around when he was in school.

"Does he think he's gay?" Jules asked.

"*I* don't think he is," Morgan offered. "But I think between whatever the bullies have said or done and the dad's disapproval, the poor boy's probably so confused he doesn't know what he is. That's just my take on it. I'm no psychologist, but I'm pretty good at reading kids."

"So he's worried about all this and makes up a story about sleeping with me to camouflage it?" Jules said.

"Maybe," Morgan said. "But I haven't seen him since last year. I don't know how things have been at his new school."

Lincoln looked at his watch. "I've got a telephone interview with some music critic from Cleveland at two o'clock," he said to Jules. "We should get on the road."

"Okay," Jules said. She put her hands on her belly, gently rubbing the small mound, and Lincoln had to smile at the thought of being an uncle.

"Morgan, thank you." He put out his hand and the teacher shook it.

"Listen, I get to Wilmington now and again. Maybe you'd like to have a cup of coffee sometime?" Morgan Gaines had turned into a fan again, or worse, a would-be suitor. "We could even do lunch if you have the time. I'd love to talk with you more about your music. I have to tell you, seeing you perform changed my life. Even in your recordings, I feel as if *you* are there in every note. I can't believe you just walked into this room today."

"I'm not sure how long I'm going to be around on this trip,"

Lincoln said, "but maybe sometime . . . That'd be nice." He kept it vague.

After they got back to the car, Jules settled into the driver's seat for the trip home. Lincoln, gratefully, handed her the keys.

"Something's not right," she said, turning off onto the road that led to the highway.

"What do you mean?" He looked around to see if they had taken a wrong turn.

"Did you *hear* him?" She glanced over as if her meaning had to be obvious.

"Him, I take it, is Morgan Gaines, but a little more to go on would be helpful."

"The way he was trying to deflect the blame for Vick's problems on everyone else. The boys at school picked on him. Walt took over where his mean daddy left off . . ."

"I didn't get that from what he said at all . . ."

"Where does he get off," she interrupted him, "saying that Walt is a stand-in for Vick's homophobic dad? Calling him *Uncle Walt* and raising those eyebrows."

"Why is this upsetting you?"

"He's got to be hiding something, Lincoln," she said. "Don't you think?"

"Jules." Her name came out harsher than he'd intended, but it stopped her rant, at least. "He didn't seem to be reaching that far to me with the things he said. I don't think he was accusing Walt of anything. And I imagine Vick did get picked on by the other boys."

She looked over at him, her expression more confused than anything else, then turned her gaze back to the road. She didn't say anything.

"Jules?" He looked at her for some clue as to what had brought about such venom for the drama teacher. "Morgan Gaines seemed pretty benign to me. I could be wrong. I'm not saying my instincts are perfect but . . . Jules-y, what's going on with you?"

"Do you think Walt's a bad guy?" She still didn't look over at him, her eyes remained locked on the road.

"No," he told her. "I don't. But it's a fact that Vick has some baggage regarding his uncle. That doesn't mean that he's abused the kid. But I'm more worried about you than anyone else at the moment. You're too wrapped up in this guy. He's married, sweetie."

She finally let out a long breath that she'd been holding in. "I know," she said.

It broke Lincoln's heart to hear the defeat in her voice. He wished he could give her everything she wanted. But he'd seen Tuni Walker at the church. She wasn't someone who would pick herself back up and move on if her husband walked out. On top of that, there were his kids to consider. And Tuni wasn't horrible. She wasn't someone a man of substance left without once looking back. She would be too easily broken, and if Walt was the man Jules seemed to think he was—the man she wanted him to be—he wouldn't leave his family.

"As soon as this is over," she said, "I've got to get back to my life in California." Her tone had acquired a new resolve.

That's my girl. Lincoln put a gentle hand on her arm. She turned and gave him the saddest smile he'd ever seen.

Chapter Twenty-eight

"Hey, Fred, it's Sam Alderman." Sam held his cell phone between his cheek and shoulder while he poured himself a glass of iced tea in the kitchen.

"Sam." The *Star-News* editor sounded genial after their heated exchange the day before. "What's up?"

"I just wanted to thank you for pulling the story. It was the right thing to do, and I appreciate it."

"Don't thank me," Fred told him. "I'd have run the damn thing in a heartbeat. But I got a call from Colin Grant, told me to pull it."

"Colin Grant?" Sam found a can of nuts in the cabinet and poured some in a bowl.

"Managing editor of the paper. He's got some relative, an old lady aunt lives in your town. She got to him, convinced him we didn't have enough to go on to put it in print. Spared your girl there the unwanted publicity."

"Who's his aunt?" Sam asked, curious. He felt disappointed that he hadn't been the one to save the day, but in the end, the result was the same. No story.

"His mom's sister," the man said. "Last name is Dukes, I think. I've seen her before when she's dropped by the paper. Anyway, she knows this Jules friend of yours and, as a favor, she asked Grant to look over the story himself. See what he thought. And he told us to pull it. That was that."

"I'll be damned," Sam said, taking a sip of his drink. He couldn't quite imagine Mrs. Dukes—the same Mrs. Dukes who talked about Jules' "true colors"—coming through and rescuing her from front-page hell. But apparently that's what had happened. "At least it all worked out."

"Always does one way or another," Fred said. "Want to hit the ball sometime? My elbow's back up to speed now, and I'm on the court a couple of times a week."

"Sure," Sam said. "Give me a call next week. I'm helping my mother out with some things right now, but I'll be back at work by then."

"Will do."

Sam put his glass in the sink and walked out of the kitchen. He heard a toilet flush and saw his mother come out of the bathroom in the hall. But he noticed as he walked by that the sink was dry. The chances of his mother forgoing hand-washing after using the john were nil. She'd definitely been hovering, listening in.

He smiled. What else could he do? She was too old to change, and it was too ridiculous to fight about. He let it go and, with nothing better to do, went outside to hose down the salt and sand from the underside of his Audi.

"Love you, Mom," he called on his way out.

"I love you, too," she called from the kitchen where he heard her cleaning up the dishes. She turned on the small kitchen television, and it sounded out the laugh track from a decades-old show he'd watched when he was a kid.

It's time for me to get back to work, he thought, as he unraveled the hose from a messy heap on the driveway.

Chapter Twenty-nine

In light of her questions about Walt, Jules found herself thinking more and more about Thomas. Why hadn't she seen his problems earlier? She could have figured things out about him if she'd let herself. Odd days when he would disappear without explanation. Times when his responses were off.

Lincoln was on the phone with the *Washington Post*. She grabbed a water bottle and headed outside for a walk.

She thought about the clues she should have taken seriously with Thomas. Once, he'd given her a box. When she opened it, she found two antique egg coddlers—small porcelain cups used for poaching—cradled like little eggs themselves in a nest of tissue paper. They were so lovely that looking at them made her spontaneously smile.

"What's this?" she asked, enchanted by his offering, and puzzled about the occasion. Had she forgotten an important date they were supposed to celebrate?

He, too, seemed confused. "You like poached eggs," he said.

"So I thought you'd like them." He'd had a nervous energy about him as he attempted to explain the gift.

That was a few months into their relationship. He'd never given her anything of note before that. A friend, another Foley artist who was into antiques, saw them, and his eyes grew large.

"Where'd you get these?" he asked. "They're gorgeous."

"Thomas gave them to me," Jules told him.

"Did he rob a bank first?"

Jules had laughed. Only later, much later after everything came to light, did she ask her friend what he thought they were worth.

"My guess would be in the eight-thousand-dollar range, could be closer to ten thousand. You should have them appraised," he said, "And for God's sake, put the damn things in a safety deposit box." The purchase of the coddlers had been the result of a manic episode.

Apparently, he'd gone to his ex-wife's apartment and taken her wedding rings, then sold them and bought the porcelain cups on a whim. After he'd settled into his medication again, he'd given them to Jules, a little fuzzy as to exactly how he came by them in the first place—but sweetly desperate for her to have them.

This wasn't the only odd episode, the only time he couldn't clearly explain incongruities in his life. But whenever something seemed off, she'd tell herself—and him—that he'd been working too hard, keeping odd hours and not sleeping enough. It frightened her how easily she'd convinced herself of this because she didn't want to see anything else.

She hadn't put the entire story of the china cups together until the final manic episode when she could no longer rationalize what he'd done. She called his ex-wife to find out what the hell his problem might be, and the woman had agreed to come by Jules' apartment. That's when Jules found out about the full scope of his illness. Before the woman left, she asked Jules if Thomas had given her a set of rings.

"What kind of rings?" Jules asked.

"The wedding kind," she said. "Mine disappeared from the drawer, and I'm sure Thomas took them sometime in the last year or so. I don't ever wear them anymore, of course, but I'd like to know what he did with them. I wondered if he gave them to you."

Jules saw the coddlers, still on the shelf, and she knew where he'd gotten the money to buy them. She gave them to the woman on the spot.

"He gave me these. I'm told they're really valuable. I'm sure this is what happened to your rings," Jules told her. "He must have sold them and bought these. Take them please. Like I said, they're worth a lot and I shouldn't have them."

The woman hesitated.

"I insist. Please," Jules handed them to her and she relented, took the porcelain coddlers. "Thank you," she said as she left, holding them gently in her hands like the fragile objects they were.

Jules thought she might walk to the cemetery, but when she reached Mount Canaan, she kept on going. Walt would probably be home. The school would have gone on summer hours. She wondered what he did in the summers. Work? Fish? After a handful of conversations with him, she felt she knew him. But in reality, she had no idea what his life was like. How often did he and Tuni make love? Did they lie in bed at night and talk about their days? Their kids? Did he grill burgers on weekends? Watch the news every night? These moments made a marriage. Jules was a recent visitor in his life, at best. She had to stop thinking there was more to it than that.

And the questions about Vick's reactions to his uncle loomed large. Could Walt really have done something to the boy? Something so bad that Vick made up a fantasy world as a distraction? Walt chose to work with kids Vick's age. Was there a darker reason why he put himself in that kind of proximity to teenagers? If that was true, then her instincts about people were worthless, because Walt seemed as decent as anyone she'd ever met in her life.

Still, she'd seen good in her own father that no one else seemed to think was there. She compartmentalized his violence toward Lincoln as storms they could weather. On the verge of motherhood herself now, she was appalled at her own complacency.

Had Jack Fuller confused her judgment of men to the point that she had no insight at all? Decades after her father's death, she'd been dangerously blind to Thomas's alter ego. God help the poor baby that would have to live at the mercy of her decisions.

Walt's house was in sight. She came to the walkway and stopped. The house looked as if different parts of it had been built at different times. The main section was small and traditional. Two levels with a porch on the front. But off to one side, an L-shaped ranch-style add-on sprawled into what would have been the side yard. A metal carport had been tacked onto the other side.

She'd decided to turn around and walk back home, when she saw Cici Johns standing behind the screen of the front door. Jules walked halfway up the walk toward the porch.

"He's not here," Cici said, her voice hard. "I'm guessing you came to see Walt."

"I'm not sure I came to see anyone," Jules said, realizing it was true. "I just started walking in this direction."

"You've been doing that a lot lately, haven't you?" Cici said, coming out onto the porch. "Only you usually make it about as far as the cemetery before you find what you want."

Jules walked up onto the porch. "I know Tuni saw me talking to Walt in the cemetery. But I'm not a homewrecker. And Walt's not a cheater. You can tell Tuni not to worry."

"I can tell her that bird over there is a rabbit, too, but she's got eyes. She can see for herself what the truth is." Cici walked over and sat on the porch swing. She looked up at Jules. "You need to leave all of us alone."

"I didn't ask to be mixed up with your family, Cici. Vick did that. All I've been trying to do is sort it all out."

Cici rocked the swing absently with her foot. She didn't say anything.

"I know she's his wife," Jules said. "And I know he's committed to his life with her. What else do you want me to tell you?"

Cici's posture seemed to settle some, drawing back just a little from the fighting stance she seemed to maintain whenever Jules came within ten feet of her.

Jules went over and sat down beside her on the porch swing.

"Let me tell you something about my brother's wife," Cici said. "After Henry died, I couldn't make the payments on the house. I could barely get what we needed at the grocery store. I called Momma and Daddy and they sent some money. But they don't have much extra to work with, and the parsonage is too little for three adults and two boys to live in.

"I asked Walt if we could stay with him, and he said he'd considered asking us. But as fragile as Tuni's nerves had been, he was worried about bringing another family, more stress, under their roof. He said Tuni had started to seem a lot better, and he didn't want to risk setting her back. It was Tuni who spoke up and said we ought to come. She told him that we were family, that you look after your own. I'm here on my feet because Tuni said that's how it ought to be."

"I'm not a threat to Tuni," Jules said again. "I never was."

"Then why are you here?" Cici asked.

"I don't know," Jules said. "Honestly, I don't." Cici was right. If she believed she had no place in Walt's life, she needed to leave them alone.

She heard a male voice inside the house talking to one of Walt's daughters. "Is Vick home from the hospital?" Jules asked.

Cici shook her head, glanced toward the door. "That's Garrett inside with Bart and the girls. Vick's got to stay in Wilmington for a while longer. Momma stayed with him for me to come home and get a shower."

"Why are they keeping him?" Jules asked.

"One of the cuts on his wrists got infected. They're telling him he has to stay because of that. But the real reason is they want to make sure he's not going to hurt himself again." Looking in her eyes, Jules saw the toll everything had taken on the woman.

"Something hasn't been right with him for a while," Jules said. "We both know it, Cici. And we both know it has nothing to do with me. I know you don't like me, and I don't blame you. But, at least, tell me you know now this business Vick made up was really a lie."

"You're right," Cici said. "I don't like you very much. But I do owe you an apology. I'm sorry I talked to that reporter and I'm glad they didn't print that story. But until I saw bruises on his neck and heard what he'd tried to do to himself, I did think it was true—what he said about you. When I saw him in that clinic after your brother brought him in . . ." She wiped her eyes with the back of her hand. "As bad as it was—you know, what he said you did—I knew it had to be something even worse for him to try and kill himself." She turned to face Jules and, for the first time, all the fire and anger had gone out of her. "What do you think happened to him?" she asked.

"I don't know." Jules took a long drink from her water bottle. Suddenly, she'd never been so thirsty in her life. "Was there any time that he came home from school, either at his old school or here, when he seemed really upset? Or when he looked as if he'd been in a fight?"

"Boys fight," Cici said. "It's what they do. I couldn't tell you one time or another when he seemed upset about that. This stuff he wants to do—be in plays and all this acting business—it hasn't made life any easier for him. But it was always what he liked the most about school, and up until lately, I thought he could handle the teasing. His daddy was hard on him, I guess, but it was within bounds. My husband never laid an angry hand on the boy. I promise you that."

Jules didn't tell her that she'd seen a father's abuse up close, and that words could do as much damage as a fist.

"And other than a black eye here and there from the playground," Cici said, "that's all I ever saw." A half smile came across her face. "And Vick always got the better of whoever started it."

Jules wasn't so sure. But if that was true, if he could physically fight back, then it would be the verbal assaults that got to him. Boys calling him gay because of the drama. Him making up stories about relationships with a woman to throw them off. Maybe it was as simple as that. Maybe nothing else had gone on.

"Cici!" a man's voice called from inside.

"I'm out here," she answered.

The man came out onto the porch, and Jules recognized him as Garrett, the youth minister who'd been praying with Preacher and Mrs. Walker at the medical clinic.

"The doctor's on the phone," he said to Cici.

Obviously a man of few words, he gave no information beyond the simple fact.

"Excuse me a minute," she said and went into the house. The man followed her.

Alone on the porch, Jules thought of Walt. He must have spent hours sitting on the porch swing that rocked beneath her at that moment. Some of those times, his daughters would join him, dangling their small feet while he kept the motion in play. Other times, he and Tuni would sit together after putting the children to bed. All around her, she saw the place where his world existed.

"Could I get you something to drink?" Garrett was suddenly there. "Tea or a soda or something?"

"I'm fine," she said. "Thank you. Your name is Garrett, right?"

"Yes ma'am," he said. "Garrett Fisher."

"I'm Jules."

He nodded in acknowledgment. He stood at the top of the steps, looking out toward the street as if he might be expecting someone. But the road remained empty.

"What do you think about Vick?" Jules asked. "You've seen him at home and you've had him in the church youth program, right?"

"Yes," he said. "I've spent a lot of time with him. Prayed with him and for him. Our sinful natures are always at war with the divine inside of us. I think Vick wrestles with this more than most. But he's a good boy. The struggle itself testifies to that fact."

Jules didn't know how to respond. A boy had tried to hang himself and this man, this authority figure in the kid's life, was spouting religious babble as if the whole thing amounted to an abstract moral dilemma.

"Aren't you worried about what really caused all of this behavior?" she asked. "That he might try it again?"

"Of course," he said with calm, somewhat condescending authority. "But I think that his spiritual well-being is a critical part of why he's made these choices. If that part of him is healed, there won't be any cause for worry."

"What do you mean by 'sinful nature'?"

"Any desires that are contrary to God's plan for our lives," he said.

Jules realized that Garrett Fisher had picked up the banner that Vick's father had carried in life. He thought Vick's involvement in theater classes amounted to homosexual behavior. Poor kid. He couldn't catch a break in the male role model department. Except that wasn't entirely true. Walt was there, but had been soundly rejected by Vick.

"His mental health issues are at the center of all this, don't you think?" She tried to stay rational.

"The mind and the spirit cannot be separated in that way, Miss Fuller." The man had a smile on his face, but his eyes didn't show it. He gave her the creeps.

Cici came back onto the porch with her purse and her keys. "I'm going to ride back over to the hospital," she said. "Blood tests they ran after he was admitted show something in his system."

"What kind of *something*?" Garrett asked.

"Drugs, maybe." Her voice dropped low. She glanced at Jules as if just remembering her presence on the porch. "They want to talk to me," she went on. "Momma's still there."

"Where's your daddy?" Garrett asked.

"He's preaching a funeral in Southport this afternoon, but Rhonda will be at the church office until he comes back and she'll tell him what's going on."

"You want me to stay with Bart?" Garrett asked.

"Tuni's upstairs. She said she's going to be here with the girls, anyway, so she'll look after Bart for me."

"Then I'll come with you," Garrett told her. "Are they sure it's drugs?"

Cici gave a slight shake of her head, as if to remind him that it was family business and Jules wasn't family.

"It's good that we cleared the air on some things, Jules," Cici said. "Thank you for stopping by." It was less of an expression of gratitude than a dismissal.

Jules stood and walked down the porch steps after them. "I hope Vick is better," she said.

"Thank you," Cici said. Then Jules overheard her as she and Garrett walked to the car. "Lord help us, if this is true."

"The Lord *will* help us," Garrett said. "He'll give us the strength to help Vick, no matter what."

Jules had already been forgotten. She found herself wishing that Vick's problems could be solved with a substance abuse intervention, but in her heart of hearts she knew that wasn't the case. Whatever Vick Johns had ingested, he'd done it *because* of his problems, not the other way around.

She watched Cici and Garrett drive off toward the highway. She hadn't gone more than a hundred yards toward home, when she heard a car slow down as it approached. Behind the wheel, Walt rolled down his window as he came to a stop beside her.

"Hey," he said, resting his elbow on the door and leaning slightly out the open window. "You walking for your health?"

"I just left your house," she said. "Don't ask me exactly why I was there. I don't even know myself."

"You get run off or you leave of your own accord?"

"Little of both," she said, smiling in spite of herself. "I talked to Cici for a few minutes. She and Garrett just left together for the hospital." She felt guilty for feeling so happy at the sight of him when misery abounded all around. "They found some kind of drugs in Vick's system."

"What kind?"

Jules sensed the school counselor in Walt kicking in.

"I don't know. That's what they're going to talk with your sister about, I guess."

He nodded, absently ran his fingers along the top of the rearview mirror. "I'll check on things at home, then ride over there," he said.

His car was the only one on the road, and so she stood on the center line by his window. He sat without any indication that he might act on his plan to go into his house.

"I've put you in a terrible position," Jules said. "Tuni saw us the other night at the church."

"She mentioned it," he said. "Several times, actually." He tried to smile, but couldn't quite pull it off.

"I'm sorry." That was one reason she ended up in front of his house in the first place, she realized. She wanted to apologize.

"But it's not your fault. I'd say it's not really anybody's fault, but hell, it's probably mine. I've been acting like I'm still in high school, working up the courage to ask you out. And I can't ask you out. God knows, I shouldn't even be thinking about you at all."

She had to launch in if she ever planned to have the talk with him. "This thing we've been doing," she said. "It's more than flirting, less than adultery. But you're right, it's not good."

"No," he said, shaking his head. "It's not."

She couldn't keep showing up at his house, and they couldn't keep finding each other in the cemetery. What did she need from him? What did she want before she left him alone once and for all? "I just need to know something."

"What's that?"

Having gone that far, she didn't know how to continue. "I've been wrong about men before," she said. "I was wrong about my father. And I was wrong again about the father of this baby. That scares me."

"I don't understand," he said. He offered his full attention.

"I need to know if my instincts are wrong about you, too. About the kind of person you are. You're the last person I should be asking, but I don't know what else to do. I'm losing faith in my own judgment. You seem decent, honest, one of the best people I've ever met. I'm asking you to tell me if I'm wrong. Please tell me the truth. I'm going to be a mother in a few months. I have to know if I can trust my gut feelings at all."

He looked at her with a kindness that she didn't believe anyone could feign. "I can't tell you I'm a good person," he said, "because right now I feel like a pretty crappy person. But spending time with you—even the little bit we've had—Jules, it's all been genuine. I haven't faked anything in that department, I promise you. And you haven't misread anything."

She listened and waited. She looked at his eyes, listened to his tone. With her father, she'd known things were wrong and had lived with them anyway. With Thomas, she'd ignored her uneasy feelings. Nothing about Walt Walker seemed wrong, nothing except his circumstances. Nothing he said or did made her uneasy.

"If I wasn't a man with a wife and family," he said, echoing her train of thought, "I'd be asking you to spend as much time with me as you could spare. But I am married. That's a fact, regardless of what I feel when I think about you. And telling you that I can't see you, that I have to stop talking with you . . . Well, that goes against everything I want. If that's decent, then I guess I'm what you think I am. But I'll tell you right now, I feel like shit."

She blinked and felt wet lashes touch her face. Nothing he said amounted to any hope at all for the two of them, but she still felt better hearing it. He looked directly at her. A man who could look you in the eye, a man who appeared as pained and sincere as Walt did, had to be entirely honest or a sociopath.

"Thank you," she said. "That's all I needed to know."

His fingers still rested on the top of his car mirror. For a moment, she laid her hand on his. It seemed like a kind of pact they were making. A pact to feel something powerful and then leave it be. After a moment, she took her hand away, stepped back from his car, and offered a small wave before she turned and walked back toward her house. After a moment, she heard him back up and turn his car around.

A few minutes later, as Jules neared her mother's house, she saw Sam's car parked near the carport. Behind her, somewhere on the other side of Mount Canaan, she heard the whoop-whoop of a siren as an ambulance came closer and closer. A bad feeling came over her, and that was when—in spite of a still-ailing foot—she broke into a run.

Chapter Thirty

As Lincoln had waited on help to arrive, he thought about Jules and Tanner. He had to stay focused on the two people in the world who made him want to live—and the baby, of course. There was the baby, too.

Three people to live for. Things were looking up already.

But the pain in his side became unmanageable and he was afraid he might pass out. If he passed out, he was afraid he might not wake up. How about that option? Marnee was on the other side, wherever that was. If there was a chance all that celebrated business about souls and the afterlife was true, he was tempted to head in that direction just to see if he could find her. A wave of pain consumed him again, and he worried that Jules would find him dead. Reason enough to keep his sorry ass among the living.

A smaller version of the pain had begun when he was on the phone with the music critic. He managed to get through the in-terview sounding coherent, he believed, but things had rapidly gotten worse. Still unsure if it was indigestion or the end of his mortal days, he weighed the risk of dying against the embarrassment of setting off every emergency scanner in the county with a 911 call that turned out to be gas. He'd compromised and dialed Sam's number instead.

At some point, he'd answered his cell phone. "Nine-one-one confirming your location," the person said. "We want to keep you on the line, Mr. Fuller." He realized Sam had the sense to call them. Good man. Who knew—way back then—that the skinny kid his father dragged from the landing that day would end up saving his life? At least, Lincoln hoped that's the way it would go.

And just then, as if by magic, Sam had arrived. Lincoln thought it couldn't have been more than a few minutes since he called him, but Sam was definitely there. *Maybe I did pass out.*

He only knew a couple of things with any certainty. Jules needed him. Jules and her baby. And Tanner was still somewhere on the earth drawing one breath after the other. This gave them a chance to find each other again someday. In his forty-two years, Lincoln had lived for love, music, and booze. The very fact that booze occupied a place in that trinity was sad. But the other two would not be taken from him. He would get better. There. He'd decided.

And just in time. He heard Jules coming in the door.

Chapter Thirty-one

"What's happened?" Jules rushed in the front door and saw Lincoln lying on the couch. Sam sat in a chair beside him with his two middle fingers laid against Lincoln's wrist. Sam looked at his watch, and she figured out that he was checking her brother's heart rate.

"He's having some bad right upper quadrant pain," Sam said. It was the first time Jules had seen him being what he was trained to be. A doctor. His very presence calmed her.

"Hey Jules-y." Lincoln attempted a smile, but he winced as pain cut the effort short.

"When did this start?" she asked him.

"During the interview," he said. "It got worse pretty fast. You didn't have your cell phone, so I called Sam."

"Dear God, Sam. Thank you for coming so fast." She went and stood beside both of them.

The sirens grew louder, confirming Jules' fear that they'd been called for her brother.

"So what does this mean?" She fought to stay calm.

"Maybe nothing," Sam said, speaking with the calm of a doctor used to keeping dire situations from getting worse. "I think we should get him to Wilmington, though. Let somebody in the right specialty who still practices medicine have a look."

"Do we have somebody who will see him?" Jules asked Sam.

"I've called a guy who comes highly recommended by people I trust. He'll meet us in the ER, then sort out from there what Lincoln needs."

"Is there anything I should bring?" Jules asked.

"Meds he's on," Sam said. "Vitamins and supplements, too, if you have them."

"Everything I take is in a pouch in the bathroom," Lincoln said.

"I'll get that," Jules said. "Anything else?"

"I guess none of your medical records are here, huh?"

"No," Lincoln said, his voice weak. "Given my situation, I suppose I should have them tattooed down my back, but I had no such foresight before this trip down."

"That's okay. They'll call your doctor in New York anyway. Your parents' records might help if they're handy," Sam said. "Family history never hurts."

"We have Mom's here," Jules said. "We got them after she died. And I think she had Dad's, too, in a file somewhere."

"If they're easy to get your hands on," Sam said. "Especially since your dad . . ." He stopped.

"It's okay, Sam," Jules said. "You can say it. Dad was an alcoholic."

"Yeah." Sam looked uncomfortable, and Jules felt badly for him. She thought of that terror-filled afternoon he had with her dad. No kid should go through that. Lincoln inherited the problem with alcohol, but not the raw meanness of the drunken Jack Fuller. Lincoln's gentle temperament, drunk or sober, had spared everyone a second generation of Fuller rage.

And about the drinking, Jules knew that she had to ask. The truth would be important for the doctor to know.

"Lincoln," Jules worked to keep her voice neutral, non-accusatory. "Have you been drinking at all?"

He looked up at her, his eyes issuing an apology.

"When was the last time?" she asked.

"Last night when I walked to the church. The whole thing with Vick . . ." He closed his eyes, opened them again. "I couldn't handle it. And I slipped up a little—at the end with Mom." He left it at that. He didn't need to say any more. She'd been amazed that he got through their mother's ordeal sober. And he hadn't been drunk. But he had been drinking. His bottles of "insurance" hadn't saved him from needing to dull the pain of watching Marnee suffer.

"You're not severely jaundiced," Sam said. "I'm no specialist, but I do know that's a good sign. This pain could be gallstones for all we know."

"Yeah, right, Doc," Lincoln said. "What are the odds of that?"

"Pretty slim," Sam told him.

Jules brushed strands of damp hair from Lincoln's forehead. "I'll go get your pills and the records."

"I'm sorry I let you down," he said.

"You've never let me down," Jules told him. "Never." Noise from the sirens seared into her ears as they closed in on her driveway, then went blessedly silent, signaling the arrival of help.

She walked into her mother's bedroom. Moments later, with manila folders and pill bottles in hand, Jules followed Sam out onto the porch.

"You ride with him in the ambulance," Sam said to her. "I'll follow in my car. If he has to stay, I can give you a ride home. Otherwise, I'll bring both of you back."

Jules had never felt more grateful in her life. Sam as Dr. Alderman, taking charge, had saved her all the panic and confusion of getting help for Lincoln.

She watched the paramedics bring him out on a stretcher. Her brother offered a forced smile and small shrug of his shoulders as they ushered him past her. In spite of the smile, he looked frightened. She'd seen him come out of bloody thrashings at the hands of his father and show nothing. This new, visible fear, terrified her. She reached out and took his hand for the briefest of seconds before they carried him out of reach.

"I don't know how to thank you, Sam," she said. "Ever since the day I saw you in the grocery store, you've been rescuing me one way or another. I've even been a real jerk a couple of times and you keep coming through for us."

"That's me," he joked. "The big hero. Sam Alderman action figures are in production as we speak."

"I'm serious," she said.

"You think I'm not?" He smiled, motioned with his head for her to get into the ambulance with Lincoln.

"I've spoken with your doctor in New York," the specialist was saying to Lincoln when Jules reached the private room they'd moved him into after his stint in the ER. Sam was still there, too.

"He was glad that you called for help at the first sign of trouble," the doctor said, "and furious with you for slipping off the wagon. He said to expect an insufferable lecture when you get back."

"I would expect no less," Lincoln said, looking miserable.

"Anyway, the pain you're having is a big, red flag. It's called pancreatitis. You've pushed yourself back, close to the edge again. Closer this time. This isn't irreversible. But this episode has put you behind the line of scrimmage."

Lincoln looked helplessly at Jules. She nodded, a small re-assurance to let him know she'd translate the sports analogy later.

"We're going to need to keep you here for a bit, simply to torture you. I want to make sure the inflammation resolves and the fatty tissue isn't progressing in that liver of yours. The hope would be that it would be getting better by now, but your little slip-ups cost you, Mr. Fuller. I'm not judging here, mind you, just stating the facts. If you drink, you will get worse. If you drink a lot, you will die."

"I understand." Lincoln looked tired, so tired Jules wondered if he might fall asleep while the doctor stood there talking.

"Things are stacked against you with your father's history," the doctor continued. "But it sounds as if he never intended to remedy his behavior. Your desire to change your habits makes all the difference. That will be a huge factor in your recovery, but you have to see it through. Of course, it would help to know what your mother contributed to this little genetic cocktail, but it's not critical. We know what we have to do."

"Mom's records are there, too," Jules said, pointing to the folders that sat stacked with Lincoln's chart on the table. "I brought them both."

"Of course," he said, "but we'd really need the birth mother's information for it to be relevant." He looked at her as if she was bordering on simple.

"That *is* his birth mother," Jules said. "I'm adopted, but he's not. Maybe that's why it's confusing."

The doctor hesitated before he spoke again. He looked un-comfortable. "The woman in those charts, Marnee Fuller, had a partial hysterectomy when she was twenty-two. Her records indicate that she never gave birth to any children." He looked from Lincoln to Jules. "I'm sorry if this is news."

Lincoln looked as if he'd been struck, but Jules knew there had to be a simple explanation. What the doctor said didn't make any sense.

"I'm adopted. They never kept that from me. I'm sure they would have told Lincoln, too. There has to be some mix-up in the dates or something. If they'd adopted Lincoln, they would have just said so."

"As far as I can tell," the doctor explained, "there's no reason to think Jack Fuller was not your biological father, Mr. Fuller."

"But that can't be right," Lincoln said, more of an incredulous mumbling than a protest. "It just can't."

"The records are very clear on Marnee Fuller's surgery and her status as a biological mother," the doctor told him. "Beyond what's on paper, I don't have any other information. No explanation."

"Could you leave please?" Lincoln's eyes stared past all of them, as if the doctor's words had become a vision. "I really need to be by myself."

"Lincoln?" Jules asked. "I don't think . . ."

"Jules, please. I love you, and I'll be okay. But I really want to be alone." Panic rose in his voice.

"At least let me stay in the room, Lincoln," Jules said, her own panic taking hold. "I won't talk."

"Please." He met her eyes. "Just for a little while. Okay?"

She couldn't leave him. She just couldn't, but Sam came in close beside her and urged her toward the door.

"Lincoln, you need support right now. You can't afford to—" she began, but he interrupted her.

"I have no alcohol here," he said, appearing to have gained some control. "And I won't do any other kind of harm to myself. I promise. I wouldn't put you through that. I just want to sort this out by myself for a few minutes." He sounded calm, but his eyes still pleaded.

She worried about Lincoln's calm demeanor. He was almost too resigned to what he'd heard. Jules didn't understand the kind of compulsions Lincoln had. But from what she'd seen, to understand them is to eventually battle them. There didn't seem to be a lot of middle ground. She'd trusted Lincoln and dismissed her concerns because she *wanted* to trust him. She'd done what was easier for her, not what was best for him. That would stop.

"And gently pass my request for privacy along to the inquiring minds at the nurses' desk," Lincoln added. "They've been hovering."

"It's standard practice to watch addiction patients closely," the doctor said. "I'll tell them to pull back—or at least to be more discreet."

Jules liked him. He didn't try to bullshit any of them. Unlike her tendencies, his goal was not to appease her brother, but to help him.

"So see, sis, Big Brother will save me from myself," Lincoln said. "Even an illusion of solitude will suffice. If I break down and cry like a five-year-old, I'd rather have an audience of strangers than you."

He smiled as if he was kidding around, but he wasn't. She knew him too well to think he could be joking. His spirit was broken, and it killed her to see it, to be able to do nothing.

"We'll go grab some coffee," she said. "My cell's on if you need me."

"Decaf," he said.

"What?"

"Make your coffee decaf." He pointed to her belly.

"Right," she said. "Decaf."

It was what he wanted, so she relented, but she felt lousy

about it. They left him to the particular hell of having Marnee's name removed from his biological tree, while Jack Fuller stayed stubbornly in place. There had to be an explanation, but as the reality of the situation settled in her mind, Jules knew that the explanation—whatever it was—would be no better than the news itself.

Jules wished it could have been the other way around. Marnee as his only parent, Jack's name erased from the picture. For Lincoln, that would have been cause for celebration.

Chapter Thirty-two

Lincoln waited for tears or nausea, the usual suspects. Maybe some combination of the two would arrive. He waited to feel the need to vent in righteous rage. None of it came. A numbness settled over him, as if some powerful anesthetic had overcome all the emotions he should have been feeling. And without alcohol or even narcotics.

He'd lobbied for the latter and was told they tended to withhold the Vicodin from people with known addictive behavior. Tylenol 3 was about the extent of it for pain, and even with that, they were stingy. And still, the blessed numbness had arrived. Go figure.

He'd always thought that the parts of him that were from Marnee could work as a potion against the parts of him that were from Jack. Marnee's DNA had been the antidote to Jack Fuller's portion of traits. But God was obviously a fan of the practical joke. And this one was a beauty, Lincoln thought. And . . . the Divine Jokester withheld the punch line for over forty years. The patience! Astounding.

Only then did the real question occur to him. If Marnee Fuller wasn't his mother, who was? He immediately put the thought out of his head. He'd have to save that one for another day. If he didn't learn to compartmentalize, he'd have to go down the hall foraging for enough cough medicine—or God forbid, mouthwash—to ingest in an effort to lose that train of thought.

He looked around for something that would quell the urgency stirring inside him. A keyboard. He wanted to play.

He pulled the rolling food stand toward him, over his lap. He pushed it down to position it correctly, then lifted his hands on top of the empty surface and closed his eyes. He could see the keyboard in front of him. As his fingers moved, he could hear the music begin.

He played for Marnee. Chopin. For Marnee, it was always Chopin.

Chapter Thirty-three

"Is there someone in your family you can talk with about it?" Sam could see that Jules' response to the revelations about Lincoln came close to full-blown shock. She'd had too much lately.

"I don't know," she said. "Mom was an only child. Maybe Dad's brothers would know. Or Aunt Noreen, his sister. But I've never talked with my uncles about anything more personal than NASCAR, and Noreen's a mean-spirited old thing. I'm not sure she'd tell me even if she knew."

"My mom might know," Sam said, pointing Jules toward the elevator.

"That's right," Jules said. "Our moms *were* really close back then, all the way back to grade school. They talked all the time when I was a little kid. If Lincoln was adopted, she'd know."

Sam didn't want to remind her that Lincoln didn't appear to be *adopted*. The only thing Sam took from what the records showed was that Jack Fuller had, at some point, had an affair, but he'd let his mother tackle that one.

"Okay," Jules said. "I guess we should ask her." She stopped walking, leaned against a wall. "Do I really want to know? Does Lincoln?"

"It seems to me that you know too much already not to hear the rest of it—whatever it is." Sam pushed the elevator button.

"Will your mom talk to us?" Jules asked. "She's never liked me much, and our families have had that Montague/Capulet thing going on now for a few decades."

"She won't keep this from you if she knows," Sam said, hoping his faith in his mother wasn't misplaced. She was no fan of Jules, but she and Marnee *had* been close, back before everything happened. Underneath all the anger and resentment at the Fullers, Rena had a big enough heart to help them. He believed that.

"Okay, let's do it then," Jules said.

The elevator opened and they went down two floors to where the cafeteria was located. Sam wondered if he should prescribe something for Jules. Something for anxiety that would take the edge off. Then he remembered the baby she was carrying. She couldn't even go for an old-fashioned bourbon to calm herself. Throw the added hormones of pregnancy into the mix, and it was a wonder he wasn't scraping her off the ceiling.

"It'll all work out okay," she said. "There has to be a reasonable explanation, right?"

"Right," he said, without much conviction.

As the elevators opened, Sam saw a gathering of Vick Johns' family waiting.

"Do you need the elevator?" Sam asked no one in particular, holding the door open

"Not just yet," Preacher Walker said. "We're going to walk across the street and get a hamburger while the doctor's talking with Vick, but my wife forgot her purse."

Cici stood there with a guy Sam recognized as the church youth minister. Preacher Walker stayed off to the side.

Jules walked over to Cici. To Sam's amazement, Cici didn't act surprised or upset to see the woman who, just one day earlier, she'd been bent on destroying in the local newspaper. In all the confusion, Sam had clearly missed a chapter of that story.

"Lincoln's down the hall," Jules told Cici. Sam went to stand with them.

"What's wrong with him?" Cici asked.

"He has a chronic condition that's flared up." She didn't elaborate, but Cici, soul of discretion that she was, didn't plan on letting it go.

"Does he have that AIDS thing?" she asked.

"Cici!" Mrs. Walker intervened as she rejoined her family. "I didn't bring you up to be rude, girl."

"I'm just asking," Cici mumbled back at her mother.

"No," Jules answered, her tone weary. "He doesn't have AIDS. Listen, how is Vick?"

"He seems better," Cici said. "At least I think he might feel a little better. The doctor says he's *delusional*, and they're trying to figure out what's making him that way. But you know kids. They all live in a fantasy world of one sort or another. I sure did when I was his age."

Sam felt sorry for her. She wanted to make her son's behavior into something normal, something that would pass with time. But everyone there knew that Vick's problems had progressed far beyond what most teenagers experienced.

"I'm sorry you're going through this," Jules said. "As a mother, it must be a nightmare."

Cici nodded, but it was Preacher Walker who spoke up. "We're the ones who should be apologizing to you, Jules." His voice, familiar from decades of sermons, tugged at Sam's childhood memories. "We all spoke and acted unkindly," the preacher said, "and—as it turns out—prematurely."

"Reverend Walker is right," Mrs. Walker said. "None of us knew the extent of Vick's problems. We jumped to conclusions about you, and that was wrong. We've discussed taking up a collection at church to contribute to your lawyer fees."

Sam saw the horror on Jules' face. He could only imagine the humiliation she would feel if they carried through with that effort.

"Thank you," Jules managed, "but that's not necessary. I'm fine. Please don't do that." Her words had a pleading quality that the Walkers must have taken to heart, because everyone suddenly went silent on the subject of a fund-raiser for Jules.

"We were just heading toward the cafeteria before we get back to Lincoln," Sam said.

"Sam, please tell your momma that I appreciate her taking over the Ladies' Summer Bazaar," Mrs. Walker said. "I just wasn't up to it with all this going on."

"Yes, ma'am, I'll tell her," Sam answered.

"We should really be going." Jules' voice hit a high register, and Sam realized she was barely holding on. He wanted to escape with her. Sam liked feeling that he and Jules were a team again, that there was a common cause between them. He was glad that Lincoln had called him.

"I guess we should hurry, too," Mrs. Walker said. "We need to be back by the time that doctor finishes."

As they turned to leave, the elevator doors opened, and Walt Walker stepped off. They all said their casual hellos, but Walt's expression, the way he looked at Jules, gave Sam the odd feeling of being set aside. For an instant he felt like an outsider— someone who had inadvertently stumbled upon a very private moment between two people.

"Did you come to see Vick?" Walt asked Jules. He looked perplexed.

"No," she said. "When I got back to the house, Lincoln was sick."

Sam caught the meaning of her words. She said, *When I got back to the house . . .* It sounded as if she and Walt had been together earlier.

"Is he okay?" Walt asked.

"For the moment," she said. "They're running some tests."

"We're just leaving to get a quick bite," Mrs. Walker said to Walt. She looked from Jules back to her son. "Come on with us. Vick's with the doctor now."

As Sam and Jules walked toward the cafeteria, Sam asked her, "Are you and Walt friends?"

"No," Jules said. "Not really."

She stopped at that, but the words seemed loaded with more than she was saying. He decided to let it go and to focus on the conversation he needed to have with his mother.

When they reached the cafeteria, Sam excused himself and went into the hall to make the call. Jules sat and waited on him, occasionally glancing his way. When his mother answered her phone, he found he didn't know what to say. Should he just bluntly ask her if she knew anything about Lincoln Fuller's birth? Would she answer if he did? He decided that a sketchy approach to the whole thing would only make her suspicious.

"Mom," he said, "I'm here at the hospital in Wilmington."

"Has something happened to you?"

"No, no, listen. I'm here with Jules and Lincoln. Lincoln called me because he was having some pain in his side. It's a long story, but they've admitted him here. Look, I've got a question to ask, and I really want you to be honest with me."

"Of course," she said, sounding somewhat offended that he would expect anything less.

"Mom, Marnee Fuller's records show that she could not have been Lincoln's biological mother. Do you know anything about that?"

Rena went silent on the other end of the line. A dead give-away. She knew the entire story—or at least the high points. He'd put money on it.

"Mom," he prompted her. "I'm here with Jules and Lincoln. They really need to know the truth, whatever it is. The doctors . . ." He decided to ramp up the pressure with a little white lie, "they think it would be helpful for Lincoln if we had a better idea of his family history."

Still silent.

"Mom, are you there?"

"I'm here," she said. "I think if we're going to have this discussion, it shouldn't be over the phone."

"Do you want me to bring Jules to the house?"

"It's not really about her," she said. "I should speak with Lincoln directly. I'll come there. It will take me about an hour to get ready and drive over there."

"Okay," he said. "I'll tell Lincoln you're on the way."

After he ended the call, he went back to Jules, told her about his mother's cryptic response.

"It's true then," Jules said. "I mean really true. Mom didn't have any kids of her own." She laid her hand on her belly, as if her own pregnant state could somehow compensate for Marnee's losses. "God, she must have been devastated. She was born to be a mom."

"She *was* a mom," Sam reminded her.

"Yeah," she said. "You're right. She was."

He laid a hand on her arm. "This has to be weird to take in," he said. "But it really doesn't change anything. I mean, you never felt like you were anything but Marnee's child, DNA or no DNA, right?"

"Never," she said. "Marnee was everything I needed."

"Did you ever try to find out about your birth parents?" He wasn't sure why he asked and wondered if she would take offense.

"No," she said, sounding unbothered by the question. "I've been curious about a lot of things in life, I guess. And people who *do* look . . . I don't think it has anything to do with how they feel about the parents who raised them. But the question itself has never been inside me. It's not even that I don't want to know. I just don't care. I never have. I guess that's weird."

"No," he said. "It's just you."

They sat in the cafeteria for the better part of an hour waiting for Rena's arrival. Lincoln had said he wanted to be alone, but neither of them knew how long they should leave him. Stunning news, news that rewrote who you *were* to some degree, had to be taking a toll on a man used to turning to alcohol to cope.

"Mom should be getting here any minute," Sam told Jules. "I think we should go check on Lincoln and make sure he wants to hear this."

"You're right," Jules said. "He doesn't even know we've talked with her." She shook her head. "Why wouldn't my mom tell him if she wasn't his biological mother? He already hated our dad. He couldn't hate him any *more* for having an affair."

"I don't know," Sam said. "I have no idea what my mom's going to say."

In the hall near the elevator, they again met Vick's family returning from their food outing.

"The doctor just called us," Cici said before anyone else spoke up. "They want to keep Vick here," she said. "We don't know for how long. The doctor thinks he's still . . . what was it he said?"

"Using fantasy to mask some real source of pain or guilt,"

Walt answered for his sister. "They're afraid he might still be a danger to himself."

Sam looked over at Jules. She was watching Walt. The dynamic between Jules and the Walkers perplexed him. They'd gone from public arguments to some strange state of détente. And he especially didn't understand the vibe between Jules and Walt.

"Is somebody with Vick now?" Sam asked, wondering why they didn't seem frantic to get back to the boy after such a disturbing pronouncement from the doctor.

"Garrett is praying with him now," Preacher Walker said. "Dr. Meadows wants to talk with us before we go back in."

"We're going to all take turns staying with him day and night until he gets through this," Mrs. Walker added.

"I'm going to stay tonight," Cici said to no one in particular.

"He needs you when he's awake during the day, child," Mrs. Walker told her daughter. "You can see him for a little while, then Garrett says he'll settle in while you get rested up for whatever comes tomorrow. You're going to flat-out collapse if you don't get some rest."

"And if Garrett's too tired, Tuni said she can come take over," Walt offered. "I just talked with her. She said the girls have let her nap this afternoon and she'll be fine."

Sam saw something change in Jules' face as she listened to Vick's family circling the wagons to cope with their crisis. Was there a small flinch in her expression at the mention of Walt's wife?

"I ought to stay with my own boy," Cici protested, but she seemed to be losing her resolve.

"I'll bring you back over first thing in the morning," Preacher Walker told her. "As early as you want. I promise."

Sam had never thought of Cici Johns as anything special in the maternal department, but something pure and fierce existed in the woman. Motherhood struck him as an alternate universe. He looked at Jules' round belly and wondered what she would be like with a kid.

"Let me know if there's anything I can do," Jules said.

They all mumbled an uncomfortable round of thank-yous before Sam and Jules stepped into the elevator to go upstairs. As the doors slid closed, the chrome reflected a funhouse image of Sam and Jules, looking for all the world like a distorted vision of the couple they'd once been.

Chapter Thirty-four

Lincoln felt as though he'd been transported to another time. In his wheelchair, a light blanket draped over his legs, he was the tragic figure in a souring operatic plot. The one destined to depart the earth while the fat lady wailed. Rena Alderman waited for him on the outdoor patio at the end of his hospital floor. Even as the sun faded, the light seemed too intense after the dull fluorescence of his room.

Rena sat across a small stone table from him, perched on the edge of a patio chair. She appeared to be dressed for an evening out. People who came to his concerts rarely fixed up as much. Sam politely excused himself, and Rena wanted Jules to leave with him, but Lincoln insisted she stay. She pulled a chair up beside him, and in Lincoln's inner narrative, the orchestra had just launched into the opening strains. No players were yet on the stage.

"Your mother was a good woman," Rena said. "I don't know why she ever let herself get mixed up with the likes of your father in the first place, but she really liked him when they were both young, I suppose. He joined the army after high school and he was stationed in Germany."

"So they dated before he left for the service?" Lincoln asked. He wondered how it was that he'd never asked his mother these questions.

"During their last year of high school, they went out pretty steady. He wrote her from overseas. I think that's what she liked most. She was at Campbell College getting her teaching certificate, and she'd get letters with foreign postage. It was all very exciting."

"But then he came back," Lincoln said.

"He came back. She'd moved home to be closer to him, and she finished her degree at the local college. Nobody had much money back then, and she didn't want to be a burden on her folks. He wanted to get married, but he'd come back from overseas drinking more, and it worried her. She kept putting him off, telling him he had to straighten up some before she'd agree. When she was twenty-one or twenty-two, I guess, she finally took a ring from him and they set a date."

Lincoln looked at Jules. She was seeing it all. He was, too. Their mother, young and beautiful. Jack Fuller wanting her, maybe still wanting—at that point—to be a better man for her. Rena seemed to slip into a different time as she told the story, her voice taking on a tone of the young girl she'd been. Lincoln almost felt sorry for the young Rena. He knew the outcome of the tale, but at that early point in the saga, Rena had no idea that, before it all played out, she and the love of her life would have a major role in the climax.

"They were, oh, maybe four months off from the wedding date when she found out he had a woman at Wrightsville Beach. Some club singer he'd met at a bar where she sang during the high season. He'd seen her on and off for a while apparently. The woman would go south when it got cold, down to places that stayed warm enough for tourists. Then she'd come back in the summer. Marnee got wind of it when a woman who taught with her at the elementary school saw the two of them—Jack and this woman—one weekend at a nightclub. When your mother confronted Jack, he confessed. She ended it with him then and there.

"Personally, I think she'd been looking for a reason to end it anyway, but she never told me that. Maybe it was what I wanted to think, because I never liked him. I always thought he was beneath her. A few months later, I think it was, Marnee started having pain in her belly. She went and stayed with her cousin in Richmond to have tests. She told me she didn't want the whole town talking about her 'female problems.' What they thought were fibroids turned out to be a spot of cancer. They caught it pretty early, thank God, but they still had to take out her uterus."

Jules moved her chair closer to Lincoln. She reached out and took his hand. He remembered doing the same thing with her when they were little. Jack stumbling around the house, loud and scary, although that was before he'd gotten physically abusive with his son. They sat in Lincoln's room, where Marnee had told them to stay and, in the dark, held hands. Listened and waited for him to leave.

"Jack came to her while she was still in Richmond. I'm not sure how he found out where she was. He came and asked me, but I certainly didn't tell him anything. Somehow he figured it out. He drove up there and begged her to take him back, said he'd cleaned himself up and wasn't drinking anymore."

"Was that true?" Jules asked. "Had he stopped?"

"Who knows?" Rena dismissed the question. "Maybe for five minutes . . . if that long."

"But Mom believed him?" Jules pressed. Lincoln saw in her

expression how much she wanted to believe in some small redemption for their father.

"She didn't buy it for a second," Rena said. "Marnee said their conversation would have ended there. She told him, 'You were with another woman, Jack. I can't just forget about that because you want me to.' Marnee wasn't stupid. She told him to leave, but then he told her the woman was dead and that much took her by surprise, I guess."

"Jesus," Lincoln said.

"The story was that the woman had taken some pills for sleeping and didn't have the sense not to drink while she was taking them. It killed her. Jack said he'd stopped seeing her already, but I don't know if I believe that. Anyway, she was dead. That much was true."

Lincoln saw the story shaping up in front of him. This other woman—this dead woman—had to be the answer to some of his questions. But he still didn't understand quite how.

"So Mom went back to him?" Lincoln asked.

"I don't think she would have," Rena said. "Dead or not, the woman had been there. Jack had cheated. Marnee told him she was sorry about what happened to the woman, but that her dying didn't change anything. But he had one more thing to tell her. I think he'd hoped to appeal to her sympathy with it, but the funny thing is, he had no idea at the time he had the one thing that would get her back.

"He said to her, 'Come with me to my hotel. I've got something to show you. I need your help, Marnee. Just come with me. After that, I won't bother you again if you say it's over.' She went with him. She told me that a maid from the hotel was sitting in a chair. He'd hired the woman to stay in the room while he found Marnee. On the bed, asleep like an angel, Marnee told me, was the sweetest baby boy she'd ever seen in her life."

Lincoln looked at Jules. She put one hand on her own belly and took his in the other.

Rena continued. "Jack said, 'God help me, Marnee, he's mine. This baby is mine and his mother is gone. I've got to give him away unless you help me.' Jack didn't know about her surgery. He had no idea how powerful he'd become. He thought the sight of the baby might drive her away for good, but it was a last-ditch plea, as if he wasn't asking for himself anymore, but for a little boy. She took one look at you, Lincoln, and she told him then and there she'd marry him."

"She was with that bastard because of me." Lincoln could barely bring his voice above a whisper. He felt like he was swimming, like no part of him was subject to gravity.

"You were all of three or four months old," Rena said. "Your real momma gone—and nothing much to speak of when she was alive, from what I heard. You had no one but Jack Fuller to count on. And Marnee knew that would never do. I would have done the same thing. Anyway, after she told him she'd marry him, she told him how it was going to be. She'd been away. No one in town knew why. And no one knew about any baby. She said they'd stay away for a while longer, both of them. Then it would be easy to say they'd run off and gotten married because you were on the way. They were going to say they stayed away to avoid scandal, but they wanted to come home.

"Then she told him about her surgery. That was her big mistake, I think. He knew he had her then. She said she wanted to adopt his baby and then, eventually, adopt another. My guess is," Rena said, "that he figured out then and there how to hold on to her forever. He didn't tell her then that he wouldn't let her legally put her name on any papers for you, Lincoln. He let her believe he would do it, but later when she pressed him, he refused."

"If I brought her back to him," Lincoln said, talking to himself as much as anyone, "why the hell did he hate me so much, I wonder."

"That one's not too hard to figure out," Rena told him. "She only married him because of you. She only stayed because of you. After a while, that got under his skin like nothing else. On top of that, when you were . . . *different*, it was easy for him to take everything out on you."

"How do you know all this then?" Jules spoke for the first time.

"I was her best friend back then. All through school. All through that time. I knew why she'd gone to Richmond in the first place. So did her momma and daddy. We were the only ones who knew about where you really came from, Lincoln. When Marnee wanted another baby, Jack lived up to that promise. They just told everybody that something had happened when you were born, Lincoln. She couldn't have more. Then they adopted you, Jules. As Jack's drinking got worse, you have to know that she would have taken both of you away from him if she could have. But since he'd refused to sign over any legal custody of you, Lincoln, she had no choice but to stay and make the best of it."

"But she loved him before," Jules said. She sounded so hopeful that it nearly broke Lincoln's heart to hear her. "Before she found out about the other woman, she was engaged to him, right? There was something she saw in him. There had to have been."

"Why do you have to defend him, Jules?" Rena asked. "Why can't you accept who he really was?"

"I saw good things in him sometimes," Jules said. "I know drinking made him into a monster, but other times, I saw him make her laugh."

"You saw what you wanted to see," Rena said, her tone harsh. "Jack Fuller had nothing but empty charm he used to his own ends."

"You've never liked me, Mrs. Alderman," Jules said. "Since we're being completely open here, do you want to tell me why?"

Rena seemed to consider before she spoke. "Exactly what you just said. That's why. When you saw that *good* in him that you talk about, it made Marnee want it to be there, somewhere, under all that meanness. It gave her false hope, and I think she suffered more because of it. It was a betrayal, I thought, for you to give him any satisfaction in this world."

Lincoln looked at the two women. "It doesn't matter," Lincoln said. "Maybe Jules did bring something out in him that other people never had a chance to see. That doesn't make her accountable for what he was at other times." He wouldn't take any more away from his little sister than had already been claimed. "Did you ever see my mother?" He changed the subject. "My birth mother." He corrected himself, because he'd never do Marnee the disservice of saying that place belonged to anyone else.

Rena shook her head. "I did read an old article about her once that Marnee found in Jack's drawer. Some arts writer in Atlanta said she had perfect pitch. Said she had the voice of a trained singer without a minute of real training. I remember he said all that natural talent was wasted in the clubs she played, but it was a treat for anyone who heard her."

"Momma couldn't carry a note if her life depended on it," Jules said. "She was off-key more than on during the hymns at church. Dad had nothing special in that department, either. I always wondered what miracle gave you what you have, Lincoln."

Lincoln felt like no one's miracle. He wanted to go back to his room. He wanted to escape into sleep if it would come.

"I missed Marnee," Rena offered out of the blue. "We buried our husbands just a day apart. Under any other circumstances, we would have been there for each other. Instead, we lost our friendship for good. We talked all the time before that awful day. I knew her as well as anyone. And I never held anything against her. It was just too painful to stay friends after . . ." She stopped. "Well, you both know what happened as well as I do. But I know that she loved both of you more than she loved her own life."

"Well, that's pretty much the bargain she made when she gave up everything and married him, isn't it?" Lincoln said. "Your husband did the world a great service, Mrs. Alderman."

For different reasons entirely, both Rena Alderman and Jules registered pure misery at his comment, and he was sorry he'd made it. But it was too late. Everything had finally been said and could not be unsaid. Not ever again.

In spite of his fatigue, Lincoln found it impossible to sleep. Jules had stayed with him for a while after Rena's revelations. Sam brought in sandwiches, but no one was hungry. They mostly sat in silence while the muted television played images of *The Andy Griffith Show*. He came close to nodding off then, but after she and Sam left, he became suddenly wired.

Jules had a key to her friend Craig's apartment in Wilmington. He was out of town, but had told her to make herself at home there. Lincoln halfway hoped Jules would invite Sam to stay the night with her so she wouldn't be by herself, but she called from the apartment to say good night, and she sounded as if she was alone.

"Are you okay?" Jules asked him. He lied and said he was fine, but she didn't buy it.

"Don't drink, Lincoln," she told him, as if his hand was on a bottle at that very second. "Please don't."

"I'm pretty sure the bar closes early here at the hospital," he said.

"My baby needs you." She ignored his attempt at humor. "Think of what Mom did for you, for both of us. I'm not enough for this kid. *I* need you. If you drink, you won't be here for us."

"I love you, Jules-y," he said in earnest. "And I love that kid already. If anything can keep me sober, that would be it."

After he hung up, he closed his eyes. He could feel the blood running through the vessels in his head, in his throat. He could *hear* it, moving through his body like wild rapids through a canyon. The very flow of his blood was keeping him awake, and he worried that he might be losing his mind.

The ridiculous wheelchair they'd made him ride in was sitting by the bed. He pushed it out of the way and put on the robe that Jules had bought downstairs at the gift shop earlier in the day. It had a pattern of triangles on it, and he imagined the points pricking at his skin as he walked. He could almost feel them.

"You're losing it, Lincoln old boy," he said to himself as he made his way down the hall.

On one of the floors below, there was a cafeteria. It wasn't the first floor, but he couldn't remember which one, so he got on the elevator and randomly pushed. What else did he have to do? He'd either see a sign or he'd ask somebody.

He got out on the second floor and started down one hall. When it dead-ended, he backtracked and turned down another hall, continued to wander. He saw pretty quickly that he was heading toward a more remote corner of the building, definitely not toward the cafeteria. A woman with a paper cup walked ahead of him in the otherwise deserted hall, so he made his way toward her to ask where she'd gotten her drink. Just as she turned to go into a patient's room, he realized he recognized her. Tuni Walker.

That made sense. He'd forgotten that Vick Johns was still in the hospital. He should go say hi to the boy. He hadn't seen Vick since he dragged the child half breathing from Marnee's truck and delivered him to a crowd of bystanders outside the clinic. The thought of it still made him shaky, and he began to rethink the plan to go into the boy's room. He wanted to help the kid, he and Jules both, but his setback made him realize that he was barely capable of saving himself.

The door stood slightly ajar, and as he came closer, his hands felt cold. His feet, too. What if he had a full-blown panic episode outside the kid's room. That would be embarrassing. He saw a sign for the elevator where the hall looped around to take him back in the direction he'd come. He'd just keep going. There was no reason to see Vick Johns. He'd get back to his room and ask the nurse for something to help him sleep. Maybe they'd let him have Benadryl.

The shortest way to the elevator was by Vick's room. As he went by, the door blocked his view into the room, open a mere sliver where it failed to close all the way. He could hear Tuni talking to the boy, her voice slurred. What she said made him stop.

"Here's your Coke," she said to Vick. "I had some rum in the car, and I put a splash in for you to make you feel better. More relaxed. It helps me relax sometimes, like those pills I gave you do."

Rum? Lincoln couldn't have heard right. Clearly he had booze on the brain. She must have said something else.

Then he heard Vick seize into a spasm of coughing.

"Just swallow, honey," Tuni said. "It'll be okay. I'll make everything okay." Her baby-doll tone didn't sound like that of an aunt talking with her nephew.

Lincoln cracked the door slightly, enough to see inside. She sat beside Vick on the bed and took the Styrofoam cup from his hand and set it on the nightstand. Then Lincoln watched in disbelief as she began to unbutton her shirt. When the buttons were all undone, facing the boy, she unclasped her bra from the front, and Lincoln saw from the side what Vick saw right in front of him. Her bare breasts, a line of tan marking where her bathing suit had been.

The boy stared at her. How could he not? Only the look on his face wasn't one of pleasure or even young lust. His expression registered terror as a predatory Tuni Walker leaned closer to him. She picked up the cup of rum and Coke.

"Here, have another sip," she said. "It'll help. I promise."

Lincoln felt nausea rising in his chest. The formerly intrusive whooshing of his blood escalated to an unbearable roar. He opened the door wider, aware that he had to do something to help the child, to save the boy from the insane woman bent on seduction. Then the sickening reality of it hit him. It wasn't the first time she'd done it. How long *had* it been going on?

The shame was that no one had understood the source of the boy's pain before. And regardless of what happened in the future, no one could undo all the harm that had already been done.

Tuni turned and saw him, registered a look of broad panic, before she let out an ear-splitting scream.

Chapter Thirty-five

Jules felt guilty about being at the apartment with Sam while Lincoln lay in his hospital room alone. Sam drove her to Craig's apartment, and she asked him if he wanted to come in. Neither of them had an agenda, but she sensed that neither of them had ruled anything out, either. It simply wasn't a night to be alone.

"He's got some beer in the fridge if you want," she called from the kitchen. "He's got quite a variety, as a matter of fact." She was starving, but all Craig had to eat was a jar of kimchi and three jumbo-sized varieties of processed cheese packages. On the counter, an impressive assortment of liquor rivaled his beer selection, taking up a third of the counter space. "We're shy on food, but he's got plenty of hard booze if you're in the mood to ramp the party up a notch." She walked back into the den where Sam sat on the couch. "After the day we've had, I wish I could join you on a bender but . . ." She patted her belly.

"No bender for me, either," he said. "I've outgrown the days when the fun part outweighs the crappy day that follows."

"Yeah," she said. "I hear that."

"I will have a beer, though. Want me to go out and grab some food? I know of a pizza place a couple of blocks from here."

"That's okay," she said, walking back to the kitchen to get him his beer. She selected a local brew with an interesting label, found a bottle opener, and went back to sit beside him on the couch.

"You sure you don't want me to make a run for food?" he said, taking the bottle. "I don't mind."

"I appreciate the offer," she said, "but Craig's got saltines in the cabinet, and I saw some Kraft singles with my name on 'em in the fridge. Unless you want something more, I'm too exhausted to even wait on pizza."

"No, I'm fine." He took a sip of his beer.

The silence that followed the exchange left a void that needed to be filled.

She thought of Walt, of the minutes that could go by as they sat together in the cemetery without any urge to speak, without the need for words. But the comparison wasn't fair and she knew it. Walt was unattainable. That changed the dynamic of both their words and their silences.

The emptiness with Sam was as much her responsibility as his. Since the night had been about honesty—about unexpected revelations—she decided that she might as well ask Sam something that she'd always wanted to know.

"Why did you ask me out in the first place?" She turned to look at him. "Especially in light of everything that had happened with you and my dad. What made you come over to me at lunch that day?"

Sam smiled, looked down into the mouth of his beer bottle, then back up at her. "My mom," he said.

"Your mom's always hated me. Why would she want you to ask me out?"

"She didn't," he said, still smiling. "That's *why* I asked you out. I was pissed as hell at her for something. I can't even remember what now. Don't get me wrong. I'd always thought you were a knockout. I'd always been attracted to you. But the nerve to invite you to a movie on that particular day had everything to do with the fight I'd had with Mom that morning. I knew it would get under her skin like nothing else."

He thought it was funny. Jules studied his face. She found nothing insulting in what he'd just told her. She wondered if she'd ever really known him at all.

"Did you go out with me for all those years so that you could keep sticking it to your mother?" Her voice sounded accusatory, but she couldn't help it. "Was I an extended revenge date?"

"God no!" He seemed genuinely appalled. "Jules, for Christ's sake, I didn't mean it like that."

"I'm sorry," she said. "You've been nothing but great and I'm sniping at you. My nerves are a little raw tonight."

"It's okay. I really didn't mean to offend you." He took another sip of his beer, closed his eyes, and let out a long breath.

Poor guy, she was really all over the place. "I'm sorry, Sam," she said again. "Really. This whole day, plus all my crazy hormones . . . That was an awful thing for me to say."

"Don't worry about it," he said. "And for the record . . ." His tone had gone serious. "I went out with you for 'all those years' because you were the most beautiful, exciting person I'd ever known. I could never quite figure you out. It made me crazy to be with you. When I wasn't with you, all I did was think about you. And none of that had anything to do with my mother. Trust me." He stopped, kept eye contact to the point that she had to look away. "Jules?"

At the sound of her name, she made herself look at him. What did she want from him? What didn't she want? She couldn't keep tugging him in and then pushing him away. He was too good a person for that.

"What are you thinking?" he asked. He looked hopeful, and it would be so easy. They would fall into patterns retained in such pleasant places of memory. Part of her wanted that for herself, even if it could only be a transient comfort.

"I don't know," she said. "I don't know what I'm thinking."

But she did know. At least part of it. It came to her in that moment with such clarity. His feelings for her were rooted in her disguise. The Jules who'd driven Sam crazy was a girl concocted from booze, tattoos and the façade of rebellion. He really *had* loved the girl she'd been inside—she believed that—but only in the context of the bizarre packaging that accompanied that person. She felt it becoming necessary to shed that outer skin. What would he think of her then? She'd accused him of betraying her with his silence about their fathers' deaths. But hadn't she betrayed him, too?

"I'm sorry, Sam," she said. "Everything's so complicated right now. Lincoln, my baby, my life in LA . . . All that stuff is still there, even though it's tempting, for one night, to pretend it's not. But you're better than a one-night stand. *We're* better than that."

"I understand," he said. And he seemed to mean it. In a way, he seemed relieved. As if on cue, his cell phone began to buzz. He fished it out of his pocket.

"Hello."

Jules could hear a woman's screeching on the other end of the line, with someone else—a man—trying to shout above the noise. Who was screaming? The loud voice trying to speak into the phone sounded like Lincoln.

"Hold on!" Sam said. "I can't hear you. Lincoln, what's going on?"

It was Lincoln! Why had he called Sam and not her?

"Listen," Sam said, "I'm with Jules. We're on our way back over." He spoke loudly, but without alarm. "Yes, that's what I said. I'm with Jules," he repeated.

Jules saw again why Sam had become a doctor. Funny, he was drawn to her wilder persona, but he was never more attractive to her than when she witnessed his steady hand in a crisis. "Let's go," she said, grabbing her purse. "You can tell me what's going on in the car."

In minutes, they were en route to the hospital.

"So what happened?" she asked, breathless from the effort.

"I don't know, exactly," Sam said. "It had something to do with Vick, and I think he mentioned Tuni. Whoever the woman was, she was freaking out. I don't think anything's happened to Lincoln. He sounds okay. But I think he stumbled onto something else."

That reassured her, although she had no idea why Lincoln would be anywhere near Vick Johns so late in the evening. She wondered if Vick had tried to kill himself again. The thought of the boy on another downward spiral made her ache. "Could the woman who was yelling have been Cici?" she asked, talking more to herself than to Sam. "Did Vick do something else to himself?"

"We'll find out in a few minutes." Sam inched just above the speed limit, but it still seemed to Jules as if they were crawling.

As much as she felt for Vick, she wondered how she would ever deal with trouble in her own child's life. How did parents survive? Poor Cici. Maybe the ability to cope came part and parcel with all the other mothering instincts. If so, Jules hoped that part of her genetic package wasn't defective. If her feelings about young Vick were a glimpse of what it felt like, she was in for quite a ride.

"Do you think I'll be a good mother?" she asked Sam.

He glanced over at her, puzzled, it seemed, by the question. "Yeah," he said. "I do."

"I've lived my life with the luxury of being selfish," she said. "I'm afraid I've waited too long to change easily. Children need *everything*. Look what Marnee did for Lincoln."

"And look what you did for Marnee," he said. "Did you resent coming here to look after her?"

"God, no," she said. "Watching her get weaker was horrible, but spending my days with her, physically caring for her . . . Emotionally caring for her . . . There was a true contentment that came with every part of that."

"There you go, then," he said. "You're wired in all the right ways, Jules. When the switch is flipped—Marnee's illness, Lincoln's illness, a baby's birth—you'll do fine. You'll do better than fine."

She hoped down to her very soul that he was right.

"You okay?" Sam asked, glancing again in her direction.

"Yeah," she said, "considering. I think I'm okay."

The yelling had not been Cici, although Lincoln told Jules that the boy's mother was on her way. The doctor-on-call was with Vick in his room, and Vick's psychiatrist had been paged. Meanwhile, two men from hospital security stayed with everyone else in a waiting room down the hall.

"What the hell happened?" Jules asked Lincoln, who looked like a refugee in his robe with a blanket draped around his shoulders. He seemed almost too shaken to speak.

"Just give me a minute to settle down," he said. "Is Sam with you?"

"He's parking the car. He dropped me off at the front entrance. It's okay, Linc. Everything's okay." She tried to reassure him.

"No," he said. "It's not."

The security guards flanked Tuni Walker, who looked as if she'd been through a spin cycle in the washing machine. Her shirt disheveled, the buttons going in all the wrong holes, and her makeup—more makeup than Jules had ever seen her wear—was smeared to nearly comic proportions all over her face. Only there was nothing funny about her. She represented a frightening spectacle. She'd clearly been crying, but by the time Jules walked in the room she sat, unmoving, like some freakish Halloween mannequin. Suddenly, seeing Jules, she came to life.

"He's lying!" Tuni screamed. "Whatever he's told you, it's a lie." The warning, directed at no one in particular, came in response to nothing, from what Jules could tell. "He's trying to protect his sister. She's the one the boy did it with. That's what Vick said. She's the one. That man is lying to get her off the hook and he's saying lies about me." Then she turned to Jules. "You can't have my husband. You hear? I didn't do anything wrong." She pointed at Jules. "It's her," she said to the guards in charge of her. "She's the one." Then she went quiet again. Her eyes again took on a malignant, vacant stare.

"Lincoln?" Jules turned to her brother.

"It was her." Lincoln spoke in such low tones, Jules could barely make out the words. "I saw her taking off her shirt in front of the kid. I saw her."

"Her shirt?" Jules knew what he suggested, but still couldn't believe it. "Tuni? She's been . . ." She couldn't even say it.

Lincoln nodded. "It's been her all along."

Dear God, Tuni Walker had been having sex with Vick. Poor kid. The thought of it made Jules sick to her stomach. "She's got kids," she said. "And Walt. This is going to kill Walt."

"At least it's an open wound now," Lincoln said. "It was worse the other way."

He was right, but that didn't make it any easier to stomach.

Two policemen came into the room, and Tuni's eyes went

wild at the sight of them. "It was her!" She pointed at Jules again. "Just ask the boy."

Jules wondered if there was any chance the police would believe Tuni, would believe that Lincoln made up his story. She found her cell phone and was about to dial Hunter when she heard one of the policemen say to Tuni, "A nurse on duty corroborates Mr. Fuller's account, Mrs. Walker."

"What nurse?" Tuni's voice sounded childlike.

"She saw Mr. Fuller in the hall and was approaching him to ask if he needed something when she witnessed his confrontation with you. We're waiting for the family to arrive. You need to remain quiet, Mrs. Walker."

"I *am* the family," she said, tears coming down her face. She'd lost her fire, her insanity. Just like that, she'd returned to her persona as Walt's timid, loving wife. "It's my family you're talking about."

It felt like forever that they waited. Sam came into the room, and Jules told him what she knew. Then he waited, too. It almost seemed as if waiting had become the point. After some time had passed—an hour, maybe less or maybe more, Jules couldn't gauge—Cici, Walt, and the rest of the Walkers arrived to claim what was left of their world.

When Jules finally saw Walt coming down the hall followed by the rest of them, she wanted to run to him, to shield him somehow from what he would find when he got to his wife. But she couldn't run to him. She couldn't protect him. Anything she tried to do would only make it worse.

"He don't treat her right," Vick called out from his room when he saw Walt at the door. "She needed me 'cause he was so bad to her all the time. She just needed somebody to be good to her."

Walt stopped, the rest of the family with him. His face formed a question that he didn't seem to have the words to ask. Then he did something that broke Jules' heart. Walt bent his head and rested it in his hand. He pressed his fingers together, squeezing hard against his temples, as if trying to erase everything, all the words and images forced on him with this new reality.

He stood there, head buried from view, with his parents on either side of him. Cici came up beside him, put her hand gently on his arm, before walking into the room to be with her son.

Chapter Thirty-six

Lincoln settled back in his hospital bed, farther from sleep than he'd been when he left it. Jules sat beside him in the recliner that would serve as her bed for the night. She refused to leave him, sent Sam home with a promise she would call first thing in the morning.

"What's going to happen now?" Jules asked. "Will they arrest Tuni?"

"I don't know," he said. "I heard one of the policemen tell Preacher Walker they'd need a psych evaluation to determine if she's mentally stable. Then they'll figure out what to do next."

Jules laughed, but it was a hard-sounding laugh. He had to agree. How could anyone be sane and do that to a fourteen-year-old kid? And her nephew at that. Not a blood relative, but the lines were too thin to draw, really. Nothing on earth could excuse it.

He wished he could turn on the television and get lost in someone else's drama, but Jules' eyes were at half mast, and he didn't want to keep her awake. He'd decided that he could mute a channel with the closed-captioned option when he saw Cici Walker standing at the open door to his room. She hadn't knocked, and Jules hadn't seen her yet. She looked like a ghost standing there.

"Come on in," he said, and Jules looked up.

"I don't want to bother you," she said.

"No bother." He sat up straighter, moved the position of his bed to sitting. "Really, come on in."

Jules stood up and went over to her. For a moment, they stood just inches apart, but not touching. Then Cici laid an open palm on Jules' belly, looked up and offered a smile.

"I don't know what to say," Jules told her.

Cici began to cry. "Why didn't I see it? I was in the same house. Why didn't I know?"

"It's unthinkable," Jules said. "That's why."

"But I knew something was wrong." She stepped back, wiped her eyes with the back of her hand. "Even before you found him that day in the woods," she said to Lincoln, "I knew something was wrong. I wanted to blame you."

Jules led the tearful Cici to the chair, then settled beside Lincoln on the edge of the bed.

"Do you know what the doctor said?" Cici asked.

They shook their heads in unison. Vick's mother had the look of someone grieving and Lincoln felt useless, propped up in his orthopedic-friendly bed.

"The drugs they found in his system were hers."

"Tuni's?" Jules asked. "She had drugs?"

"Prescription drugs," Cici said. "Her stuff for anxiety. She told him they would help him relax because he was all nervous about what they were doing. The drugs were probably why he tried to kill himself, the doctor told me. They make teenagers suicidal sometimes. And Tuni filled his head with garbage about Walt, saying he treated her like dirt. She turned Vick against his own uncle."

"What was she planning to do?" Jules asked. "Did she think no one would figure it out?"

"I don't know." Cici took a tissue from the bedside stand. "She might have tried to get him to run away with her. Who knows what she was hoping would happen?" She shook her head again, looked at Lincoln. "I've got to get back to Vick, but I just wanted to thank you again, Lincoln. You've saved the boy twice. Lord knows how he'll come back from this, but he'd be in a lot deeper if it wasn't for you. I know people in our town haven't always treated you the best, but no one will ever hear me do anything but sing your praises. I hope you get better. Jules says it's not the AIDS thing, and that's good, right?"

Jules started to say something, but Lincoln touched her arm, shook his head to stop her.

"That is a good thing," he told the woman. Cici's efforts were earnest. Her heart was headed in the right direction, even if her reasoning was thick as a stump.

"I'll spend the rest of my days in your corner," she said. She put her hand to her heart as if taking an oath.

Lincoln had long considered any serious boxing match with the hometown crowd to have ended after adolescence. Apparently, there were still a few battles to fight. Cici made for a sturdy—albeit ill-informed—ally.

"And Jules," Cici said.

Lincoln saw his sister flinch at the sound of her name.

Cici continued. "I'll tell you again I'm sorry. I've said it, but it doesn't seem like much considering what you went through. I can't take any of it back. But I'll never say another word against you as long as I live. My brother was right in everything he told me. And when things settle down some, he could probably use a friend."

Lincoln guessed that was Cici's way of offering her blessing for Jules to have a relationship with Walt. He wished it could be that simple for his little sister. But nothing was simple about what they had all just discovered.

Cici said her good-byes and went back to be with Vick.

"That was unexpected," Jules said.

"Everything that's happened since Mom died has come out of left field," Lincoln said. He lowered the bed to a half recline.

"It's been a hell of a day," Jules said. "We haven't even had a chance to process the stuff Rena told us. I wish we'd known so we could have talked to her about it. Why do you think she didn't tell us?"

"She got to choose you," he said. "She decided to bring you into her life. But I landed in her world by surprise. Maybe she never wanted me to think I was less of a choice. That's just a guess, I don't know. With all she sacrificed, I feel like she earned the right to play it any damn way she wanted to."

"I told Sam that it was a shame she never had kids because she was born to be a mother. He told me that she *was* a mother. He was absolutely right. No one was ever *more* a mother than Marnee."

"God knows what I would have been, *who* I would have been, if she hadn't claimed me," he said.

"Just think about *me*," Jules said. "I would have been some-where without you." And after a long pause, she added, "I don't know what I'd do if I didn't have you."

Lincoln didn't know if the last part reflected on the fact that Marnee gave them to each other as siblings, or commented on the state of his health. Either way, he was needed. "I'll be a good uncle to that kid," he said. "I promise."

"Since the slot on the birth certificate will be left blank in the 'dad' section," she said, "I'm sorta counting on it."

Later, he watched her sleeping. Curled up on the recliner with a blanket he'd put over her long after she'd moved from light dozing to deep slumber, she made small sleep sounds that he would recognize blindfolded. In a pitch-black room full of sleeping people, he could find his sister. Marnee had done that. She'd made them into a family.

He settled back, watching a silent TV, hoping that sleep would find him, too, eventually.

Chapter Thirty-seven

"It's the middle of the night," Rena said when Sam came in the door. "Where on earth have you been? When I got home from the hospital, I thought you'd be coming before too long."

She was in the den, awake and waiting for him. Just like when he was in high school. Funny, if he stayed home with her for more than a few days, all the old patterns returned.

"I didn't mean to worry you," he said. "Why didn't you call my cell phone?"

"You're a grown man," she said. "I don't want to be overbearing."

"So you sat here worrying? Just call me next time. I stuck around to give Jules a ride, then got caught up in some other stuff that happened." He didn't want to tell her about Tuni Walker. He didn't have the stomach to repeat it. But she'd find out and then be mad that he kept it from her.

"Actually, the police were called," he said, measuring his words carefully. "Vick Johns is still in the hospital. Lincoln walked into the kid's hospital room and found Tuni Walker doing . . . inappropriate things in front of him."

"Who? In front of Walt?" Her face registered confusion.

"No," he explained, "in front of Vick." Sam felt disgust wash over him again, mirroring the look on his mother's face. "Tuni made a big scene when Lincoln found them. Hospital security got involved, and they called the police."

"But the boy accused Jules?" Rena still seemed confused. Why wouldn't she be? It made no sense.

"Apparently, that was to cover up this business with his aunt. It may have been going on for a while with Tuni."

"Oh, my Lord," Rena said. "She's his *aunt*. By marriage, but still . . ."

"Still . . ." Sam said, putting his keys on the front table and sitting down across from her in the den. "She's got real problems. They'll do a mental evaluation first, and then go from there. If she's sane enough, they'll arrest her."

"What an awful ordeal for the Walkers," she said. "I can't imagine . . . But you shouldn't be spending your time involved in all this, Sam," she said. Then, after a moment's hesitation, she asked, "Are you going with her again?"

Going with her. Sounded like a steady date to the school sock hop. And *her* meant Jules, of course. It always meant Jules.

"No," he said. "I'm not." Sam didn't know which surprised him more. That he could say that with certainty, or that he felt okay about it.

He'd looked at Jules while she stood in the hall of the hospital, watched her calm Lincoln and comfort Walt. She'd acquired this aura of womanhood. Motherhood, he supposed. Not just her round belly, but her demeanor. The expressions on her face. The girl he'd known in high school was strangely absent from the woman he'd been with all evening. The change made her more attainable, no less beautiful, but less a part of him. Less a part of who they'd been.

"I've been her friend, Mom. She's really needed a friend, lately."

"She's pregnant, you know. I could tell."

"I know."

She didn't say anything else. Sam imagined that she must have drawn blood, biting her tongue.

"Thank you for coming over tonight, for telling Lincoln and Jules the truth about what happened," he said. "I know that was hard for you, but it meant a lot to both of them." Then he added, "It means a lot to me, too."

"I felt like I was betraying Marnee. All these years, I haven't really thought about all that. Even though we didn't stay close, I always respected her. She was my closest friend for a long time. I'd hate to go against her wishes."

"After they saw her medical files, the truth couldn't stay hidden any longer. Marnee would have wanted them to understand the choices she made."

"You're a good boy, Sam," she said, rising, he supposed, to head toward bed. "Sometimes, I think you're too good. That the rest of us don't deserve you."

"There's more than a bit of maternal bias in that opinion, I'm afraid," he said, smiling.

"Oh, I almost forgot," she said, turning to him before she left the room, positioning her good ear so she could converse across the room. "I saw Rob Standard at the drugstore yesterday. He wants you to call him. I guess he's living in Raleigh now."

"Yeah, he's been there a couple of years." Rob was a friend from high school. The only other kid from their class besides Sam to go to med school. "He wants to get me into climbing," Sam said. He told her mostly just to tug her chain. "He's got some plan for us to work our way up to climbing Mount Rainier out in Washington State."

"Oh, I can just see you tromping up the side of some mountain," she said, dismissing the notion that he might be serious.

Was he just kidding? How could she find it so unbelievable?

"I'm not joking," he told her. "He has a whole regimen planned for starting with some easier climbs here on the East Coast and working up to Rainier by next summer."

"Good Lord," she said, beginning to sound concerned, "you've got more sense than that, I hope."

She honestly didn't believe he would do such a thing. She apparently thought he'd spend the rest of his life going to work, visiting her once or twice a month, maybe meet a woman she could tolerate, and for some real excitement, play tennis a couple of times a week. It was time he made some plans to get out of his comfort zone.

"Did he leave his number?" Sam had the number, but he couldn't stop himself from egging her on.

"No." She looked wary. "Samuel Alderman, you are not seriously planning to go climbing up mountains in your precious spare time, are you?"

"Why not?" he said. "Maybe it's time I did something to challenge myself. Don't worry, Mom. I'm going to be fine."

He got up to go to his old room for the night, kissed her forehead as he passed by, then made his way down the hall without looking back.

Chapter Thirty-eight

Lincoln stayed in the hospital for two days, but had come home the day before. Without the need to get dressed and drive to Wilmington, Jules didn't know what to do with all her nervous energy. She had cleaned every room in the house, then cleaned each one again.

"For God's sake," Lincoln said, "go run some errands, or just drive to the beach. But you need to get out of this house."

He sat at the piano and worked on a new arrangement of a piece he was scheduled to play with the Cleveland Orchestra.

"I need to take these dishes back to Mrs. Dukes," she said. He was right, a drive would settle her nerves. "You'll be all right?"

"Go, go," he said, waving his hand to dismiss her as he looked down at the score with a furrowed brow.

"I'll be back soon." She grabbed the clean dishes that were sitting on the kitchen counter, along with her keys.

"Don't rush," he called after her as she went out the door.

Jules knocked on the older woman's door. Mrs. Dukes lived on Broad Street in a house that her grandfather had built a decade or so after the Civil War ended. Jules knew this because every-one knew it. It was part of the collective knowledge of growing up in Ekron. As she approached the massive columns of the expansive front porch, she felt as if she should have arrived by horse and carriage.

"Well, Jules," Mrs. Dukes said, opening her front door. "Good Lord, come on in out of the heat," she said. "I swear it gets worse every summer."

"I can't stay," Jules said, feeling bathed in the shade of the foyer.

In her hand, she held the empty Pyrex and the other dish she'd come to return. On the bottom of both dishes, small pieces of masking tape had "Dukes" written on them.

"These were delicious," Jules said, handing them to her. "Es-pecially the casserole. Thank you."

"I'm glad you enjoyed it. Come on into the kitchen. Sorry I look such a sight, but you caught me in the middle of cleaning the oven."

"I shouldn't stay, I just . . ."

"No, no, no . . ." the older woman protested. "Don't turn around and leave. I have half a lemon pie in the refrigerator, and I've been hoping for a partner-in-crime. Let me just wash up a bit and we'll have a piece."

Mrs. Dukes soaped her hands and arms where black smudges from the oven brushed against her. Then she set about finding the pie and cutting them both a slice.

"It'll do that baby good for you to put on a pound or two," she said pointing for Jules to sit at the table. "You're so busy looking after that brother of yours, you probably don't stop to eat. You need somebody to look out for you."

To her horror, Jules felt tears spring to her eyes. Pregnancy hormones had turned her into a regular sap, and the woman's plainspoken display of motherly concern brought Marnee's absence into bold relief. With all the drama subsiding, Jules realized she would need to get on with the process of grieving.

"Oh, I'm sorry. I never did know when to hold my tongue," Mrs. Dukes said, leaning in and laying a sympathetic hand on Jules arm. "You look just fine, dear. I'm an old busybody."

"It's not that," Jules told her, struggling to compose herself. "You just reminded me of Mom when you said that. That's all."

Mrs. Dukes nodded. Of course she understood. She'd lost her own mother at some point in her life. Too bad, Jules remembered, she would have no grandchildren of her own.

"If you need a substitute granny sometime," the older woman said, as if reading Jules' thoughts, "my offer still stands. I'll be over in a jiffy. Over at your place here, that is. It would take a bit more prodding to get me out to California. Are you thinking you might stay around for a while?"

"I don't know, really. I haven't done much thinking at all lately. Only reacting to everything."

"Well, there's certainly been a lot to react *to*. I heard about the latest business with Tuni Walker. Sickening stuff. I can't believe what happens in this world."

"It was horrible," Jules said, all too aware that just days before, everyone had thought she was capable of the horrors now attributed to Tuni. "I think she's got some emotional problems."

"She would have to now, wouldn't she?" Mrs. Dukes said, shaking her head. "The preacher and Alice have kept to themselves since word got out that Tuni had been taken off by the authorities. I hope they'll let the people in the church offer some comfort. It's not their fault. Any of us could have seen that something wasn't right in that situation if we hadn't been so busy looking in the wrong places."

Jules understood that the last part was an acknowledgment

of the false accusations against her. None of that mattered anymore. Even though the nightmare had occurred so recently, it already seemed like part of another life.

Ever since she was young, Jules had been reacting to things that happened around her. Maybe the time had come when she would be able to choose the sort of life she wanted. The life she would build for her child.

"I feel so sorry for that little Vick," Mrs. Dukes said. "And for Walt and the girls. There are no winners in this situation."

"No," Jules said. "You're right about that."

"I'd like to do something for them," the older woman said as she collected the empty plate in front of Jules. Jules realized she'd eaten a whole piece of pie without noticing.

"I don't know what on earth would help at a time like this," the woman continued, talking to herself as much as to Jules.

Back at her mother's house, a paper sack full of small potatoes sat on the porch outside the front door. For as long as she could remember, neighbors made a habit of leaving whatever excess they had from their gardens outside Marnee's front door. Even with Marnee gone, someone had continued. Jules wondered if they did it specifically for her and Lincoln or out of habit? When she and Lincoln went back to their lives in New York and LA, would the sacks of corn, green beans, and potatoes still come? The arrival of such bounty on that particular day seemed to confirm for her that baking was the thing she ought to do.

She took the potatoes inside, began to rummage through cabinets in Marnee's kitchen. She clanged and clattered about looking for the rectangular baking dish that Marnee had always used for her scalloped potato recipe. It was nowhere in sight. Still, Jules liked the sounds that came from all her looking. It reminded her that work waited for her. It would be good to go back to the soundstage someday soon.

"What the hell are you doing?" Lincoln came into the kitchen, his hands covering his ears.

It was a good sign if he was acting restless. Still, she worried about a relapse.

"Somebody named Lois left a bag of new potatoes on the porch," she said. "I'm surprised you didn't hear her."

"I was listening to music with my headphones for a while," he said. "Maybe she came by then. Why are people still leaving this stuff here? If they know us at all, they know I'm sick and you don't cook."

"The note said her garden came in early and she's going out of town," Jules told him, still looking for the casserole dish. "And as of today . . . I cook."

"You've taken the potatoes as some sort of sign that you should cook?" He put ice in a glass, then poured himself tea from a ceramic pitcher that sat on the counter by the sink.

"I thought I might bake something and take it to Walt and the girls. I'm looking for the right baking dish. That brown one that Mom used for her scalloped potato and ham casserole."

"There are dozens of baking dishes here," he said, looking at the collection she'd pulled out in her search. "Why do you want that one?"

"Because it's what she used," she said, searching through one of the high cabinets. She didn't know how to explain. It seemed important to take the dish to Walt in just the right way. That was all she knew.

"And you're planning on baking this thing from scratch?" Lincoln asked.

"Yup," she said, closing one cabinet and opening another.

He leaned on the white countertop, his hand around the sweating tea glass. "Let me get this straight. You're going to put ingredients together and transform them with heat into edible matter? I don't believe it."

"Stop it." She smiled. "I'm not an idiot. And potatoes are already *edible*, jerk. I'm going to make them delicious. I can follow a recipe as well as you can."

"You're forgetting that I won the 4–H county pie bake-off in fifth grade," he said. "Don't mess with a gay former 4–H baking champ. You will lose every time."

In the strong afternoon light, the white counter gleamed behind him, giving him a kind of celestial aura. When had Marnee remodeled the kitchen? When had she replaced the speckled linoleum that Jules remembered from growing up with the smooth Corian surface? Things changed. Things that defined your life altered and shifted while you weren't paying attention. Sometimes you didn't even notice until you missed them. She opened up another cabinet, and scanned for the dish she wanted.

"Mom would be pissed at you for tearing up her neat kitchen," he teased her.

But she had no intention of letting him get to her. "Put your blue ribbons back in the drawer, Mr. 4–H. I'll cook and I'll clean up my mess. You're not invited to help with this one. I found Mom's recipe and I'm on a mission. I just need that brown rectangular glass thing she always used."

Maybe in her new life, a life where she would make clear choices for herself and her baby, Jules would choose to bake. From her kitchen, she could produce cookies, casseroles, and various concoctions for her kid's bake sales and school potluck dinners. And she could start by baking for Walt. She would make scalloped potatoes and ham—the very thing Marnee always baked when the world spiraled out of control. All Jules needed was that dish made out of the brown glass. She turned, and Lincoln held it out to her.

"Where'd you find it?" she asked, taking it from him with two hands as if it might be something fragile instead of the heavy tempered glass that it was.

"Where she kept it," he said, pointing to a deep drawer beside the oven. "But that's all you get from me. My services have been rejected. I will, however, stick around for the entertainment value. I can't wait to see this, baby sister." He sat down at the table. "So does the fact that Walt's wife was carried off in a paddy wagon have anything to do with your newfound compulsion to bake?"

"It was a *padded* wagon," she corrected him, "and no, this is just what people do when there's trouble," she said, still not looking at him. "I'm being a good neighbor."

"Is that what it's called?" He murmured this last part under his breath, but she heard him anyway.

She kept her focus on the tasks at hand, set about pulling out everything she would need. With the ingredients, the recipe, and the dish, anything was possible.

"What are you thinking, Jules?" Lincoln asked.

"About what?" She didn't want to get into it with him.

"About Walt."

She turned to him. "I'm thinking that he's hurting," she said. "And I'm thinking I'd like to help if I can. That's it. I'm not scheming. I don't plan to seduce him with food. I understand that there's too much going on right now in his life for that."

"I'm not worried about him," Lincoln said.

"I know. And I love you for worrying about me. But I'm going to be all right. For the first time in a long time, I actually believe that. So how about you?" She got out the measuring cup. "You're feeling better?" She wanted the question to sound offhand, a casual inquiry, not a show of obsessive hovering.

"Well enough to go home next week," he said.

She stopped what she was doing, settled back against the counter. It had to happen. One of them had to end the suspended existence they'd been inhabiting.

"Are you sure you're ready to go back? To be living alone?"

"Tanner said he'd come stay with me," Lincoln said.

Jules worried even more about that. "Tanner?" Lincoln's ex-partner was a sweetheart, but also someone who tended to be the life of the party. "You could end up worse off than you started if you fall for him again, you know."

"I know what Tanner is and is not capable of offering, Jules-y. I just need a way to transition back into my life. Dr. Lange has recommended someone for me to see, a psychiatrist who works with addiction. And Tanner can be there with me on the home front. I'm not looking for more than that. I promise. Besides, I deserve to enjoy my life a little bit, don't I? If nothing else, Tanner knows how to orchestrate a good time."

"You need to remember that having a good time means something different than it used to." She didn't want to lecture him anymore about his drinking, but Lincoln had run out of chips to play when it came to screwing up that part of his life.

"Tanner barely drinks at all," he said. "That was one of the reasons we split up. He said he couldn't stand to watch what I was doing to myself."

"You never told me that," she said.

"Why would I? You were already worried enough without knowing that booze was tanking my relationship. He wants to help now, and I'm going to let him. You could take a lesson from that, Jules. Maybe think about moving closer to New York so that I can do the brother-uncle thing from the front row."

She nodded. "We'll see," she said, still holding the glass pan. "I'll figure out what I want to do. But first, all I want to do is make this thing." She propped Marnee's recipe up on the counter where she could read it, then set about baking her first casserole.

Chapter Thirty-nine

"Hello?" Tanner's voice sounded sleepy. Lincoln knew he'd woken him. Tanner believed in the restorative power of naps. Maybe Lincoln would decide to take up the habit.

"It's me again," Lincoln said. "You have a minute?"

"Sure. What's up?"

Lincoln heard him sitting up, taking in a deep breath to get the oxygen to his brain.

"Is your offer still open?" Lincoln asked.

Tanner stayed silent for a moment, as if considering the question. "It is," he said, finally. "Why? Has your response to it changed?"

"It has," Lincoln told him.

"Why?" Tanner asked again. He had the right to sound suspicious.

Lincoln had called the day before to tell his former partner about his setback. To tell him about his stay in the hospital and about what he'd learned from Rena Alderman. That's when Tanner had made the offer: "If you're done with drinking," he'd said, "if you really mean it, I'll move back in. I can look after you for as long as you need me. Then we can go from there and decide what we want."

Lincoln had turned him down. Maybe he'd wanted to keep his options open for alcohol, or maybe he hadn't wanted to think about leaving Jules and going back to New York.

But it didn't matter anymore. Something changed when he saw his sister in the kitchen. As he watched her single-minded effort to make something for Walt Walker—to make it in just the right way, with just the right dish—he'd felt something give way inside himself. She was taking control of at least a small part of her world, and it made her seem fearless somehow— determined to forge ahead with a reinvention of her life. He decided the time had come to shed a few fears of his own.

"Lincoln?" Tanner prompted him, and Lincoln realized he hadn't answered the question. Why the about-face?

"Because I don't have a single blood tie on this earth that I can name," Lincoln said. "And the last one I had is one I never wanted to claim. And it doesn't matter. I had a wonderful family, anyway. My mother made me and Jules her family. And today, even with Mom gone, it's all still there. Everything she put in place for us. And it occurred to me that you're part of my family, too. I'm not making any pronouncements about what I want our future to be. But you're part of something I don't want to dismiss."

"I don't understand half of what you just said," Tanner told him, his voice catching. "But you got to me anyway. And it sounds like a good reason to let me help you."

"That's what I thought, too," he told Tanner.

After they'd ended the call, Lincoln looked around his old room. He looked closely to see if there was anything there from his past that he should take with him when he went back to New York. Southerners were supposed to be all about keepsakes.

But what Marnee had given him, he couldn't leave behind if he tried. Regardless of how lightly he traveled, everything important that she'd offered would be right there.

He lay back on his old bed, the afternoon still bright outside his window. And with the smells of potato casserole reaching every corner of Marnee Fuller's house, he closed his eyes to take a nap.

Chapter Forty

Jules waited outside the Alderman front door. She'd had too much of everything once her baking project began, so she made not one casserole, but three. One, she and Lincoln could have for dinner. The second, the original one she'd planned on, sat in the car in the brown dish. That one she would take to Walt. She'd planned on taking his by first, but, at the last second as she approached his house, she'd lost her nerve and headed for Sam's house. The third one would go to Sam and Rena.

"You look like Jules," Sam said, opening the door. "But with that dish in your hands, you must be channeling someone else."

"I baked," she said.

"I'll be damned." He smiled, motioned for her to come in.

"I can't stay," she said, "I have another delivery. I'm a regular casserole Santa Claus now."

It felt strange to be inside the Alderman house.

"So is the cottage all ready for the season?" she asked. Small talk seemed ridiculous, but suddenly it was all she could manage.

"I'm going back to work day after tomorrow," he said. "I've taken longer than I planned with . . ." He stopped.

"With everything that happened to me," she said. "You stayed to help. I know that, and I really appreciate it."

"We're friends," he said. He meant it. She could see that he had come to some resolution about it, and she was glad.

"You've been a really good friend through all this," she said. "With my questionable skills in the kitchen, this is a weak show of gratitude, but I tried."

He took the dish from her, put it on the counter as they walked into the kitchen.

"So what's next in Sam Alderman's life?" she asked.

"Mostly," he said, "I need something different. Something to get me out of the limbo I've settled into over the last few years. Hanging around you again has helped me see that."

"I don't know how," she said. "I've done nothing but drag you from one crisis to another since I've been here. I need to do just the opposite. To settle things down."

"It's funny," he said. "I was thinking that about you. You'll be a great mom."

"Thanks." She felt self-conscious, wanted to shift the focus away from her life and back to his. "What do you want to change?"

"I don't know," he said. "I've turned into this divorced man using his vacation time to fix up the family cottage. It's been a phase, I guess—a regression back to being a little boy again after Laney and I split up. But it needs to end. I want to challenge myself."

"I guess we've all gone through times in life where we've lived as people we didn't really want to be," she said.

Rena walked into the room. She looked at Jules, and in the place of the old anger that had always been directed toward Jules, there was something else. Almost a sadness.

"I brought you a casserole," Jules said. "Mom's scalloped potato and ham recipe."

Rena nodded, looked vaguely distracted. "She used that brown dish for that recipe. The same one, every time." It was an offhand comment as she took the casserole from Jules.

Jules glanced at the clear, oval baking dish. "You're right." It struck her how well Rena had known Marnee in their younger years. She thought of that dish—the *right* dish—waiting in the car to be taken to Walt.

"She always used this one for cobblers," Rena went on, touching the edge of the glass lightly. "When she was first married, she made cobblers constantly. Whatever was in season. Peaches, blackberries, apples. Cobblers. You'd think she'd invented them."

It seemed to Jules that after opening up to them at the hospital, Rena had discovered an ocean of memories about her old friend.

"She bought that particular dish at Belk's in Charlotte. I wasn't with her when she got it, but she showed it to me when she got home. It seemed wildly expensive at the time," Sam's mother said. The thought of Marnee and her new dish had brought something close to a smile to the older woman's face.

"When you're done with that," Jules said, "why don't you keep the dish? You know, so that you have something . . ." Something of Marnee's. Jules wondered if it would be pleasant or sad to have something that reminded her of a friendship lost so long ago.

"Thank you," Rena said. "I'll enjoy it."

Sam witnessed the interaction between the two women with something akin to awe, it seemed to Jules.

"Oh." She remembered the note. "There's a thank-you note taped to the bottom. I found it on Mom's bureau. She wrote it to you after you visited. She never told me you came by."

A tender smile came over Rena's face. It made her look younger. "We decided it would be our little attempt at subversion," Rena said. "No need to stir the pot with Jack's family. I'm sure she wouldn't mind you finding the note, but sometimes it feels good to have something you keep just for yourself."

"I understand that," Jules said. "Sounds like it meant a lot that you came by. I guess she didn't get a chance to mail it." Then added, "I didn't mean to pry by reading it. I just didn't know what it was when I saw it there."

Rena nodded, but quickly looked away, and Jules wondered if she was going to cry. "So when is that baby of yours due?" Rena asked a moment later, appearing fully composed.

Sam must have taken in Jules' look of astonishment, because he came to her rescue. "You're what? About four months along?" he spoke up.

"Yeah, about that," Jules said. "A little more, now."

"Would you like something to drink?" Sam asked. His mother seemed to be lost in her own thoughts.

"No thanks," Jules said. "I should go."

"Jules," Rena spoke up again. "I appreciate the dish. We'll enjoy what you made, and I like having something nice of Marnee's. It's special to me. She was a good person."

"She thought the same of you," Jules said.

"You think so?" Rena asked, hopeful and clearly unsure.

Jules didn't know. She never heard her mother talk about Rena Alderman—not after their husbands were gone. But Jules did exactly what Marnee would have wanted her to do.

"Yes, ma'am," she said. "I do."

As she drove back toward Mount Canaan, she realized she'd gone out of her way over the years to make life hard with Rena Alderman. Making peace was as simple as kindness, sometimes.

Walt's older daughter answered the door. The little one stood behind her big sister, and there wasn't a smile between them. Jules didn't even know the girls' names. They'd been "Walt's girls" and that was all. They both looked like Tuni—all dark hair and big eyes. Twins separated with years rather than minutes.

"Is your daddy here?" she asked.

Blank stares gave way to both girls shaking their heads. So Walt wasn't around. "Aunt Cici and Vick are out back, though," the little one finally said.

The warm casserole sat in Jules' hands. She held it with palms flat on the bottom like some Eucharistic offering.

"Could you girls take this to the kitchen and put it in your refrigerator for me?" Jules said. "It's for your supper."

"Is it too hot?" the little one asked; she must have been about seven or eight.

"No," Jules assured her, wondering how the girl thought *she* could hold it with her bare hands if it was just out of the oven, "it's had time to cool down." Maybe the two of them didn't think she was really human.

The big one took the dish from Jules, and they both walked toward the back of the house, leaving Jules at the front door with no good-bye and no invitation to enter. She decided to walk around to the backyard and find Cici. This little trip to see how the Walkers were doing wasn't going the way she'd planned.

"Cici?" Jules saw the woman kneeling among a patch of small plants. She looked up as Jules approached. Only after she saw Cici did she see Vick at the far corner of the yard, pulling weeds out of the ground with gloved hands. If he heard her, he didn't acknowledge it.

"Hey, there," Cici said, turning to face Jules. She brushed a strand of hair from her eyes with the back of her hand and left a small smudge of dirt at the arch of her brow. "I wondered when you were going to come around."

Jules didn't know how she should take the last part. But Cici didn't appear to be going for confrontation. Maybe she thought she and Jules had become friends of sorts. Maybe they had.

"I brought something for you to eat," Jules said, settling on a garden bench near where Cici worked. "I didn't know what else to do."

"There's not much else *to* do," Cici said, standing up and coming over to sit beside her. And then, in a lower voice, she added, "And that's about right anyway, 'cause it sure feels like somebody died."

"How's Vick?" Jules asked, echoing Cici's lowered tones.

Cici stared out at the yard toward her son, and for a second Jules thought she hadn't heard the question. But she'd heard it. She swallowed hard. "He seems pretty good, considering," she said, finally. "They've got him on something that keeps him a little zonked, but we're supposed to taper that off soon. I don't know. The two of us are staying with Momma and Daddy right now. Bart's still here 'cause space is tight, so that's not going to work for long, but with Tuni's things everywhere and the girls constantly asking where their momma's gone . . . It was too much for Vick to be living here."

As if he sensed they were talking about him, he stood up from his weeding and walked in their direction.

"Hey, Ms. Fuller," he said, when he'd reached them.

"Hi, Vick," she said, not knowing what should follow. He seemed different, not quite aware, and she remembered what Cici said about the pills.

"Aunt Cici!" Walt's older daughter called from the back door. "Garrett's on the phone."

"Excuse me a minute," Cici said, and got up to take her call.

"I'm real sorry," Vick said, when his mother was out of ear-shot. "It was wrong. All the things I told people."

"You were dealing with a lot that we didn't know about, Vick," she told him. "I wish things had been different for you."

"Saying it was you, wasn't right," he said again. "I don't know why I did that."

"You just need to think about getting better," Jules told him. "You should concentrate on putting it behind you." Jules felt helpless talking with him, rendered incapable of anything beyond platitudes for the child.

Under his breath, with sounds that were barely words, he said, "Sometimes, I thought about it being you instead of . . ." He stopped. "That helped some. I guess that's why I said it. I ought to apologize for that part, too."

Jules' face went hot. She had no idea how to respond to the boy's admission. He was looking at her, waiting for something. Some kind of absolution.

"You did what you had to do to get along, Vick," she said. "No one blames you for that. No one blames you for anything. Not even for the things you thought about. Nothing that happened was your fault. Okay?"

He nodded, looked relieved through the veil of medication that clouded his eyes. He also looked old—too old to have his whole life ahead of him.

Cici came back out of the house. When she reached them, Vick said, "Momma, I think I'll go to Paw-Paw's and lay down, if that's all right."

"That's fine, Vick," Cici said. "I think that's a good idea."

As he walked away, Jules understood that the carnage of Tuni's actions lay scattered throughout the entire family.

"What have you told Tuni's kids?" Jules asked when Vick had gone. She hadn't even thought about that until Cici mentioned them asking about their mother.

"Jessie, the little one, is convinced that Tuni's run off again like she did that time before," Cici said. "Mica, the oldest, knows it's more than that. I know Walt's told them their momma's got a sickness in her brain and can't talk to them right now. I don't know how he's going to handle it down the road. If they decide she should go to trial, we'll have to tell them the whole truth about what happened, I guess. Part of me hopes they just decide to keep her in the loony bin, but Lord knows who pays for that. Walt's got his hands full as it is."

"How's Walt doing?" Finally. The question she'd been wanting to ask.

Cici shook her head. "He's acting the same as ever," she said. "But I've seen him taking capful after capful of that milky stuff for his stomach. When something hits him hard, it always takes a toll on his gut. It's the only way you can tell. My guess is he's barely keeping any food down, but he'd never let on, so I don't know for sure. We'll all be all right," she said, "eventually. All except Tuni, that is. And like I said, God knows what's going to happen to her. Not that I care much. She deserves what she gets and then some. As for the rest of us, it's just going to have to run its course."

Jules registered a disappointment that surprised her. As much as Jules had told herself and Lincoln otherwise, she *had* been hoping that an avenue would open up for her and Walt. Sitting in his backyard, seeing the fallout from everything that happened, she understood how naïve—naïve and self-indulgent—those hopes had been. He watched a marriage he'd planned to honor for a lifetime get blown to hell, with his nephew turning up as a prime casualty.

"I'm still not sure how long I'll be around," Jules told Cici. "But if there's anything I can do for any of you . . ."

Cici looked past her, across the yard toward the back door. Jules followed her line of sight and found Walt standing on the stoop at the top of stairs that led down to the backyard. She wanted to go to him, but she didn't. She wanted to make things better for him, but she didn't know how.

She thought about how she'd seen him at the hospital as he came out of the room with Tuni. His eyes, red-rimmed and swollen. His face alone told her how the ordeal had broken him.

Nothing she could do would ease his trouble. Then or now. She'd made him a silly casserole.

"Hey," he said as he walked across the yard to reach them. Cici was there, but his greeting was for her.

"I need to wash up and check on Bart and the girls," Cici said, standing up.

"Make sure they put the casserole in the refrigerator," Jules told her as she walked away. "It shouldn't sit out for too long."

"I'll do it right now," Cici said, and made her way inside the house.

Walt sat down in the spot Cici had vacated. He didn't say anything right away, but to her surprise, his silence calmed her. Humid air settled in a thick blanket on her skin, warmed her very bones. Rain would follow, and that was okay, too.

"Did I hear you brought food?" Walt asked, finally.

"My first attempt at one of Mom's recipes," she said. "Scalloped potatoes and ham."

"Sounds good." Small talk, but the sadness in his voice gave him away.

"Can I help you with anything?" she asked, giving him an opening. "I saw your girls at the door. They have to be lost. What can I do?"

He didn't answer right away, and she wondered if she'd overstepped, pushed him when he wanted to keep it to himself.

"I should have seen something," he said. "I lived with the woman, slept in the same bed. I don't know how I missed something that wrong." He was looking out toward the sky, toward the line where sunshine abruptly gave way to a cloudy mist in the distance. "Truth is, she was always a little off. Always somewhere between woman and child. I got used to it, I guess. A little more of one or the other didn't register. Vick's anger toward me . . ." He stopped and looked at Jules. "She told him that I was bad to her. That I neglected her. Belittled her. And I have to wonder if that part of it wasn't right. Did I?"

"No, Walt." Jules kept her voice firm. "Tuni's illness belongs to her. You didn't cause it, and you can't make it go away. The fact that you didn't see the extent of it just shows how good she was at disguising it. For the sake of your sanity, and especially for your girls, you have to let go of that responsibility."

He let out a deep breath. She couldn't tell if he planned to accept what she said or not.

"It's going to be a long road back," he said. "For me, Mica, and Jessie." He named them, rather than calling them "the girls." He was preparing himself to respond to them as individuals, and to let each one grieve or heal in her own way. "I don't know how we'll do it right now, what the next steps will be. But I'm not free to live the way I'd like. I wish I could say it was different, but it's not."

He was talking about her, about *them*. He said what she already knew. In his present crisis, there would be room for family, for friends and neighbors. But not for a woman in his life. Not yet.

"I understand," she said. She laid her hand on the small roundness of her belly. She had adjustments to make, too. The complications seemed endless.

"It's funny," he said, looking at her stomach. "I know what you looked like before you had a baby showing, but I can't seem to see you that way in my mind."

"Well, I haven't been much to look at these past couple of months," she said, thinking of her makeshift outfits and un-kempt hair.

"But you *have* been." There was conviction when he said this, and she turned and looked at his face. "That first weekend, when you came back to stay with your momma, I saw you. After that,

I made note of you all the time—same way I did when you were sixteen, I guess." He smiled. "But these last months, when you were in a room or when you were across the street . . . I'm not proud of it. Maybe in my gut I knew something was way wrong with Tuni and that's why I gave myself permission. I don't know. But the minute you were anywhere nearby, it knocked the wind out of me. Every damn time."

She felt her legs go weak. She wanted to melt into him, but she couldn't. He'd already said as much.

"It's funny," he said, smiling. "Even when I have a dream, I see you like you are now, all round in your face and in your belly."

It was an offhand comment. She wondered how often she'd been inside his dreams.

"What *did* you look like before?" he asked, as if it might be important for him to see it again in his mind and remember. His voice carried none of the playful inflection implied in the question. It was as if he needed to integrate his flawed memory of her with what he saw in front of him.

"I don't know," she said, feeling the blush go up her neck and into her cheeks. When had she turned shy? "I was skinny," she said. "I've always thought I was too skinny."

"Nothing wrong with skinny," he said. His words sounded gentle.

What did he mean? And what did he want?

Small rumbles of thunder sounded in the distance, but it seemed more stern than menacing. She could feel the air changing.

"What are you planning to do about the baby?" he asked, as if it had just occurred to him that the round belly would some-day yield a small human being. "Are you going to have it here or in Los Angeles?"

"With everything that's happened since I found out I was

pregnant, I haven't had a chance to make real plans, although the woman subletting my condo is getting anxious to know if she can stay there or not. I guess I've always thought I'd go back to LA as soon as I could, but over the last few days . . ." She hesitated, considered how she should word her thoughts. "I've been thinking about the other options. I've gotten all the work I need in Wilmington, and the doctor I've seen is there. I'm closer here to Lincoln in New York."

Walt looked to be holding his breath, waiting for her to say something else. But she couldn't. It wasn't her place. Not under the circumstances.

"And there's me." He said it for her.

"And there's you."

"And then it gets complicated, doesn't it?" He looked toward his house. A house filled with Tuni Walker's shampoo and shoes, dresses and pictures. A house filled with her children. "Like I said, it's going to be a while before my life gets put into any sort of predictable order. It's going to take time before Jessie and Mica will understand having somebody else coming in and being part of our lives. I can't ask you to stay for me. It wouldn't be right. Much as I want it. Truth is, I can't even say how long it will be. It's just going to take . . . a while."

A while. One of those vague Southern expressions. It meant everything and nothing all at once.

"I know," she said. "I've known it all along. And it's not your fault. It's just the way things are."

"So where does that leave us, do you think?" He seemed out of ideas and without any notion of what might come next.

What he didn't realize was that she'd spent her whole life not knowing exactly what would come next. In a lot of ways, she found it a source of comfort.

"Neighbors," she said. "That leaves us neighbors."

"For how long?"

Soft rain landed on her arm. Warm rain. Warmer than it ever felt in Los Angeles. It was a quiet Southern rain that didn't make her feel she had to take shelter, to flee it. She closed her eyes for a moment and let it fall, damp on her skin.

"That's just the thing," she said, turning to look into his troubled eyes. "I was thinking I might stay exactly as long as it takes for us to know. I was thinking I might stay for a while."

He didn't smile, but she saw the relief in his expression, the easy way he let himself breathe. He ventured no closer than they'd been, but, even so, something passed between them.

"You were skinny," he said, as if the memory had returned, fully intact.

"Yeah," she said. "Always was . . . Until this." She looked down at herself.

And then he reached over, put the tips of his fingers lightly against the rain-dampened shirt that covered her belly. He'd touched her that way before, and it had seemed like a final gesture. A good-bye. But this time, it felt like something else. Not a beginning, but a promise. Light as his touch was, she felt it go through her. And for that moment, it seemed like enough.

Epilogue

Sweating and spent, Jules felt the slick miracle of baby flesh against her arms as the doctor handed the child to her. Slight weight settled against Jules' bare skin, as her baby girl squirmed and rooted, in search of milk.

Jules looked at her daughter and it came to her. *Clara May.* It wasn't God's voice, but Marnee's. Marnee. Messenger of God. Unseen, but felt as plainly as hot and cold. So Julie Marie entered into motherhood of her own. Lincoln was with her. Walt, too, waiting somewhere outside the doors.

Jules kissed her daughter for the first time, and claimed for herself the old, old love, declared new again in Clara May.

A+
AUTHOR
INSIGHTS,
EXTRAS, &
MORE...

FROM
**JEAN
REYNOLDS
PAGE**
AND
AVON A

The Importance of the Reader

I had the good fortune when I was just out of college to work as a publicist in New York with a number of modern dance companies. Among them, The Merce Cunningham Dance Company was one of my favorites—both in terms of my interaction with the company and in terms of the dances in the repertory. I remember hearing Merce Cunningham say in an interview—and I'm paraphrasing here—that the particular bias that any viewer brought to the performance was an important part of the creative life of each dance. In other words, when a dance is filtered through the mind and the experiences of the person watching, it becomes something different to each person.

I feel that way about books and I see my books as being completed in a new way each time someone reads one of them. An interesting thing happened once at a book club I visited. One of the members mentioned that I had not described the physical appearance of the main character in any great detail (I believe this discussion was about my first book, *A Blessed Event*). The person asked me what visual image I had of her.

"Before I answer," I said, "I'd love to hear how all of you saw her."

Without realizing it, each person described someone who looked very much like themselves. I loved this. To me, it meant that the readers identified with my main character and brought to her story the extended detail of their own experiences. In this sense, I see writing books as a kind of collaboration with the reader. I see the discussion questions included in my books as a way to explore the story with the added layer of the reader's experience. So with this in mind, here are a few discussion points to get things started.

1. When Jules finds out she is pregnant with Thomas' child, she decides that, because he has repeatedly chosen to go off his medication for bipolar disorder (and as a result of this has exhibited dangerous behavior), she will not tell him about the baby. How do you feel about this decision? Do you think she made the right choice in order to protect her child or should he be told that he is a father in spite of the potential risks?

2. Lincoln and Jules had different experiences with their father, Jack Fuller. How did Jack's abuse affect the people the two siblings became in their adult lives? How is Vick's experience similar to Lincoln's? How is it different? Why was the boy vulnerable to the particular type of abuse that he endured?

3. Walt tells Jules that she reminds him of a rodeo clown, something seemingly frivolous and fun, but with a fiercely serious purpose behind the charade. Jules believed that if she maintained the outward trappings of someone wild and unpredictable, she would shield Lincoln by offering herself as a distraction. She wanted to protect her brother, first, from the anger of their father, and later, from the disapproval of the community. Do you think there were any additional, perhaps more self-serving, purposes for Jules' disguise? If so, what were they?

4. Jules is initially upset with Sam for keeping the truth from her about the day their fathers died. Do you think she was justified in being angry with Sam, but not with Lincoln? Is it always better to know the truth about painful situations, or are there sometimes good reasons to stay quiet in order to protect someone?

5. What should happen to Tuni? Is she a victim of some sort of mental illness? Should this be taken into consideration, or are her actions beyond any such justification?

The Boundtrack™

In the A+ pages of *The Space Between Before and After*, I included the playlist of songs used as inspiration in the process of getting to know my characters. My husband and I began calling it my "Boundtrack™". Of course, I thought I'd invented the wheel, but I've since discovered a number of writers who use music as part of their writing life. It makes sense. Music evokes memories and emotions in a writer that can help bring context and credibility into a developing protagonist.

Sharing the music in the A+ section seemed to resonate with readers before, so I thought I'd use this space once again to share the songs that have been part of this book. As I looked over the list, I realized that the songs had a certain progression that followed the events of the novel. For this reason, I will list the songs, not grouped by character, as I did in The Space Between Before and After, but rather, following where each song fits in the narrative.

So here is the Boundtrack™ for *The Last Summer of Her Other Life*.

"Not As We" by Alanis Morisette: (Jules) In the early moments of the book, Marnee is there and then gone. This song was probably written as a break-up song, but when thinking about Jules and how she felt at the loss of her mother, the song captured, for me, all of the confusion of becoming a motherless child. Regardless of your age, when your mother dies, you are alone in a way that you have never been before.

"You're Missing" by Bruce Springsteen: (Jules and Lincoln) Written in response to 9/11, this song captures the feelings Jules and Lincoln have as they live in Marnee's home without her. They are surrounded by the possessions that have existed beyond their mother's lifetime. I remember so well in my own mother's home, feeling as if she'd gone to the store or to visit someone. Her house was *waiting*, as Springsteen says. I was waiting, too.

"Sugar Mountain" by Neil Young: (Jules) Particularly in the early parts of the book, Jules is struggling with what she feels to be prolonged adolescence. Her move to Los Angeles has helped her maintain this existence. As she finds herself pregnant and without a mother on whom to rely, she realizes that it is time to grow up. For her baby's sake, she must become a full-fledged adult. Regardless of the point you have reached in your life when you step out of childhood for good—in Jules' case, thirty-eight and under extreme circumstances—it always feels as if you're leaving *too* soon.

"One Headlight" by The Wallflowers: (Sam) When I first began writing this book, I imagined that Sam and Jules would get back together. He's a great guy, but he's at a crossroads in life. A few chapters in, it became clear to me that Jules was someone who fit in with his desire to break out of his life "in the middle", as the song puts it. The reference to "me and Cinderella" in the lyrics helped me to get a handle on Sam and Jules. She's the exciting fairy-tale in his past. He wants to recapture that, but she's becoming someone else entirely.

"Searching For A Heart" by Warren Zevon: (Jules) In spite of her history with Sam, Jules has a smoldering attraction for Walt that extends back to her first awareness of her own sexuality. The double whammy for her is that, as an adult, she is equally drawn to his integrity and his maturity. As she comes to terms with her response to Walt, she realizes she's falling in love. These feelings for this married man are unwelcome, but she can't just wish them away. Zevon says of love, "You can't start it like a car, you can't stop it with a gun." How brilliant is that? Possibly the best line about love I've ever heard.

"Boogie Street" by Leonard Cohen: (Walt) I'm still not sure what Cohen and collaborator Sharon Robinson intended "Boogie Street" to represent, but whatever it is, Walt finds himself in the thick of it. This song took me to Walt's unbidden, unexplained pull toward Jules. All the raw feelings that he didn't want, but couldn't deny.

"Hide and Seek" by Imogen Heap: (Lincoln) I put this song with Lincoln, but really, it took me through one particular scene in the book: when Lincoln finds Vick in the woods. The song has a powerful, disorienting quality about it that suits Lincoln's panic and all of the questions that race through his mind as he acts to save the boy. Somehow, the song portrays not only the emotions, but a strong sense of place as well.

"Cathedral" by Crosby, Stills & Nash: (Lincoln) Another "scene-oriented" inclusion. Lincoln goes to the church in the aftermath of finding Vick in the woods. The urge to stop all of the images and the feelings in his head drive him to seek comfort. The church is a place where Marnee took him for protection. His other comforts in life have been music and booze. All three come together in a manic effort on his part. There is a desperation in this song that fits Lincoln's mindset—the anger and fear left over from his own childhood that he relives through Vick's torment.

"Heroes" by David Bowie: (Jules and Lincoln) After the incident of Vick in the woods by their house, Jules and Lincoln realize the full desire to help Vick rather than blame him. This is a turning point—particularly for Jules who is already questioning her ability to be a good mother once her own baby is born. There is a certain liberation captured in this song that mirrors the way Jules and Lincoln felt as they set off for the drive to Vick's old school. They felt empowered by their decision to do this one, small thing.

"Sideways" by Citizen Cope: (Walt) As Walt's feelings for Jules progress, there is a defeated quality in the acknowledgement of his emotions. Falling in love with Jules does not fit in with the image of the person Walt sees himself to be. He's a married man, committed to the promises he made. This song conveys the complexity of this situation with surprising simplicity.

"And The Healing Has Begun" Van Morrison: (Jules and Walt) As I worked on the final scene of the book, this song (one of my favorites from way back) kept going through my head. It was almost as if I saw the scene unfolding before me and heard this in the background. It has a yearning, yet resolute, quality about it. Walt and Jules can't quite have what they want—yet. But they will get there.

"Southern Rain" by Cowboy Junkies: (Jules) One thing Jules realizes during her time back in North Carolina is the richness of the landscape and the relationships that occur within it. While she loves her work, her life in Los Angeles has had a diminished quality about it. She had a relationship with a man she later realized she never really knew. This song brought to mind the feelings that reemerged about Walt, but also the texture and emotions of her ties to her Southern home. It is the place where, for me, the novel comes full circle. She understands that she wants to raise her child in the place where Marnee raised her.

As I did with the playlist from The Space Between Before and After, I have a link on my website jeanreynoldspage.com that will take you to the iMix of the Boundtrack™ for *The Last Summer of Her Other Life* on iTunes. I hope you find the songs as inspiring as I have.

Photo by Andy Ziskind

Jean Reynolds Page

JEAN REYNOLDS PAGE is the author of *A Blessed Event, Accidental Happiness*, and *The Space Between Before and After*. She grew up in North Carolina and graduated with a degree in journalism from The University of North Carolina at Chapel Hill. She worked as an arts publicist in New York City and for over a decade reviewed dance performances for numerous publications before turning full time to fiction in 2001. In addition to North Carolina and New York, she has lived in Boston and Dallas. She currently lives with her family near Seattle.